For Laura

Michèle Stapley

The Death of Art

by Michèle Stapley

Published by:

GRENWOD Publishing

ISBN 0-9745553-2-0

Cover art by Michèle Stapley

Book design by Studio Street Graphics

Published by Greenwood Publishing

Printed in the U.S.A. by
Morris Publishing
3212 East Highway 30
Kearney, NE 68847
1-800-650-7888

For my husband, Sam,
always supportive, always patient

Acknowledgements

I received wonderful assistance from my three daughters: Suzie Zetz, with her masters degree in psychology, who patiently shared her professional insights; Julie Jones, graphic designer, who designed the cover and basically did everything else to the book but write it; and Jacqui Nyetrae, who spent hours proofing and correcting for age-appropriate behavior and dialogue. Much love and appreciation to each.

I am especially grateful to Tom and Ann Morrow, the honest-to-goodness owners of the real *Celebration of Fine Art*, who kindly allowed this project to go forward. I hope my descriptions of the show do it justice, for it is truly a beautiful and unique celebration of art. I can assure the reader that no murder has ever taken place on the premises, and that the nighttime security system is not at all as I have described it.

Thanks to many artist friends—as well as the Morrows and the Long Gallery—who gave me permission to mention their names for no other reason than for the sheer fun of it: Robin Branham, Brad Brenner, Graydon Foulger, Dan Hill, Daphne Keskinis, Roger Lundskow, Jan McLaughlin, Beth Page, Penny Benjamin Peterson, Martha Pettigrew, Kirk Randall, Dorothy Ray, and Bill Shaddix.

Thank goodness for experts. Particularly helpful were Marilyn Andreini, R.N.; Lt. David Kelly, Sgt. Doug Ewing and Sgt. David Norton of the Phoenix Police Department; and last but certainly not least, my editor, Jim Veihdeffer, owner of Words In Action, who tidied up the manuscript with wit, wisdom and diligence.

The Death of Art

PROLOGUE

She had been waiting for over an hour, parked on a gravel road alongside the freeway ramp exactly as he had directed. The rain, which was coming down in a chilly drizzle, was turning the dust on her windshield into squirming blotches of Arizona mud. She was glad she wasn't driving in the traffic that was swooshing past her on I-10 because her wipers were a mess, just like everything else about her car. Perhaps by the time he arrived the rain would have moved on and then she could drive away safely. She would head north to Phoenix a rich woman.

What a day! God, they were good. She smiled as she remembered the last salesman they conned, the one with the paunch and the electric blue tie. He had almost drooled—she could see the saliva pooling in the corners of his mouth—when she slowly slid the tips of her fingers down the neckline of her silk blouse to the low-cut center. His gaze never wavered so she let her hand linger a moment before she slipped her finger under the fabric, lightly stroking the skin between her breasts and releasing the tease of perfume. When she leaned more closely over the counter he tried so hard to get a better look and to breathe in more of her scent that her partner made the switch without even the possibility of detection. The hardest part was to keep the flirtation going until the end when she said, no, she didn't think she was interested, but they might come back later. Then she thanked him for his help, brushed his hand lightly, and glanced demurely into his moist gray eyes.

A brittle draft pushed in from the window and down the back of her neck causing her to shiver under her thin jacket. She had dressed for a day trip to Tucson, expecting good weather and an early evening. Where the hell was he? He told her six o'clock and here it was, quarter past seven. She could feel the dampness come up from the floorboards and chill her feet through the soles of her sandals. Exasperated, she turned on the ignition to get some heat and immediately station KUPD blasted its heavy metal like a gunshot through her ears, unsettling her as much as the cold. She snapped the radio off, breaking a long red fingernail, and leaned back in the seat. No time to get jumpy now.

What if he couldn't make the deal? What if he tried to cut her out? No, she thought, he was too clever for that. He would find a way to make the deal and then he would split it with her, just like he said. And the reason he'd do that was because he'd never get a better accomplice. She knew she was good. She had talent. Her first time, and no glitches, not one. Her adrenaline had kicked in and she had moved through the show with total confidence. She was perfectly in tune with him. They were like dance partners, moving together beautifully with the music and captivating one audience after another.

She was good even when they reversed roles. Then she would button up her jacket, push her long blond hair behind her ears and put on those oversized black-rimmed glasses. It wasn't just the props, though. She could actually make herself almost invisible. All she had to do was remember high school, when she had crooked teeth and tacky clothes and was twenty pounds overweight. That's when she learned how it felt to be ignored, and that's just how she made herself feel when he was grinning that cute grin at some sexy salesgirl. Anyone could tell the girl was just plain tired of dealing with all the old, leering customers and that she simply enjoyed being lusted after by a hunk. Unfortunately, this particular hunk was not the slightest bit interested in anything but the switch. And she, Lydia,

2

completely ignored, made the perfect switch, timing it to the precise moment he brushed an imaginary strand of hair from the salesgirl's expectant face, telling her that her ears were the most marvelous, delicious shade of pink.

The rain stopped. The heater had warmed her but now she was hungry. She wanted a burger and fries. Even with all the money in the world she would want a burger and fries. But the thing she really craved, what she thought about all the time, what motivated all of this and everything else she had done, was a large two-story house, one with a fireplace and French doors and a pool and a spa. It would be in one of those ritzy gated communities in north Scottsdale. Of course, she also wanted a fancy car. She wasn't sure what kind, not having the sort of friends who owned any, but she had seen advertisements for Porsches and Jaguars. She would get herself one of those.

She watched the car stop and saw him get out and pull up his collar against the chill. He walked carefully, avoiding the puddles that had formed in the gravel at the side of the road. He opened the door on the driver's side and motioned her to move. A blast of cold, wet air invaded the car so she quickly swung her legs over the transmission hump and wiggled into the passenger seat, letting out an impatient "shit" and tugging at her short skirt. She hated the cold. She hated the smell of the wet desert and the clammy feel of the vinyl seats. She hated the traffic with its dizzying glare of headlights. Her head was beginning to pound.

He sure took his time settling behind the wheel. For one thing, he left his gloves on, so it took him a long time to loosen his tie. Finally, collar opened, he purred like a damn cat and pulled a parcel out from under his coat, placing it on the dashboard between them. He grinned at her, stretching his arm across the back of her seat and gently pulling at her ear. "Such a pretty, pretty shade of pink!" he said, mimicking himself and resting his gloved hand on her shoulder to play with a stray curl.

Even though it was fun to watch him pour on the charm, to play the game, she refused to smile and wondered if he would ever try to con her. Of course she had let him seduce her, because that's what she wanted. She didn't particularly like the rough part that went along with it, but she knew how to protect herself. No one was going to mess with her, ever.

She looked back and forth between him and the package, trying to decide where to focus her attention first. Her aggravation won out, so she turned and faced him, pissed at his smug expression, and demanded, "Where the hell have you been? I've been waiting in this dumb car, freezing to death, for almost two hours."

"Relax, honey, relax. It just took longer than I thought. A little mix-up. You know how things are."

"Don't *honey* me! And no, I don't *know how things are!* All I know is I did my part perfectly, with no mix-up at all." She tilted her head defiantly and crossed her arms over her chest, waiting for the compliment she knew she deserved.

He never stopped smiling as he tugged at her ear again. "You're right, honey. And you know what? You were perfect. You were amazing...in fact, you were absolutely brilliant."

Mollified, she allowed herself a little smile. "You were pretty good yourself, pretty damn good." She uncrossed her arms and gave a double thumbs-up and a hearty "Yesss!"

Her eyes felt like they were pulled by magnets to the dashboard. She twisted forward, eager now to examine the package, and that's when she noticed his shoes. "What the hell are you wearing those for?"

But her distraction was momentary and her eyes returned to the package. The proof of her talent, the keys to her beautiful house, were right there, glowing in the golden ribbon of light from the nearby traffic.

She was still smiling when she felt something warm and smooth around her neck. It got tight very quickly but she didn't try to pull it away at first because her fingers were busy untying the parcel on the dashboard. Suddenly, with a fright that came too late to save her, her eyes and mouth opened wide and her hands jerked to her neck in panic. She thrust her shoulders from side to side in an effort to shake free from the restraint, at the same time trying to pull his gloved hands away from the back of her neck. But her arms didn't go where she thrust them and instead made futile, pawing motions in the air. Several times her fingers plucked at her neck searching for slackness in the noose, but there was nothing to grab.

Her arms became heavy and fell into her lap. She smelled his leather glove as his hand slipped over her nose and mouth and forced her head back against his shoulder. His breath was warm on her cheek, and somehow comforting. She leaned back and thought it curious that the headlights on the highway were growing dimmer. They got so dim she couldn't see them at all.

PART 1

ONE

Even though the big white tents appeared each January, they were in such contrast to the few remaining miles of desert that motorists driving north on Scottsdale Road to their luxury homes in the foothills were always surprised to see them. They knew the tents would stay in place until Easter, just long enough to become a familiar landmark and a convenient destination for their winter visitors. But then, the disappearance of the tents in the spring would be a surprise as well.

Everyone called them "the big white tents," but the actual event was the Celebration of Fine Art, its purpose made evident by the life-size and monumental sculptures fork-lifted into the wide grassy area planted between two of the huge tents and visible from the road. A third tent, farther back and parallel to the road, connected the other two, all three forming one enormous U-shaped structure.

For the three days between the raising of the tents and the official opening of the art show, dozens of pickups, trailers and vans jammed into the parking lot in the back of the far tent and disgorged an amazing variety of artwork, equipment and furnishings. Chaos reigned as artists lugged their possessions, or pushed them on dollies, through the tent's only entrance, across the wide lobby, and down either the north or south tent, to their assigned booths. They quickly painted the freestanding walls which served to partition one booth from the next, set up their own lights, and arranged their displays of paintings, sculpture, pottery or jewelry. Some chose to lay wall-to-wall carpet on the asphalt floor they could call their own for the next ten weeks. Others preferred the ambiance of a throw rug, usually faux Oriental and purchased from Home Depot. Finally, the booths were finished off with the artist's name in bold letters and perhaps a few potted plants.

Late the third night, when the last of the artists finished setting up, passing motorists might notice the lights going out one by one until the tents were left in darkness. A security light shone in the sculpture garden until ten o'clock, when a timer turned it off. From that point on, there was only a chain link fence and one security guard protecting the property, which was closed to the public at night, but always open to any artist who wished to come to work.

It was for that purpose that Art Russo drove this rainy night down the long gravel driveway. He maneuvered his brand new pickup to avoid the worst of the puddles and thought how much he liked the smell of creosote when it rained. Back in New Jersey he had hated the rain, but now that he had retired to Arizona, with all its glorious, sunny days, he found himself looking forward to each rainstorm.

The gravel crunched loudly under his tires as he made the turn skirting the edge of the dark and silent desert. The parking lot was almost empty, but he immediately spotted Derrick's Silverado and uttered a quiet "damn." He hoped he wouldn't have another confrontation with that pain in the ass tonight because he needed to finish the sculpture that Mrs. Nielsen liked. She was going to bring her husband to see it in the morning.

This was the first time Art had come to the tents at night and he was amazed at how different everything appeared. Glowing with natural light during the day, at night the huge space looked as dark and hollow as a cave, with only a few scattered lights left on by the artists still at work. The tent flaps, which were always pulled wide open to allow access to the sculpture garden, were now closed and laced shut. The entrance lobby and adjoining café, normally bustling with activity, were populated tonight by a drowsy security guard who was leaning back in a chair with his feet up on the customer service table, watching television in the murky darkness. He didn't bother to look at Art. He just waved his hand and said, "Don't forget to sign in." Art found the clipboard, signed his name and noted the time. It was 10:15.

From the direction of the lights, Art knew that there was only one other artist working farther down in the south tent and he didn't bother to find out who it was. Eager to get to work, he walked directly to his booth and turned on his lights. Against a backdrop of dark gray walls stood his sculpture, beautifully spotlighted and professionally displayed on the wooden stands he had made himself.

He immediately turned his attention to the figure of the old man reading. It was modeled in clay—to be cast later in bronze—and he was concerned about the thickness of the sculpted base. The figure, 15 inches tall, sat on a fairly massive, rough-textured slab, but now, as he rotated the turntable to examine it from all sides, he was convinced that he had made the slab too thick. Whatever adjustment he made had to be right the first time if he wanted to close the sale in the morning.

Just yesterday he had sold *Mother and Child*, a bronze that was the same size and scale as *Old Man Reading*. It would have made an excellent guide, but since it was gone he looked for the photographs Eldon had just taken of it. Then he remembered that he had left the photos in his truck.

The guard was still at his post, feet up and motionless, so Art slipped out quietly, not wanting to disturb him. He saw that one car had left the lot.

He took long quick strides on the wet gravel, zipping his jacket against the wind, which was now whipping the rain to the east. He found the photos on the front seat and pushed them under his jacket for protection. When he passed back through the entrance he got a better view of the guard, who was snoring softly.

It was much darker when he walked back down the aisle and he wondered why in the world someone had turned off his lights. Apparently the other artist had left, too, because now the whole south tent was dark.

There was only the faint, eerie glow of the television set to guide him for the first few yards.

A gust of wind whistled sharply through the laced flaps and rustled down the aisle. The canvas roof began to rise and fall with the wind, causing the metal framework to creak and groan like the mast of a great ship. There was another sound as well, but Art couldn't figure out what it was or where it came from. He stood still, momentarily disoriented. Then straight ahead he saw the little darts of a penlight playing along the jewelry display case in the booth next to his. He held his breath and approached quietly, certain that the noise of the tents would cover his footfall. He was positive it was Jess. Oh, how he'd love to catch him this time, drag his skinny ass out to the parking lot and give the kid a whooping. It would actually be a kindness, he thought, knocking some sense into him instead of getting him fired.

Art approached slowly, feeling his way along his own familiar walls. When he reached the light switch he said, "Okay Jess, what's going on here?"

Before his fingers could flip the switch something crashed down on his arm and he staggered sideways, dropping the photographs. The assailant grabbed him by the neck and shoved his head violently against the wall, knocking a small bronze sculpture to the ground. Dazed, Art watched a gloved hand pick up the sculpture while the penlight danced little zigzags on the floor. What strange-looking shoes, he thought. Then he saw the sculpture high above his head and watched helplessly as it came crashing down. He was aware that his knees had buckled and that he was sliding, in slow motion, down the wall and onto the asphalt.

Later, when the rain and wind had moved on and the last of the clouds were slipping away, he looked up briefly from the cold, wet grass and saw Jesus Christ, beautifully sculpted, pale and majestic against the dark sky. Then he closed his eyes and prayed over and over, "Jesus, oh, sweet Jesus."

TWO

Detective Antonio Manuel Jesus Bannigan, known to his friends as Tony, planted himself in the middle of the lobby and surveyed the art show with one slow turn of his head. At 6-foot-2, it was relatively easy for him to look past the café and out to the sunlit sculpture garden. He watched the officers at work and said, to no one in particular, "Strange place to dump the victim."

His partner, J.D. Harris, looked up and nodded. "Yeah, well, that's where they found him, all right, right there, by that big white statue. He was lying on his back, head and face all bloody. Still breathing. But Doc says he's as good as dead. They took him over to St. Clare's."

"But why *there*, by the statue of Jesus Christ?" Tony shook his head in disbelief. The officers were now yellow-taping a large circle, about thirty feet in diameter, all around the statue, working carefully in the wet grass.

"Is that who the statue is? *Jesus Christ?* For Christ's sake!" J.D. took a step to the right so he could peer through the crowd, a necessary maneuver for someone 5-foot-5. He thrust his head forward and squinted hard into the light. "You know, you're absolutely right. That *is* Jesus Christ. Holy shit!"

"J.D.!"

"Sorry. No disrespect intended, honest." He paused and grinned mischievously. "You better not tell your mother about this one."

"Let's just leave my mother out of it." Then a broad smile lit up his face. "But you're wrong, you know. Dead wrong. She'll go to town when she hears about this."

Tony could see his mother's eyes grow bigger and bigger as she listened to the story of the man lying half-dead at the feet of Jesus. She'd make the sign of the cross and then she'd look up at God to ask why He didn't take better care of His people. Then she'd get to work in earnest and pray a rosary for the victim. She'd pray for the victim's family as well. And if he knew his mother at all, she'd even pray for the creep who did it. That last part irritated him.

"Anyway," J.D. continued, "see where they're running the tape over to the tent? It looks like he was assaulted inside the tent, in his booth or whatever they call it, and then dragged outside."

"Who found him?"

"One of the customers. An elderly lady." J.D. fumbled with his notes. "Francie Nielsen. Says she brought her husband this morning to order one of Russo's sculptures. Russo wasn't in his booth so they walked back through the sculpture garden to wait in the café. They took the gravel path—see how it cuts through the grass over there? —and that's when she nearly tripped over the poor guy. Screamed pretty loud, I guess. She's still shook up. They're in the office now, with the Morrows."

"Who are the Morrows?"

"They own the place."

"Bet they're thrilled. Who else was here at the time?"

Tony Bannigan's eyes scanned the café while he asked the question, carefully observing the people assembled there under the supervision of Officer O'Neill. Some were sitting at little tables, drinking coffee. Others were standing in twos and threes near the opening to the sculpture garden, watching the police at work. No one was talking. One of the women was sobbing.

"We counted forty-five. Mostly artists and staff. A few customers. The place had just opened. Anyway, the artists and customers are there," he said, pointing to the café, "and the Morrows are in the office with the staff and the Nielsens. We haven't let anyone come or go. But it really wouldn't matter much. Doc says it happened last night. None of these people were here then. At least, we don't think so."

J.D. handed Tony the clipboard with the sign-in sheet from the previous night. "You might be interested in this."

Tony looked it over carefully, memorizing the information. Gretchen Schmidt came at 9:10 p.m. and stayed until 10:20; John Amory was here from 9:20 until 11:05; Taylor McGrath signed in at 9:30 but never signed out. Art Russo, the victim, was the last to sign in, at 10:15. Why so late, Tony wondered.

"What about the security guard? Where is he?"

"The Morrows called him and he's on his way. He told them he didn't see or hear a thing."

Tony handed the list back to J.D. "Let's try to locate these folks. We're going to want to talk to them all." Then he turned his attention back to the layout of the tents.

On the left of the entrance was a long, skirted table where brochures were handed out and where, he was told, the security guard sat at night. Hell of a security system. He'd bet a buck or two there was booze stashed under those skirts. Behind the table, a short set of steps led up to the trailer that abutted the tents and served as a sales office. The artists' booths started farther back, where the aisle turned the corner into the south tent. He could see paintings, illuminated by overhanging spotlights, on some of the walls. Easels, storage bins, shelves of pottery, and stacks of frames were visible.

On the other side of the entrance was another table where tickets were sold, and behind that, the restrooms, and then, farther back, the same configuration of display walls that turned the corner and led down the north tent. He could see more paintings, sculptures, equipment, and work tables. One hundred artists. One hundred booths. One hundred places where things could be hidden. And probably one hundred hammers, drills and other assorted objects capable of bashing in a skull. He sighed and wondered if a miracle had happened and the weapon was found. Fingerprints would be nice.

It took just a few seconds for his long legs to move him past the skirted table and up the office steps. He popped his head in the door and quickly picked out the elderly Nielsens, a well dressed couple in their 70s. Mrs. Nielsen was crying. Mr. Nielsen was patting her arm. Tony nodded at them. "Sorry you had to be the ones to find him. You can go home now if you want. We'll call you later if we need anything." They looked relieved and left in silence, holding hands tightly. He then asked the Morrows to start collecting all the information they had on the artists and staff, especially Art Russo—his application form, bio, sales records, anything at all. "Does he have any relatives?" he asked.

Yes, there's a daughter, they told him. In New Jersey. Mrs. Morrow was just about to call her.

~~~~~~~~~~~~~~~~~~~~~~~~~~~~~~~~~~

It was almost noon and Kate was still wrapped in her long chenille bathrobe, comfortably burrowed between the pillows of her sofa. She dangled fuzzy slippers from her toes and munched a chocolate chip cookie. The Sunday *New York Times* was spread out over the coffee table, except for the book review section which she had saved for last, a treat to savor with her final cup of coffee.

Outside, the snow was falling silently on the rhododendron bushes, covering their leathery leaves with thick piles of white fluff. She looked at the scene for a moment and decided that the view out her window was the most perfect and exquisite background for the tall vase of irises that stood on the bookcase beneath the window. Martin had sent them to congratulate her on her new position, and she thought how perfectly they reflected Martin himself, tall, elegant, precise. She had placed the bouquet between her two most treasured possessions: her father's sculpture of Snuffy, her childhood cat, and a black and white photograph of her mother as a young woman.

Haphazard stacks of psychology texts were still stuffed into the upper shelves of the bookcase, together with all the reference material she had used for her final research paper, "Longitudinal Study of Antisocial Personality Disorder." Below, novels and mysteries lined up in neat rows and shared shelf space with the handsome art books she had inherited from her mother.

She kicked off her slippers, tucked her long legs under her robe, and licked the last crumb from her fingers. She told herself that she really had to repair her chewed off fingernails before she began work at the clinic tomorrow. Maybe now that grad school was over she could actually break the habit. She was sure that nothing, absolutely nothing, could be as stressful as the oral comprehensives and final exams she had just endured.

She answered the phone on the fourth ring and stared blankly out the window as she tried to absorb what a woman named Mrs. Morrow was telling her. None of it made any sense at all. Mrs. Morrow repeated the information while Kate watched the snow pile higher on the rhododendron bush until one of the leaves tipped under the weight. As soon as it dumped its snow, the leaf sprang back up, waving like a bright green mitten. She stared at it vacantly until it was covered with new snow, and then thanked Mrs. Morrow for the call and hung up the phone. "Jesus, oh, sweet Jesus!" she moaned, stumbling toward her bedroom.

She hastily pulled piles of clothes from her closet, far more than she could possibly need, and stuffed them into her suitcase. She threw on a pair of jeans and a sweater. Barely looking in the mirror, she pushed her dark hair back from her face and forced it into a lopsided ponytail. Make-up was useless because she couldn't stop crying. She started to put on jewelry, then wondered why, gave up, and threw it all into her purse. Car coat or blazer? She decided on the blazer and began absentmindedly stuffing handfuls of Kleenex in her pockets.

She called the airlines and then ordered a cab. What should

she do about tomorrow? She flipped open her laptop and zapped out an e-mail:

Martin honey - Daddy's been hurt...he's in the hospital ...am flying to
Phx now ... will call/e-mail tonite...tell clinic i won't be in tomorrow -
kisses, Kate

Walking down the aisle to Art Russo's booth, Tony heard part of the conversation J.D. was having with the crime scene team. Why did he always have to sound so damn stupid? Tony was sure he did it just to be irritating.

"These are real nice statues, you know?" J.D. was saying. "Look at this one. *Very* nice. And that one over there, the naked lady with the pretty tits. Holy cow. But look at the price—a thousand bucks! Nice, but not *that* nice."

"They're not *statues*, dimwit," the gal with the camera replied. "They're *sculptures*. Statues are in churches and parks and cemeteries. These here are sculptures. And that one there, of the nude—you don't call it a naked lady, dimwit—that nude is worth more than a grand if you ask me. Look how expressive the posture is, the curve of the back, the way the head..."

"*Look how expressive*"...J.D. did a perfect imitation. "Gimme a break."

Tony interrupted, impatient with the banter. "Okay, what do we have so far?"

"Lots of fingerprints all over the statues ... the *sculptures*. Looks like everyone in the city of Scottsdale has touched these things. We got luckier with footprints. See that partial over there by the sculpture stand? Nice, muddy print, but it's hard at this point to tell if it's significant. A lot of people have been walking around here this morning. But we'll check it out."

"What else?"

"It appears Art Russo was bashed against the wall and hit with some sort of heavy object. There's blood here on the wall, smeared all the way down, where he must have dropped. Then, whoever did it dragged him over to the nearest tent flap— that one there— unlaced it, dragged him outside, dumped him by that big white statue, came back in and then laced the tent back up again. No prints on the tent opening."

Tony studied the tent flaps. They could only be laced or unlaced from the inside. Along the edge of one side, short loops of cord were sewn, one above the other. To close the flap, each loop had to be threaded through a corresponding eyelet along the edge of the other side, and then pulled down over the next eyelet, like a chain stitch. That meant they had to be laced closed from the top down and unlaced from the bottom up. Right now, all the flaps were unlaced, pulled apart, and tied back with bungee cords to the steel posts that supported the tent.

J.D. frowned. "There's only one reason anyone would go through all that trouble and drag the guy outside: because he needed more time. He didn't want the guard to find the body during the night."

"I'll talk to the guard," said Tony. "You finish up here. And let's hurry it up so these people can get back to work." He looked at the sculptures again. The naked lady did have pretty tits. But he really liked the one of the little boy fishing.

THREE

The guard arrived and an interview space was arranged in one of the artists' booths near the office. Two wicker chairs faced a wall of abstract watercolors that Tony tried to ignore. The guard's name was Gary. "Gary the Guard" he was proud to call himself. He was a bland, round man in his 60s, bald, with a beige mustache and dressed in a brown polyester uniform with heavy black shoes. He sat down stiffly and looked at his laces.

"Never heard a thing. Never saw nothing neither."

"Ever see Art Russo come in at night before?"

"Don't think so. But you can check the sign-in sheets to find out. I don't match faces and names much. Just make sure they got one of them ID badges on when they come in."

"Badges?"

"Yeah. All the artists have 'em. Wear 'em all the time. Have to have 'em on when they come in at night."

"So you check their badges and then make them sign in?"

"Yeah. Something like that." Gary the Guard lowered his eyes. "You gotta understand, I don't look at them real careful."

"Do you ever go out to the sculpture garden?"

"Don't have to. The security fence goes all around the tents, and that includes the sculpture garden. And all the tent flaps leading out

17

to the sculpture garden are laced up at six o'clock when the show closes."

"Last night, do you remember Art Russo signing in?"

"Yeah, I mean, you know, I just remember some guy coming in a little after ten. I was watching an old movie on TV. Oh yeah, and it was still raining, I remember that."

"You watch TV all night?"

"Yeah. Nothin' else to do."

"Did you see Gretchen Schmidt leave? That was about five minutes later."

"Yeah, I remember her signing out. Boy, she's somethin' else, know what I mean?" His whole face lit up as his hands rose, drawing curvy lines in the air.

Tony ignored the gesture. "Let me ask you this, Gary. Didn't you think it was strange that Art Russo never signed out? For that matter, neither did Taylor McGrath."

"Oh, about Taylor, he just came in to pick something up. His wife was waiting in the car. Couldn't have been here more than five minutes. I told him not to bother signing out. He was in a real hurry."

"But do you ever check up on the artists after they get here? Make rounds...patrol the place?"

"Every hour on the hour. I turn on the up-lights and walk all around the place."

He pointed to the overhead beams where several giant light canisters were directed up at the white canvas roof. "When there's artists here, they got their own lights on, so I don't need anything but a flashlight. But later, when everyone's gone, I put the up-lights on when I make the rounds. Then I turn them off again."

"Well, on your rounds, say at eleven, did you see Art Russo in his booth?"

"Come to think of it, no, I don't remember seeing him except when he came in."

"So you don't check the sign-in sheet to see if everyone's accounted for?"

18

"Not my job. Anyway, some of 'em refuse to sign in and some of 'em forget to sign out. I can't *make* 'em do anything, you know."

"You mean there could have been other people who came in through that entrance last night that aren't on this list?" Tony was trying to be patient.

"Not without me knowing. It's real easy to hear a car drive up 'cuz the gravel makes a whole lot of noise out here in the desert." Gary the Guard studied his shoelaces a minute and then looked back at Tony. "You know, sometimes the artists don't sign in because they're already here. I mean, sometimes artists just *stay* when the place closes at six, so they never actually leave and come back in. See what I mean? And since they haven't signed in, they don't sign out, neither."

"These people who stay, or who don't like to sign in, who are they?"

"Well, Eldon Melrose, for one. He's the photographer. He takes pictures of paintings and stuff for the artists. Usually he waits for the show to close, takes the paintings down from the artists' walls, brings 'em over to his booth where he got special lights and stands and stuff. After he shoots the pictures he brings the paintings back, hangs 'em up, and that way the artists' walls stay looking good while the show's open. Says the lighting's better at night, too. Anyway, he's here a lot, doing all that photography, and he never signs in or out. Never."

Tony was an amateur photographer himself, so he'd make sure to take a good look at Eldon's booth. He might pick up some pointers, or maybe even get some inspiration. He could use some inspiration. He hadn't taken pictures in months.

Gary shifted his ample rear end onto the other cheek and checked the laces of his shoes again. His round face was flushed and little half moons of sweat appeared under his arms.

Tony encouraged him with a smile. "So tell me, who else comes at night and doesn't want to sign in?"

Gary cleared his throat, looked up at the ceiling, cleared his throat again and looked down at his shoelaces.

"Well, only two, really. Derrick Hughes, for one." He pointed to the next booth, where a huge wooden sign with the name **Derrick Hughes** burnt into it western style was hung against a khaki-colored wall. Bronze horses, cowboys, cattle and Indians sat atop rough-hewn sculpture stands. Not bad, if you liked western stuff, thought Tony.

"He's one of those hot shot I-dare-you-to-try-'n-make-me-do-somethin'-I-don't-wanna kind of guys. Always wears those stupid western clothes, boots, cowboy hat, big huge silver belt buckle. Tough guy, always strutting around. Walks like he just got off a horse. Thinks he's John Wayne, for god's sake. He's only a sculptor. No big deal."

He leaned forward and lowered his voice. "I wouldn't want the Morrows to know, but I'm scared of that guy. He's tough, has a temper, too. I don't want to mess with him if I can help it. So I don't even ask him to sign the sheet anymore."

Tony nodded and Gary seemed relieved that this confession of inadequacy was over and accepted. He took a deep breath and continued.

"Then there's Jess. He works maintenance, part time. He comes at night when there's some job to do that would disturb the customers during business hours. He's what you call antisocial, know what I mean? Just plain antisocial. Anyway, he never signs in and I just leave him alone."

He leaned toward Tony in confidence, lowering his voice once more. "One of the artists, Peter Sterling, accused him of stealing a ring from his jewelry display case last week and there was a real big stink over that. They found the ring later, but Jess was really ticked. He won't talk to any of the artists anymore. Hates 'em all. Like I said, just plain antisocial. He'd be fired by now except his mom's a friend of the Morrows.

Tony closed his notebook and stood up. "Once more now, just so we're clear, last night you saw nobody else here— not Jess, the antisocial maintenance guy, not Derrick, the cowboy, not the photographer, what's his name? Eldon— only the people on this list?"

20

"I didn't say that."

"Well, then, who was here?"

"Derrick hung around for a while."

"What time did he leave?"

"I don't remember. Not real late, though."

"Didn't you hear him leave?"

"I don't remember. It was pretty noisy with all the wind and rain."

"Okay, Gary. One last question. Do you sneak a little drink now and..."

"No sir. No, I don't! Against my religion. I'm Mormon. No way, don't drink at all."

He stood up and leaned closer to Tony, certain that an important confidential relationship had been established. "John Amory, now he's a drinker. I think he comes down here every night just to get away from his wife and enjoy a few beers. Poor old guy. Don't know how he paints at all between the beer and the arthritis. Comes in almost every night and lots of times I walk him out to his truck. Last night I walked him out on my eleven o'clock rounds. Real nice guy, though, even if he does drink. Real nice."

"Now wait a minute. When you walked him out to his truck at eleven didn't you see Art Russo's truck still there? Didn't you think it strange that there was a truck parked outside and there wasn't anyone left inside?"

"No, not really. Sometimes artists leave their cars here overnight. Don't know why they do it, but they do."

"Well, how many vehicles were out there at eleven o'clock? Just yours and Art Russo's?

"I think so. Yeah. Two trucks, that's all."

Tony thanked Gary the Guard and walked down the south tent again to check on the progress in Art Russo's booth. They were taking the last of the photographs, removing the yellow tape and getting ready to leave. As he moved farther down the aisle he noticed the sign on the sea green walls in the next booth: **Peter Sterling ~ jeweler**. He checked his notebook to refresh his memory: 'Peter Sterling - ring stolen - accused Jess.' Now those were two guys he'd especially like to interview. But most of all, he'd like to interview Art Russo himself. Before he died.

FOUR

It was 8:30 in the evening before Kate found her father in Room 216 of the intensive care unit at St. Clare's Hospital and Medical Center. She recognized him by the muscular arm resting above the sheet and the powerful bulk of him under it. His head was bandaged so that only his mouth and jaw were visible. A ventilator tube came out the side of his mouth and smaller tubes draped and coiled out from several blinking machines and found their way down his arm, disappearing here and there under a variety of tapes and bandages. One of them made it all the way to the back of his hand, which lay at his side, perfectly still.

She touched his fingertips and whispered, "I'm here, Daddy. I'm here." His fingers didn't move. She couldn't remember his hands being that still. They were always smoothing, rubbing or patting the nearest object at hand, or else they were firmly gripped around some tool or utensil. He used his fingers to explore the texture, the shape, the heft of things the way most people used their eyes. And as far back as she could remember she had understood that he was happiest when he was working with clay, down in his basement work-room, where he disappeared every Saturday morning.

His hands were strong, but what a gentle touch he had. She remembered how he would rub the top of her head or play delicately with her fingers as if to discover who she was underneath, and how her mother would smile when he patted her fanny or rubbed her feet. She used to say that he could knead the dough for pasta as art-fully as he laid the bricks for the front walk.

But the most vivid memory of all was when he kept stroking the casket at the cemetery and how he wept when he couldn't touch it anymore. She was only ten, but that's what she remembered most about that day.

For a few minutes she tried to make sense of the blinking num-bers and graphs displayed on the little blue machines, but her eyes were moist and everything blurred. Then, abruptly, her shoulders slumped and she dropped down into the chair beside his bed, let-ting the strap of her purse slide down her arm to the floor. Her head fell back and tears flowed and she didn't make a move to wipe them away.

"Mrs. Russo?"

She bolted upright and instinctively pushed her hand into her pocket for a tissue.

The woman repeated, "Mrs. Russo?"

"No, not Mrs., *Miss*. I'm his daughter, Kate."

"Why don't we go down the hall, Kate. There's a little waiting room where we can talk, and maybe you could even get some rest. You look exhausted."

She led her down the stark white corridor to a tiny room where three straight chairs lined up on one wall and a large vinyl recliner on another, all pale blue, the same color as the walls. A triangular Formica table fit into the corner and held a box of tissues and a few old magazines. Someone had tried to cheer the place up with a blue and pink watercolor print but it did no good whatsoever. She thought of all the people who had gathered in this ugly little room over the years and all the hours they must have spent waiting, pray-ing, hoping.

"Please tell me, how is he? Has he been conscious at all? Is he in any pain?"

She stopped, frustrated and confused and feeling stupid with her questions. "I'm sorry. I can't think of the right questions to ask. I don't want to know about last night, about…the assault. I just want to know how he is now." She dabbed her eyes and pushed stray strands of hair off her face. "I don't even know who his doctor is. Are you the doctor?"

The woman smiled. "No, I'm one of the nurses. Dr. Sayed will be here soon and he'll answer all your questions. I want you to know that your father is getting the best care possible. He really is." She patted Kate's hand and repeated, slowly and gently, "He's getting the very best care. We're all looking after him."

Kate believed her. Right now she had no way of evaluating the hospital or the doctor or the staff. But she did know there were some people you could really rely on. She had learned that from her own experience, not from all the psychology classes she had taken. Martin told her repeatedly— he even mentioned it to all her friends right in the middle of her graduation party— that she relied too much on her own experience and, worse of all, on her intuition. It wasn't professional, he said. To hell with that, she thought. Right now, what else could she rely on?

"Just make yourself comfortable…people seem to like the recliner. I'll send the doctor in as soon as he arrives…it should be just a few minutes." The nurse left the room and closed the door softly.

The overhead fluorescents hummed annoyingly and the blue walls got on her nerves, so she opened the door a crack and turned off the lights. Settling back in the blue recliner, she blotted her face and took a series of deep breaths. She closed her eyes and forced her body to relax. In a few minutes she saw little blue machines with blinking eyes and tube-like arms appear from nowhere and line up, like toy soldiers, around her father's bed. As long as they were there, guarding him, she knew he would be safe but…

She drifted lightly in and out of her dream until the door opened wider and revealed, in the bright pillar of light, the shadowy silhouette of a tall man.

"Miss Russo? May I come in?"

"Yes, of course." She pointed to the light switch. "Go ahead, turn it on. Please, come in."

He was dark complexioned and almost handsome, with thick brown hair and large brown eyes.

She swiveled her legs over the side of the recliner and sat up straight, feeling pathetic, like a little girl in a doctor's office, still clutching a handful of damp tissues.

"I'd like to ask you a few questions, if you don't mind." His voice was calm and professional.

"You want to ask me...his medical history?"

"I'm sorry, Miss, I'm not the doctor. I'm Detective Bannigan from the Scottsdale Police Department. Tony. Tony Bannigan. And there are some questions I need..."

"You're what?" A detective...in the hospital? "Look, my father's in critical condition...and I'm here waiting for the doctor... and you walk in, just like that, and want to ask me questions?" She stared at him, her mouth open, nose running.

He continued in a careful, measured tone of voice. "I know this is a terrible time for you, but we want to get the guy who did this to your father. I'll just take a minute, all right?" His heavy eyebrows shot up, as if to solicit her agreement, and formed wavy horizontal creases across his broad forehead.

Before she could answer, he sat down in the chair by the door and took out a notebook and pencil. Then he looked back at her, with his eyebrows still raised, waiting for her response. She was sure he would want to talk about the awful thing that happened to her father and she wasn't ready for that. Maybe later, but just now she couldn't deal with it.

"I'm sorry, Detective, not now. I told you, I'm waiting for the doctor." She blotted her face. "I said, not now, please. Please, just leave." She pointed to the door and he left.

Two hours later she stepped out of the elevator into the lobby and immediately spotted Detective Bannigan standing by the

Information Desk where she had parked her suitcase. He stood erect, like a soldier at ease, legs apart, hands behind his back. She was going to find it difficult to be polite to this man who seemed so determined to intrude into her private life. Why couldn't he just leave her alone, at least for tonight?

He acknowledged her approach with a nod, and brought one hand forward as if to ward off any complaint. "I'm not going to ask you any questions. Honest. That can wait. I just thought you'd like your father's keys, you know, the keys to his house and to his truck. You'll be staying at his house, won't you?"

"Truck? He's got a truck? God, I hate trucks," she said as she reached for her suitcase. "Yes, I'll be staying at his house, but I sure don't know how to get there from here. I was just going to call a taxi tonight." It hadn't even occurred to her that she didn't have the keys to the house.

"Don't worry about the truck, Miss. It's real nice—a Ford F150. Brand new, automatic and everything. Easy to drive. I'll have someone bring it over here right now, and if you want you can just follow us to his house."

She was picking up her suitcase and trying to absorb the idea of having to drive a truck when her purse started ringing. Dang! She fumbled for her cell phone, irritated as usual by the silly tune it played. A comb fell out first, then her sunglasses.

"No cell phones in the hospital." The information clerk stood up and glowered at her, pointing emphatically to the door.

Dropping her suitcase and stuffing the comb and sunglasses in her pocket, she glared at the clerk and scurried out the door, finally extracting the phone, stamping her foot in frustration and pulling the strap of her purse back on her shoulder.

She had barely said hello when a crisp voice at the other end demanded, "Is that you, Kate? Are you in Phoenix?"

"Martin? Yes, hi, I'm in Scottsdale…at the hospital. I was just talking to the doctor and he said…"

He cut her off. "What hospital?"

"St. Clare's, the name of the hospital is St. Clare's."

"For heaven's sake, get him to the Mayo Clinic."

"No, no he can't go to Mayo...he can't be moved...no, St. Clare's is fine, really. The doctor said..."

"I'm serious, Kate, get him to..."

"Look, not now, okay? I gotta go. They're getting Daddy's truck..."

"He has a truck? You hate trucks. Ever since..."

"Well, apparently he just bought it...it's brand new, the detective said. They're driving it over right now."

"The detective? What detective? What's a detective doing there?"

"Detective Bannigan. I don't know why he's here. Look, I gotta go. I'll call you later..."

"For heaven's sake, be careful driving."

"Of course I'll be careful, Martin. I'll be fine. Yes, yes...I love you, too." And she hung up.

Detective Bannigan was standing next to her now, suitcase in hand, apparently ignoring the conversation. He quickly loaded the case into a shiny blue pickup that had pulled up to the entrance. A uniformed policeman got out and held the door open for her. When she stepped up into the cab Detective Bannigan said, simply, "Just follow us...we'll get you there in no time."

Once more tears welled up and cascaded, unchecked, down her cheeks. She was ashamed of the self-pity, but her mind was automatically ticking off all the things that were overwhelming her. Her father was in the hospital, critically injured. She was thousands of miles from home. She had to drive a damn truck. And there were policemen in her life—a *detective* breathing down her neck.

Actually, once she drove out of the parking lot and down the street, she found the truck wasn't so terrible after all. The new car smell had mingled with her father's familiar after-shave and was somehow reassuring. Propped up high, she could see all around her, not like in the little Honda she drove at home. For some reason it made her feel competent, capable, resourceful, even powerful. It was only when she drove up a little hill and the row of street lights revealed a series of familiar stucco walls draped with bougainvillea that she was brought back to her new reality, to her father's house in Scottsdale, Arizona, where she would stay for however long it took for him to get better.

Detective Bannigan followed her to the door and waited for her to turn on the lights.

"If you'd like, we can walk around and check things out to make sure everything's okay." His eyebrows shot up, forcing the wavy creases to return to his forehead.

Why couldn't he just go? All she wanted was to be left alone and go to bed. "Do you have to?" she asked, trying not to be rude.

"No, of course not. I just thought it might make you feel safer..."

"No, I'm fine, really." Just go!

"You sure?"

"Positive," she said through clenched teeth, forcing her face into a smile. She waited for him to turn around and then she closed the door firmly. Right away she opened it a crack and called out "thanks for your help." When she closed it again, this time more softly, she bolted it securely.

She had been at the house only once before, at Christmas time. That was less than two months ago. They had put the tree over there, between the patio door and the corner fireplace and had decorated it with colorful Mexican ornaments. She had loved it. Martin had joined them for a few days and he didn't like anything about Arizona, not the sunshine, not the desert, not even the ornaments from Mexico. After Martin returned to New Jersey her father had asked her, in all seriousness, "You're not really going to marry him are you? Isn't he just a little bit of a prick?"

At that, she had marched out of the room, packed her bag, and left in a huff. She was thirty-six and old enough to pick a husband. It was the first time ever that her father had made her angry and she had stayed angry until today. Now, of course, she was sorry she had lost her temper. Now, all she wanted was for him to get better and she wasn't so sure that was going to happen.

Dr. Sayed had not been very helpful. He had tried to explain the injuries, but he was so careful in what he said that Kate was left with more questions than answers. A CAT scan had found a subdural hematoma and the neurosurgeon had operated. They were concerned about mid-brain damage and were watching him carefully for any evidence of increased cranial pressure. "The brain is a pretty unforgiving organ," Dr. Sayed had told her, but then he added, "We are always hopeful, and you should be, too."

She wanted to be hopeful, but when she returned to her father's room and held his hand, whispering that she loved him and that he was going to be okay, he gave no sign that he heard her. None at all. It was hard to be hopeful after that.

She did not want to call Martin back. He would only continue the argument and she was tired. All she wanted was to take a shower and go to bed. So she turned off her cell phone and opened her laptop instead.

Martin honey - i'm exhausted...past my bedtime...they're taking good care of daddy. The house is fine and so's the truck...will tell you more in the am - kisses, Kate

FIVE

Tony Bannigan waited patiently in the lobby of St. Clare's Hospital convinced that Kate Russo would arrive soon. He was pretty sure she had gone to bed early last night—there was a two-hour difference between New Jersey and Arizona—and that she would be eager to see her father as soon as she got up. Visiting hours started in less than an hour, but Tony had already checked on Art Russo's condition in ICU. No change there. Although he was hoping Art would regain consciousness, it didn't look good. Tony knew that sooner or later he would have a homicide on his hands.

The interviews yesterday had not been very fruitful. Gary the Guard was right about John Amory. He was a gentle, middle-aged alcoholic whose arthritis had impaired his physical condition to the point where he was disqualified as a suspect. Today Tony would talk with Taylor McGrath and Gretchen Schmidt, the other two artists who had signed in Saturday night. Of course, there were three others—the ones described by the guard—the ones who often came at night but never signed in. Of those, he had already interviewed Jess, the maintenance worker.

Jess was a skinny, unpleasant young man, jumpy, sullen, and reeking of cigarettes. He had an alibi that could easily be checked and J.D. was following up on that now. Jess also had a record:

petty theft, possession, street stuff, for which he had done some time. Jess didn't like any of the artists and he was furious about the recent accusation of theft by the jeweler. Tony recognized a loner when he saw one and doubted that Jess was strong or vicious or motivated enough to bash someone's head in.

He watched an attractive, middle-aged woman come in through the hospital's double doors. She looked at the visiting hours that were posted near the entrance and then at her watch, and took a seat in the lobby not far from Tony. The magazine she picked up apparently didn't hold her interest and she thumbed through it distractedly, glancing at her watch every few minutes. Her face was familiar. Of course! He had seen her yesterday in the sales office at the art show when he had met the staff. Her name was Connie, if he remembered correctly. Well, well...perhaps Art Russo has a girlfriend.

The doors opened again. He recognized Kate immediately, but only by her navy blue blazer and long legs. She looked altogether different. Yesterday she was a mess, her hair pulled back in an untidy ponytail, tissues stuffed in her pockets, face all red and blotchy. Although he couldn't see her face very clearly from where he was sitting, he sure liked the way her dark hair, cut just above her shoulders, bounced up and down as she walked.

She, too, looked at the sign and then at her watch. Instead of entering the lobby, she turned down the hall to the cafeteria. He decided to give her time to get settled before he approached her. Perhaps she wouldn't be so prickly this morning.

He knew from years of experience that people responded in a variety of ways when violence suddenly invaded their lives. It all depended on their personalities and their relationship with the victim. Some screamed obscenities, others needed to be hugged, and a few seemed to withdraw into their own worlds. Dysfunctional relationships got exaggerated. Family members often blamed each other. Sometimes they blamed themselves. You never knew. It was best to be tolerant and patient and a little detached. Let them get over the initial shock and then, maybe, they'd settle down enough to be helpful.

He got a cup of coffee and a bagel and headed toward her table. She was sitting at the back of the cafeteria, studying the front page of the newspaper with such intensity that he had to cough to get her attention. She raised her head quickly and he found himself looking into the largest, clearest and most amazing almond-shaped eyes he had ever seen. They were hazel, almost green, with clearly defined lids that were fringed with long lashes. He didn't pay much attention to the rest of her face, except to notice her high cheekbones and a sprinkling of freckles across her nose.

He could tell by the way her eyes didn't quite focus on his that she really didn't want to talk to him, but that she would probably tolerate his presence. That would have to do.

"Sit down, Detective. I know I have to talk with you sometime, so it might as well be now."

"Reading about our Governor?"

"Governor? Dang! I was just trying to figure out who she was." She explained, a little embarrassed, "I like to cover the captions and see if I can guess who the people are and why they're in the paper. I thought she was a lawyer..."

"That's pretty good, actually. She used to be Attorney General and now she's our Governor."

Kate studied the photo again and folded the paper carefully, front page up, displaying her short, uneven fingernails. They seemed to belong to the Kate Russo of last night, he thought, the Kate with the tissues and red eyes and ringing cell phone.

And then, as if on cue, the cell phone rang inside her purse. What an irritating tune it played. This time she found it quickly and whispered into it, "I'm at the hospital and no cell phones are allowed. I'll have to call you back...yes, I love you, too."

She gave him a brief, apologetic smile. He liked her smile as much as he liked her eyes.

"I keep forgetting to turn the dang thing off. Sorry."

He wanted to delay the few questions he had so he could look at her eyes some more and maybe get a little conversation going.

"What do you do for a living, Kate?"

"Nothing, actually. I was supposed to start a job today."

"Doing what?"

He saw her bristle slightly. "Are these questions necessary? I don't want to be difficult but I don't see how the details of my life could possibly be important to your investigation." She frowned and looked down at her coffee, displaying once more the rows of luxuriant lashes.

"Sorry," he said. "I was just making conversation. I was simply interested in what it is you do. After all, you know what I do..."

"Detective, this is not exactly a social occasion. Could you please just ask your questions so I can get upstairs and see Daddy?"

Daddy? He didn't know any grown woman who still called her father Daddy. He couldn't decide if it was charming or childish.

"Right. Well, from what we've learned so far your father was well liked and respected. We can't find any enemies or a motive, so it's possible the attack may not have been meant for him specifically. He might have just gotten in the way of something else that was happening. Apparently he doesn't have a record or anything."

At this, Kate sat up straight and glared at him as if it were improper to even mention her father and a record in the same sentence.

Tony continued. "And if that's the case, our investigation will go one way, but if it was a personal attack we'd look at other things. So right now we're just going through a process of elimination."

"My father has no dark past, if that's what you want to know. Some people think everyone with an Italian name is a part of the Mafia or something. They're just stupid, of course." She looked at him defiantly and he wondered what had made her so sensitive.

"Your father might be a great guy, Kate, but even great guys can have enemies." He smiled at her, attempting to keep a casual demeanor. "So the question is, do you know of anyone who might want to harm him? Someone with a grudge? Someone jealous? Someone...?"

"No. Absolutely not. Everyone loves Daddy. Really. He has lots of friends. Worked hard, was a stonemason. And he's a churchgoer, a member of the St. Vincent de Paul Society, for heaven's sake. He lived in the same house in New Jersey for over twenty-five years, ever since my mother died..."

"What about lady friends, romances, love affairs that could have caused problems?"

"Really, Detective! You don't think some woman..." She shook her head and took another sip of coffee. "Actually, if you must know, there was one girlfriend I knew about. He saw her on and off for a few years. It didn't work out." She shrugged her shoulders. "She wanted to move to Florida and play golf. Not exactly my father's preference."

"Then why did he move here?"

"He was retiring. He had some health issues and thought the warmer climate would help. But mostly because there's an active art community in Scottsdale and he wanted to start sculpting on a professional level. It's been his hobby for years."

"Any lady friends out here?"

"I doubt it. He never said anything to me."

"Well, sometimes fathers don't share everything with their daughters."

"He never kept secrets like that. I'd know."

Tony must have appeared skeptical, because she sat up straight and got that testy look again. "Look, Detective, I can't read peoples' minds or anything, but I do have certain insights. My father and I are close, and besides, I'm pretty intuitive—I just got my master's in psychology and..."

"...and that's why you try to analyze people from their pictures in the newspaper?" He was just teasing, but as soon as he said it he knew she would take it as sarcasm. And he was right.

She immediately flipped the newspaper over, smacking the photo on the tabletop. Then she got up and left the cafeteria with long deliberate strides, her hair bouncing with each step. Wow, he thought, admiring the view. But immediately a second thought intruded: stay professional, you jerk.

He watched as she got in the elevator right behind the attractive woman who had been waiting in the lobby.

Taylor McGrath and his wife were in their booth at the far end of the north tent. A couple in their 50s, they looked alike, dressed alike, and Tony would soon discover, talked alike, finishing each other's sentences as they apparently had done for years. Taylor worked at the easel, painting western landscapes from photographs he had taken. Utah, Tony guessed. His wife sat at a little desk with a stack of brochures, a guest book, a checkbook and a variety of file folders. An amicable division of labor.

They decided to go to the café for coffee where it was possible to talk out of the earshot of customers who were strolling around the tents. Tony looked out to the sculpture garden, so cheerful in the sunshine, and for the first time noticed the plump nudes with little gold fig leaves which stood on pedestals not far from Jesus. He couldn't help smiling.

"What brought you here Saturday night?" Tony began.

"We had sold a painting and were going to ship it..." he said,

"...but we left the customer's address on our desk..." she said,

"...and since we promised to mail it first thing in the morning..." he said,

"...we drove back to get it." The partnership had spoken.

"Did either of you see John Amory?"

"Yep, sure did," he said. "He was painting when I passed by his studio."

"But I didn't," she said. "I stayed in the car. It was raining and there was no point in both of us getting wet."

Tony looked at the wife, wondering if she were the observant type. "What exactly did you see while you were sitting in the car? Did anyone leave, go in, anything?"

"Nothing special. I just looked at the cars parked there and thought how strange it was for people to work so late. They should be home with their families and..."

"How many cars—or trucks—were there?"

35

"Oh, let me see. Four altogether, I know that. Three trucks and one car, I think.

"Four besides yours?"

"Yes. I saw four...vehicles."

Four? The guard would have one, of course, and so would John Amory and also Gretchen Schmidt. That's only three. Art Russo hadn't arrived yet. So whose was the fourth?

"Could you describe the...vehicles?"

"Oh, no. I don't know anything about...vehicles. Taylor is the one who knows about things like that," she said.

"And I didn't even look at them. Just ran in quickly, to get out of the rain," he said.

"So, you saw no one but the guard and John Amory?"

"Sure didn't."

"Did either of you know Art Russo?"

"Sure didn't. We're here to sell as much artwork as we can. We don't socialize much. People here are real nice..." he said,

"...but we stay close to our studio. We've never even been over to the south tent..." she said,

"...and we always bring our lunch, so we don't meet people in the café..." he said,

"...and we never go to the wine and cheese parties the artists have every few days." The partnership had spoken again and Tony got the picture. The only thing that surprised him was that artists could be so dull. Of course, it was nice to eliminate one more suspect.

SIX

After he left the McGraths, Tony crossed the lobby and headed down to the south tent. It was a half-hour before he was scheduled to meet with Gretchen Schmidt, the only other artist who had signed in Saturday night. He slowed down as he came to Art Russo's booth. It had been all cleaned up and the sculpture looked very handsome. The man definitely had talent, Tony thought as he bent close to examine the bronze head of a young woman with windswept hair and a sweet smile. Then he looked again at the boy fishing and thought about his son.

Something on the floor caught his eye. A corner of paper, almost black, stuck out from under the freestanding wall. He nudged it out with his fingertip. It was a photograph of a sculpture, a mother holding a child, and it was obviously the work of Art Russo. But Tony noted that there was no mother and child sculpture on display.

A group of customers leaving the jewelry booth next door distracted him. He quickly glanced at the sign to recall the jeweler's name and slipped the photo between the pages of his notebook.

"Peter Sterling? Do you have a few minutes to talk? I'm Detective Bannigan, Scottsdale Police."

Peter smiled brightly, a charming male model kind of smile. He was perhaps 40 years old and was dressed in an expensive golf shirt and pleated wool slacks. Tony noticed his Rolex watch and guessed that his shoes were Italian. Expensive Italian. Everything about him, including his haircut, looked elegant, in a casual sort of way, and he had the kind of boyish grin and easy manner that Tony always associated with a sense of entitlement.

"Yes sir, I'm Peter Sterling. Frankly, I'd rather sell you some jewelry but I'd be happy to talk to you about Art — I guess that's what you want to talk about." He was carefully returning items to the display case. "But I can't tell you much because I just got back this morning."

"I was looking for you yesterday," said Tony. "Strange you weren't around on a Sunday. That would be a good day for sales, wouldn't it?"

"Yeah, but I was out of town. Went down to the Tucson Gem Show."

"Well, then, perhaps you can just tell me about Art, what kind of a guy he is, and what kind of friends he had, or enemies, if there were any."

"All I can say is that he's a really great guy. Helpful, too. I'm not handy with electricity and stuff so he put my lights up for me." He pointed to his complex overhead lighting system, which included everything from pinpoints to floods. "And then he laid Vicki's carpet for her. See what a nice job he did?" He pointed across the way to a carpeted booth with large acrylic paintings and a long work-table crammed with colorful jars of paint and a half-dozen coffee cans stuffed with brushes.

"Vicki's a single mom and her little boy spends most of his time here. The darn kid gets under foot a lot, but Art, he was always kind to her and little Zach."

"Was there anyone who caused Art any trouble? Customers? Other artists? Anyone at all?"

"Sure. The same guys we all have trouble with. There's always a few of them wherever you go. You know the kind."

"Well, who for instance?"

"Derrick's one. He just makes everyone's life miserable. But he was really nasty to Art. They're both sculptors, you know, and Art's been selling his stuff faster than Derrick has. I suppose Derrick just didn't like the competition. Cut into his paycheck."

"Ever hear Derrick make any threats?"

"No. Derrick doesn't say much. He just breathes intimidation. But you really ought to talk to him. It wouldn't surprise me a bit if..."

"Anyone else?"

"Well, there's Jess. He's one of the maintenance guys. Trouble, just trouble. You ask him to do something and sometimes he does it and sometimes he doesn't. He hates everyone, but he seemed to be especially nasty to Art. I could never figure that out. But you ought to check him out as well. He's been in trouble before, I think."

"I hear you accused Jess of stealing some jewelry."

"Yeah, a ring. That was a mistake, I admit. But he was slinking around here that morning doing god-knows-what so I figured he had the opportunity. Apparently I must have dropped the ring myself because I found it a few hours later, under my workbench."

Tony looked over at a small workbench covered with tiny drills, a lighted magnifying glass and what looked like dental instruments. Next to it, several small machines were bolted to a heavy board that lay across the floor along one of the walls. At the end of the display counter there was a small skirted card table where Tony supposed supplies were stored.

He knew Gretchen Schmidt would be waiting for him so he thanked Peter and was about to move on when Peter unlocked the jewelry case and grinned up at him. "Hold on a minute, Detective. Wouldn't you be interested in a little piece of jewelry for your wife? Earrings? A ring?"

Tony smiled back and shrugged. "No wife." Not any more. And not ever again.

As he moved on he thought how wrong Kate had been. Apparently there were at least two people who didn't like her father.

A few booths farther down the aisle he met up with Gretchen Schmidt. Gary the Guard's description of her fell considerably short of the mark. She was at least six feet tall and looked like a Viking princess. Her white blond hair was arranged in tiny braids that wrapped around her head like a crown. Little tendrils escaped the arrangement and formed long, delicate bangs. Her shoulders and hips were broad, her waist tiny. The most alluring part of her was provocatively covered by a long, low cut tunic, which clung to her hips and thighs. She wore black tights and had apparently kicked her shoes into the corner by her backpack. Her eyes were baby blue and her lips the color of wine.

She was, very simply, amazing to look at. And her paintings were almost as amazing. Oversized florals, somehow erotic, were painted on dramatic backgrounds of deep emerald, or crimson, even black.

Right from the outset Gretchen seemed eager to help, to make Tony's job pleasant. She smiled a lot, with just the tiniest touch of flirtation, and constantly fiddled with her hair and the ID badge that rested precariously on her left breast. When she showed Tony the painting she had finished late that Saturday night her blue eyes searched his face anxiously for approval. Quickly disappointed, she frowned, saying, "I guess it's not really very good. I have trouble with tulips."

Tony knew he had failed some kind of sensitivity test, so he forced himself to examine the bright purple tulips very carefully. Finally he managed a comment on how transparent the flowers looked. "Really? You think so?" That seemed to be all Gretchen needed. Her smile returned immediately.

First, Tony asked her about her car. She drove a Camry. Next he asked if she had seen anyone in the tents Saturday night. No, only the guard. What about Art Russo? No, she hadn't seen Art. But she sincerely hoped that he would recover, he was such a nice man.

"But you signed out at 10:20 and Art was here at 10:15. Didn't you have to pass by his booth on the way out?"

"Well, yes, but he wasn't there." She looked confused, as if she had given him the wrong answer. It seemed to Tony that she wanted to help so badly that she was searching her memory for a better answer. Finally, she said hopefully, "I went to the ladies' room before I signed out. Does that help?" She raised her hands, which were streaked with paint, as an explanation.

"Did you see Jess that night?"

"I don't think I know Jess. But if he was here, I didn't see him. Sorry."

"Did you see Eldon that night? I'm sure you know Eldon, the photographer."

"Yes, everyone one knows Eldon, but I didn't see him either. He's here a lot at night, but I didn't seem him Saturday. I'm really sorry."

"What about Derrick? Do you know Derrick? Did you see him?"

She turned back to her painting and said quietly, "No, no one."

Then she dipped her brush into a saucer of crimson paint. When she bent over to apply the paint to a half completed watercolor, he got an eyeful of her charms. She saw him look at her so she smiled at him sweetly. "I hope I helped and I really hope Art gets better. He's a very nice man." Then she bit her lip, frowned intently, and slid the brush with one stroke across the length of the paper.

Tony's next stop was Eldon's booth, which was the very last one at the end of the south tent. It looked more commercial than the others, almost like a retail shop.

His display walls were painted black and featured a shiny silver sign that read **Eldon Melrose ~ Photographer**, and in smaller letters underneath, **by appointment only**. The walls were divided into four sections and Tony looked carefully, eager to examine the work of a professional photographer.

The first section was devoted to photographs of artwork: paintings, sculpture, even jewelry. The photos were good, but not carefully done. Tony thought that the focus was soft and that the three-dimensional objects had not been carefully composed within the format.

The next section was labeled 'Special Events.' Tony didn't recognize any of the celebrities, but there were shots of dinners, banquets, openings. They, too, were competent for an amateur, but not really professional. And what was the point? Was he trying to sell the photographs? Sell his services?

On the third section of the wall hung a large framed collage representing an Arizona sunset. Upon closer inspection he discovered it was made up of postage-sized snapshots of dozens of nude models, none of them particularly attractive. The pictures were not especially pornographic or even very interesting.

The final section of the wall was covered in black felt and had overhanging halogen spotlights. A small black stand was placed in front of the wall. Tony imagined this was where Eldon photographed the artwork after the show closed at night.

But Eldon himself was nowhere to be found. So Tony took out his notebook and wrote 'Eldon' as a reminder. Then he wrote 'Derrick' and finally, remembering the attractive woman at the hospital this morning, he added 'Connie.' Oh yes, and he wanted to get with J.D. about that extra truck in the parking lot.

But right now he was calling it quits. He was going to have dinner—with his mother.

SEVEN

Tony was relaxing in the living room of his mother's house while she was in the kitchen doing the dishes. They had just enjoyed a dinner of green corn tamales and a large salad. He wasn't allowed in the kitchen except on holidays when he prepared his famous *chiles rellenos*; otherwise the room was reserved for the women of the family.

His mother, Inez, was not only a wonderful cook, but believed cooking was akin to godliness. As if to emphasize this point, the Virgin of Guadalupe stood on a table in the corner of the kitchen, flanked by a vigil light and a vase of artificial flowers. A photo of his father, Police Officer Ryan Bannigan, killed when Tony was in high school, stood beside the Madonna.

Inez Bannigan was a handsome and sturdy woman of 60. Her hair was still black and she wore it in a no-nonsense bun at the nape of her neck. She never wore slacks, even to clean her house, which was often untidy and cluttered but always immaculate. The living room furniture was a con-glomeration of things bought secondhand or at discount stores over many years of penny-pinching and she was completely satisfied with the results. Framed black and white photographs that Tony had taken of street corners and storefronts in south Phoenix hung, slightly crooked, over the sofa.

Inez was brought to this county as a little girl, but her education had been limited and she spoke with a noticeable accent. Each morning she read the newspaper carefully, and she even formed a book club with several of her neighbors because she wanted to be as well informed and as American as her children. Sometimes the results of her efforts were amusing, as she would occasionally twist newly learned words and expressions beyond recognition. In this regard she tolerated correction, but never, ever, laughter.

She arranged to have dinner with each of her children once a week. Sophia, a law student, came on Tuesday. Angela, a schoolteacher, came with her husband and their daughter, Angelina, on Saturday. Monday was Tony's night. Then on Wednesday, everyone gathered together, often with aunts, uncles, cousins, assorted widows, friends and neighbors.

There were special rules regarding dinner at Inez' house. These were observed conscientiously by family and friends alike. The two most important rules were that grace be said before anyone picked up a fork, and that all dinner table conversation be courteous. Absolutely no business or politics were to be discussed until coffee was served.

"Tonio," his mother called out from the kitchen, "you want coffee?"

"Yes, Ma, I'd like some coffee." He already had far too much coffee today but he knew his mother loved to chat after dinner, asking him questions and delaying his departure.

She joined him in the living room and right away, as expected, came the questions.

"The man who was hurt—hurt and left by the statue of Jesus. How is he?"

"Pretty much the same. Still in a coma. I don't think the doctors are too hopeful."

He told his mother all about his cases—all, that is, that was public knowledge. It was just what his father used to do. She simply wanted to know who to pray for, their names, ages, and special circumstances. She considered this to be her full-time job.

"I've been praying very hard for him. I tell God that Jesus looked after him that whole night, so He should keep looking after him. He shouldn't desert him now."

44

"I'm sure God will take your advice, Ma." Then he added, "The man's got a daughter, so you ought to pray for her, too."

"A daughter? How old?"

"I don't know. Around thirty-five, I guess. She just flew in from New Jersey."

"Oh, from far away. Poor thing!" Inez had never been east of Arizona, so New Jersey might as well have been another country.

Her eyes got teary. "I know how she feels. All alone, her father so sick."

Tony waited for the story that was sure to come. With his mother, there was always a story.

"Before you were born, Tonio, your grandfather was very sick, dying, in Merida, Mexico. I was the only one who could go to him. When I got there I didn't know anyone. I stayed in his little house and cared for him the best I could. For three weeks I took care of him. So hard it was."

"What happened to him, Ma?"

"He got worse and worse. I didn't know how to find a good doctor. Then of course he died. I had to find a priest and a church and a coffin and a cemetery. So hard it was."

"I'm sorry, Ma. I guess I don't remember hearing that story."

"That's a long time ago. But this girl, what's her name...?"

"Kate."

"Well, Kate's story is a little like mine, no? You understand, she is having a hard time, too, just like me."

Suddenly her eyes widened and her eyebrows shot up, forming wavy creases across her forehead. Then she smiled, one of her knowing, mischievous smiles.

"Is she pretty, Tonio?"

"Oh, Ma!" he laughed. "How'd you know?"

"You must invite her to dinner, Tonio!"

"I can't do that, Ma!"

"The early bird gets the girl, Tonio."

"The *worm*, Ma. The early bird gets the *worm*."

"Who gets the girl, then?" his mother asked, seriously.

He hid a smile. There was no use explaining.

"You'll invite her for Wednesday dinner. Everyone will be here. I'll cook something special and she will be happy, you'll see."

"Ma, I can't do that!"

"Why not? She's not what you call a suspect. Not even a witness." Inez had a very limited police vocabulary but she enjoyed using it as often as possible. "What harm is done? We won't talk about what happened. Not a word! You know the rules. We'll just talk about happy things." She stood up, signaling the end of the discussion.

"You'll do what I say, okay?"

"Sure, Ma," he lied. There was no way he'd invite Kate, and even if he did, he knew she wouldn't accept. It was very clear she was in love with someone at the other end of her damn cell phone.

Tuesday morning Kate left the hospital and headed for the art show in her father's bright blue pickup. Mrs. Morrow had called her last night and suggested that she act as her father's representative while he was in the hospital. It would give her something to do and she might even sell some of his work.

After careful consideration she decided on a simple schedule; she would visit her father in the morning, spend most of the day at the show, and return to the hospital in the evening. When she e-mailed Martin about her plans, he replied immediately that she hadn't gone to graduate school just to become a salesperson. She should spend her time finding a better doctor for her father, and figuring out how to get him out of that tiny hospital and into the Mayo Clinic.

So this morning she told Dr. Sayed that she might be interested in getting a second opinion. He said that would be fine with him, that he understood her concern and would even give her some names if she wished. But then, she thought, whose will be the better opinion? Dr. Sayed was rated among the top five in

Arizona for trauma cases, according to the research she had done on the Internet. And St. Clare's, though small, was regarded as one of the best facilities in the county. Finally, she made a conscious decision, based on the intuition Martin so despised, to trust Dr. Sayed and St. Clare's, even though it was apparent her father's condition was not improving.

At least this morning the detective hadn't disturbed her. She had enjoyed a leisurely cup of coffee in the cafeteria, reading the paper and successfully guessing that the couple on the front page was a local politician and his girlfriend, and that there was some kind of scandal. Detective Bannigan might make fun of her, but so what? Some people did crossword puzzles. She did people.

As she drove east to Scottsdale she saw the big white tents from a distance, shining brightly against the deep purple of the McDowell Mountains. Large paloverde trees and ocotillos and occasional saguaros dotted the desert landscape on either side of the tents. Morning shadows stretched diagonally inside an enormous sculpture garden where she could see several bronze horses galloping past a pair of chubby marble nudes. Gracefully swaying poles supported discs of burnished silver that twinkled in the morning sun and floated over the bright green grass.

The entrance to the tents was at the back, wide and inviting and flanked with blooming potted plants. Heavens, it might still be snowing in New Jersey, she thought, and here she was, in jeans and a blazer, enjoying the sunshine and the geraniums and the desert mountains.

At the office she was given her official badge, *Kate Russo, Representative*. Then Mrs. Morrow toured her around the lobby and café and escorted her down the south tent, past displays of bright impressionistic paintings, delicate enamels, intricately woven baskets and bold abstracts. There were watercolors, wood carvings, tapestries, and all these things came in such a variety of sizes and shapes and colors that Kate could barely take it all in.

Halfway down the aisle she stopped short and caught her breath. Scattered in front of the dark gray walls of her father's booth were at least a dozen sculptures on display stands and turntables, each lit with its own overhead spotlight. They were wonderful! She had always loved his work, but to see it here, so nicely presented, was thrilling.

Kate knew immediately that this new work was better, freer, more emotional than anything he had done before. She could see the expressive movement of his hands right in the finished work, the way each push and pull of his fingers was evident. The figures seemed to have a life of their own because their gestures and body language had been captured with such accuracy and affection.

After Mrs. Morrow left, she examined each piece carefully, smiling at the simple titles: *Girl with Dog*, *Boy Fishing*, *The Chef*. She especially liked *Old Man Reading* and *Nude Bather*.

The booth looked right out to the sculpture garden. She could see two bronze children sitting on a bench, and a marble lion poised to jump down from its tall pedestal. Over to one side, a dignified Indian scout shaded his eyes into the sun. Several rotund nudes cavorted with glee, and oh, what a lovely Christ figure stood in the center, tall and majestic and serene.

The sunlight was intense, the sky a piercing blue and the grass shimmered in the breeze. Visitors strolled around, sipping soft drinks and examining the artwork, while a handful of children crawled all over the huge bronze alligator that slithered through the nearby grass.

Kate walked over to the bench and sat down next to the life-size children. She looked over at the statue of Jesus and thought that He too would enjoy this day, the scenery and weather and all the artwork on display. She wanted to pray, but the words wouldn't come, not here, not after all these years. So she just whispered quietly, "Jesus, sweet Jesus, please don't let him die."

She jumped when the phone rang. It was Martin. She tried to describe the beautiful day, how the tents gleamed white against the mountains and the sculptures cast purple shadows in the grass and her father's work had taken her breath away. But in the end she said yes, she had talked to Dr. Sayed about getting a second opinion...no, she didn't know what she was going to do about her job at the clinic...and yes, of course she loved him.

EIGHT

Peter Sterling looked up from his workbench, removed his visor, and smiled a welcome. He was so attractive and charming that Kate guessed he had little trouble selling the outrageously handsome jewelry that was arranged in neat rows in the display cabinet. One of the rings, squarish rather than round, caught her attention and she wished she had long polished fingernails so she would have an excuse to buy it.

She was still peering into the cabinet when, out of the corner of her eye, she saw a little boy's head pop out from under a long skirted worktable across the way.

"Mommy, I want my juice!"

The mother, young, tan and athletic, handed him his juice and smiled over at Kate.

"Hi, I'm Vicki. I'm so sorry about your dad. I hope he's okay. He's been real helpful and he's been so nice to Zach." She looked down at the little sneakers protruding from under the table skirt.

"That's his fort. A very well supplied fort, I might add. He's got blankets and pillows, cars and trucks, stuffed animals and soldiers — you name it. But he's really happy there, in his own little world...and at least I know where he is." She wiped her hands on her big black apron, creating fresh new streaks of acrylic colors over the

49

old. "So how *is* your dad? Will you be working for him until he comes back?"

"I plan to. I don't really know what I'm supposed to do, but I guess I can learn. I think I want to start by rearranging some of the sculpture. His work is so beautiful but the arrangement doesn't seem well balanced or something. I really don't know much about these things. What do you think?"

"I think you're absolutely right," said Vicki.

"And I agree," said Peter. "Your father was thinking about making some changes anyway. We can help you do it right now if you'd like. No problem at all."

It didn't take long for the three of them to decide on a plan, and they quickly rearranged the booth. They pushed the smaller bronze pieces together and moved the little desk and chair to the side, next to two empty sculpture stands. The two clay pieces changed places, and the most important sculpture, a portrait of a young woman with windswept hair, was placed in the center. Finally, the spotlights were redirected and the sign was lowered a few inches. Kate was pleased with the results. What good neighbors she had.

"Wow, is everyone as helpful as you two?" asked Kate, admiring the new arrangement.

"Sure. Well, almost," said Vicki. "Just stay away from Derrick. You can't miss him, all gussied up like a cowboy. Nobody likes him, and he doesn't much like anybody, either. He certainly didn't like your dad."

"And let's not forget Jess," Peter added. "He's a good-for-nothing creep, does maintenance. Don't know why he bothered your dad, but he sure did."

Derrick and Jess. She would have to remember the names. It was strange and a little frightening to think there were people who hadn't liked her father. She never thought that could happen... wasn't that what she had told Detective Bannigan?

Then Peter, in his charming way, grinned again, saying "But don't worry. Everyone else is terrific. Just like us."

"Miss Russo? I'm Francie Nielsen." An elderly lady, nicely dressed in an expensive but out-of-style cashmere jacket, approached Kate and patted her on the arm. "Mrs. Morrow called to tell me you would be here today. You see, my husband and I were here Sunday morning to order one of your father's sculptures. This one here." She pointed to *Old Man Reading* and paused. "I'm so sorry about what happened to your father. I do hope he recovers. What do the doctors say?"

Kate didn't know how to respond. She wasn't sure herself what his condition really was, so how could she explain it to anyone else? Mrs. Nielsen apparently mistook her hesitation for unspeakable sadness.

"Oh, my dear, you must have hope, you know. It's very important to have hope. And positive thoughts. Good thoughts, full of hope." She patted her arm some more before looking around the booth and exclaiming, "I see you've moved things about. Yes, very nice. Much better. You know, I really do like the one of the old man reading, but my husband always preferred this one, *Girl with Dog*. Is that an Irish setter? Yes, I do believe it is. A girl with an Irish setter. It reminds him of our granddaughter, Molly. I just don't know; which one do you like best?"

"Well, I..."

"The *Old Man Reading* is nice, you know, but I'm not sure if I like the bottom part. Do you? I mean, it looks a little heavy to me. But I love the posture. Your father does posture very well."

Kate was at a loss for words. It seemed the woman was just rattling on and Kate didn't know when or if to jump into the conversation.

"Last year, you know, we bought a Martha Pettigrew, and the year before that we bought a Dan Hill. This year we were going to buy a Derrick Hughes but when we saw your father's work we liked it so much better. He does posture so well. I'm just so sorry about your father..."

Kate managed a small 'thank you'. Would Mrs. Nielsen never stop talking about her father? Apparently not. She started right up again.

"...You know, when I saw him lying there, all bloody and dirty, it was just terrible." She dabbed at her eyes. "He looked so awful! I almost had a heart attack. Such a nice man, and to be all bashed and bloody like that, it's such a shame. I do hope he gets better, dear, but you have no idea how awful he looked..."

Mercifully, Vicki walked over and interrupted, escorting Mrs. Nielsen to the café and leaving Kate standing among her father's sculptures, stunned and trembling. She sat down and tried to get the image of her father, bashed and bloody, out of her head. Had Mrs. Nielsen been the one to find him? Where exactly did she find him? Actually, she didn't really want to know. She looked out at the sculpture garden and watched the visitors strolling around without a care in the world, and thought maybe she shouldn't even be here. How could she forget about her father's condition even for one instant? Martin was right. She should be looking after her father, not distracting herself here.

The moment she bent down to pick up her cell phone to call the hospital, she spotted a pair of snakeskin cowboy boots pointed in her direction, one foot tapping very slowly. She looked up and there was a real live cowboy standing right beside her, lean and mean. He was dressed in very tight jeans and a black western-styled shirt. His huge silver belt buckle was at eye level, so she had to lift her head to see his face. A soft gray cowboy hat sat low on his head and he glared out from under it with cold gray eyes. This had to be Derrick.

Her visitor didn't say a word as he carefully surveyed the newly arranged booth and then examined her with the same scrutiny and contempt. He frowned, turned on his boot heels, and ambled off, with swinging arms and a rolling gait. Everything about him said, "Don't mess with me." But she certainly wasn't going to let Derrick, or anyone else, scare her away.

A calm resolve replaced whatever she had felt just moments ago. She would stay and learn how to sell her father's sculpture.

She couldn't just sit in the hospital all day long. This was better. This was healthier. This was more productive. So this was what she was going to do.

A new customer wandered in, gave a cursory look around, and started asking questions about the 'pre-cast' list that was posted next to *Girl with Dog*. Since Kate had no idea what the list was for, she could only stammer vague explanations until the customer got impatient and simply walked away with a shrug.

"Dang," she thought, "I just lost a sale!"

It was then that she realized she didn't know what she was doing. She didn't know how to talk to customers, how to make a sale, or even how to describe her father's work. She didn't know where he kept his records or how much he had sold. She didn't know what the 'pre-cast' list was for. And what about his brochures? Should she give one to everyone who came into the booth? How could she tell a real customer from someone just strolling by?

When she reviewed her situation more calmly, she realized that the first thing she had to learn, in case the emotional Mrs. Nielsen returned, was how those 'pre-cast' lists worked, because they obviously had something to do with the ordering process.

The records her father had kept in his little desk eventually yielded some answers. It seems he sold bronze sculptures right from his inventory, like *Mother and Child*, which was listed as his very last sale. But he also took orders from his recently completed clay pieces, *before* they were cast in bronze. Apparently he wanted to have enough advance orders to pay the foundry cost, which was quite high. She figured that at the foundry he would order enough pieces to satisfy all the advance orders, plus any additional ones he might want for inventory.

On each of the two clay pieces her father had a 'pre-cast' list with room for ten names. There were already five orders for *Girl with Dog*, but no orders yet for *Old Man Reading*, which he must have just finished—his tools were still on the turntable stuck into mounds of clay. Everything else on display was bronze. She would have to check his studio at home to see if he had any more inventory.

Then later, at the office, she learned how to fill out the sales forms. Now, she thought, she had at least a basic understanding that could get her through the rest of the day. Tonight, she would study his brochures carefully so she could represent him intelligently. He deserved that much.

Tired, and ready to end her first day, she was preparing to leave when Mrs. Nielsen suddenly reappeared, chipper and smiling, as if their previous conversation had never taken place.

"You know what, dear? I decided to order both, one for my husband and one for me. We can afford it, so why not?"

Why not, indeed, Kate thought, as she wrote Mrs. Nielsen's name on each of the lists and filled out the sales forms. Now there was one order for *Old Man Reading* and six for *Girl with Dog*.

NINE

Zach finished his orange juice and looked through one of the tiny windows his mother had made for him in the canvas cloth that covered her table and made up his fort. There were three windows, each on a different side. He didn't need one on the fourth side because there was nothing interesting to look at and that was the side where he liked to arrange his vast army when he took a nap. He would line up his soldiers and animals and trucks on both sides of the throne he had just made for the new King.

He watched Kate carefully for a few minutes, wondering if she were as nice as the old man who used to work there. Zach liked him a lot, even though they had never spoken to one another. A couple of times the man brought him little boxes of raisins, which he didn't much like, but the raisins made great cannon balls when his soldiers needed them, and he used the boxes to make fortresses and bunkers and even a nice throne for the King.

He hoped the new person would bring him something even better than raisins. He thought popcorn would be good. Almost every afternoon he could smell fresh popcorn but no one ever gave him any. Popcorn would make better cannon balls than raisins — and then he could eat it.

He arranged his pillows in a row, lay on his back with his blankie and looked up at the stars his mother had glued to the bottom of the table. There were big gold and silver stars, and tiny ones in red and blue. He liked the blue ones best and began to count them. He always fell asleep before he counted them all.

When he woke up from his nap he was very hungry. He was glad he didn't have to go pee because then he would have to leave the fort and walk to the restrooms with his mother. She always took him with her to the ladies' room, which made him feel like a baby.

The opening to the fort was in the corner where two sides of the canvas skirting came together. He stuck his head out and demanded a snack. His mother was busy talking to someone, so he knew he would have to wait. He peeked out the second window and scanned the sculpture garden. The sun was so bright it made his eyes hurt. The enemy was still there, of course. He could see them all; the tall Indian and the galloping horse and the evil alligator were all staring at him. Strange silver space ships were lined up, ready to fire at his fort. He felt sorry for the children who were sitting so still on the bench near the alligator. He had never seen them move. Ever. They were probably scared to death.

Finally, a brown paper bag was set inside the fort along with a small carton of milk. He hoped it was a peanut butter sandwich. And please, no carrot sticks. He never ate them anyway. They made good rifles for his soldiers, but after a few days they weren't stiff anymore, so he had to put them in his pockets and try to flush them down the toilet. If they didn't go down, he hid them by throwing lots of toilet paper on top of them. Maybe they'd go down when the next person flushed.

After devouring his peanut butter sandwich and gulping his milk, he looked out the third window. He saw the man who always smiled and who frightened him because he looked like a robot with his goggles on. Sometimes he took off his robot eyes and then he looked better. But the man was the reason why Zach was worried about the King.

He had discovered the King when he snuck over to the man's fort. It was a much smaller fort than his but he thought maybe there was another boy hidden there, and if they became friends the two of them could battle the enemy together. But once he got there, there was no boy. There were a lot of plastic boxes, but no toys. But the wonderful thing he found in the other fort was a big soldier. It was so much bigger than any of his soldiers that he called him the King. The King was dark brown and was guarded by a wolf that sat at his feet. He had a smooth round crown on his head and a bird sat on his shoulder, probably a hawk who could fly out and spy on the enemy.

The King was pretty heavy, and Zach needed two hands to carry him across the aisle to his own fort. He almost dropped him twice. But he finally got him under the canvas, and now the King stood on a raisin box throne, tall and strong and guarded by all the soldiers and animals in his army.

The problem was that he couldn't tell his mother any stories about the brave new King. If she knew about him she would make him return the King to the smiling man with the robot eyes, and then Zach would have enemies on two sides of the fort.

So Zach decided to keep the secret to himself. But he was so afraid that the man would find out the King was missing and would try to get him back, that he ordered all his animals and all his soldiers to guard the throne bravely during the day. At night, he wrapped the King in his blankie and hid him under a pillow.

Tony sat at his desk and wondered if they would ever find the weapon. He even wondered if they would ever find the perpetrator. They had no fingerprints and only part of one shoe print. Rain could destroy a lot of clues and it was always difficult to come up with hard evidence in such a public place, but these were only excuses and they were running out of time.

"I'm sure he's going to die," he told J.D., "and when he does, we'll have a homicide on our hands and we won't know where to start."

"He can't die," said J.D. "Your mother's praying for him. You said so yourself."

J.D. was an avowed agnostic, mainly because he liked the sound of the word, but also because he didn't like to get dressed up to go to church on Sunday. He loved to tease Tony about his mother. Of course, he never had the nerve to tease Mrs. Bannigan to her face. If he did that he'd never get invited to dinner again.

"I just can't imagine anyone lying in wait in a dark tent in order to kill Art Russo. I mean, how would anyone even know he'd be there at 10:15 at night? Unless, of course, he was going to meet someone, but that doesn't seem to make much sense. But it is weird that he came in so late. And it's weird about the Jesus thing, too. I keep wondering if there's any significance to that, but the more I think about it the more I think, no, it was probably just the easiest place to dump him, the biggest statue to hide him behind."

He drummed his pencil on the desk. "And then there's that extra truck in the lot. We know the truck was there when the McGraths came at nine-thirty and that it was gone by eleven o'clock when the guard escorted John Amory to his car. The doc seems to think the assault happened right about then. So we've got to find out whose vehicle that was." He wrote 'extra vehicle' on a yellow post-it and stuck it to the side of his computer monitor.

J.D. added, "You know what I find strange about this? Everyone seems to like Art Russo so much. I spoke to dozens of artists yesterday and they all said he was a great guy. No one seems to have a motive."

"That's not entirely true. Peter Sterling told me that Derrick was jealous of Art's sales, and that Jess didn't like him, either, although he didn't know why. By the way, did you check out Jess' alibi?"

"Sure did and he's okay. Says he was home like a good little laddie, nice and quiet-like with his mommy. And according to his mother, they rented some movies and stayed home that night. She's a real nice lady, by the way."

"So how did she ever get a son like him?" Tony wondered.

"Now, now, Tony, You ought to know better than that. You're not nearly as nice as your mother..."

Tony interrupted. "Seriously, you know what I think? I think this whole thing has something to do with all that jewelry being right next to Art Russo's space. Maybe someone was trying to break in...if not Jess, then someone else. And Art could have surprised him...or her." He thought of Gretchen, 6 feet tall, who was just as physically capable of committing the crime as any man.

"Yeah, but that's not expensive jewelry, is it? I thought it was just costume stuff. I mean, in a place like an art show you don't expect the kind of jewelry that would inspire a heist or motivate a murder."

"Actually, I don't know a damn thing about the jewelry," Tony admitted. "But that's at least something we can look into. I do know that Peter Sterling said he was down at the Tucson Gem Show last weekend, and there's lots of expensive stuff bought and sold down there. So let's just see what we can find out."

"By the way," said J.D., "I heard that Kate Russo is down at the art show now, working in her father's booth."

Tony stopped drumming his pencil and sat up straight.

"How did you find that out?"

"I was talking to the Morrows today...suggesting that they lock the place up around eight or nine o'clock from now on. Anyway, that's when they told me about Kate."

Tony hoped she would have the sense, after what happened to her father, to leave the show before dark. Maybe he should see her again, just to tell her to be careful. Yeah, that's what he should do. But right now he had to concentrate on everyone's least favorite artist.

TEN

Derrick entered the interview room, swung one of the straight-backed chairs around to face him, and sat down, fixing his boots in imaginary stirrups about as far apart as if he were on a horse. He rested his hand on the lower rung of the chair like he would on an old saddle. His hat remained planted on his head in accordance with cowboy custom.

"I don't have to be here, you know, so this better be quick. I know my rights. And, frankly, I don't like cops."

Derrick glowered at J.D.—and J.D. knew why: he was not only short, he was also insignificant looking, and bigger men often tried to intimidate him. But J.D. had learned to stare right at their crotches, rather quizzically, and this usually unnerved them just enough to establish a level playing field.

Of course Derrick did not glower at Tony who was standing up, all 6-foot-2 of him, leaning casually against the wall with his hands in his pockets.

"So, Derrick, I see you've got a record of domestic abuse, like to rough up the ladies," Tony said, just for openers.

"You don't give a rat's ass about domestic abuse. Just get to the point. I got better things to do than come here and talk to you."

"Okay, then let's start with where you were Saturday night."

"Out drinking," was the rapid-fire response.

"The guard says you were in the tents."

"Maybe I was. But I left real early. And then I went out drinking," he said quickly.

"Where? And who with?"

"All around...Eldon," he shot back.

"Eldon, the photographer? How long have you two been friends?"

"Didn't say we were friends. Just said we were out drinking," was the instant reply.

"Okay, then, where'd you go?" Tony asked just as quickly.

"Dos Gringos, then Martini Ranch."

"Whose car did you drive?"

The questions and answers, which had been zipping back and forth like a ping-pong ball, suddenly came to a halt. Tony could see the hesitation. Derrick looked like a kid in school who didn't know the right answer. He pushed the brim of his hat farther down over his forehead, gave it a tap, and finally said, "Mine, we drove mine. I mean, I drove mine."

"We can check that out, of course," said J.D., staring at Derrick's zipper.

"And of course we will," said Tony as he grabbed an empty chair, flipped it around and pushed it to within a few inches of Derrick's before sitting down.

"So, Derrick, I hear you're at the tents a lot at night. What are you doing there?"

"What do you think I'm doing there? I'm working, of course. I got a big sculpture going. Ten horses. Three cowboys. Lots of action. It's eighteen inches high and thirty-six inches long. Big piece. Complicated piece." He paused, "Expensive piece, too."

"If you're just there working, why don't you want to sign in, like everybody else?"

"Why should I? I got a right to be there, they say so in the information packet. Says right there, artists can come in anytime they want. I'm from out of state. I don't have any other place to work during the show. Anyway, why should I sign in just for some nerdy little guard? You tell me, why do I need to listen to him?"

"Because the owners want it that way."

"Them? They're just happy if I sell a lot so they get their cut. They want me working and selling, working and selling. Well, that's just what I'm doing, working and selling. Not like some of the other two-bit sculptors who dawdle around, making their stupid stuff. Just a bunch of assholes, that's all they are..."

"Is that what you thought of Art Russo?"

"Don't put words into my mouth. I never even mentioned his name." He pushed his hat back to where it was before. "But if you were to ask me, I'd tell you I didn't much like him. He was trying to steal my customers so I had good reason not to like him, but I didn't hurt him, either. Like I told you, I was out with Eldon Saturday night."

"You figure you lost some sales because of Art? How much money would that amount to?"

"I don't know the exact amount. Probably one or two sales. Maybe three, four, five grand."

"That's a lot of money, Derrick. Some people would say that's a motive to get him out of the way."

"For a couple of grand? Are you crazy? You know how much I make each year? Believe me, a couple of grand's nothing, not a damn thing!"

"Really?" J.D. allowed his eyes to wander up to Derrick's face before coming back down. "We can check that out, too, you know."

Derrick glowered at J.D. but since he couldn't make eye contact he looked at Tony briefly and asked, "Are you guys finished, yet?"

"For now. We may want to get with you again, so make sure you hang around Scottsdale."

"Maybe if you do your job right you won't have to waste my time again."

Tony stood up to end the interview, amused that J.D. was still keeping the playing field level. They both watched Derrick swagger out of the building and across the parking lot, head held high and rolling slowly from one foot to the other. Just like he got off a horse,

Gary had said. Then he climbed into his black Silverado with its gun rack and *Wild Life* Idaho license plate and drove off.

Tony had arranged to meet with Connie, the nice-looking lady he had spotted in the hospital lobby—and Russo's girlfriend?—at the Scottsdale Cheesecake Factory. She didn't want to be interviewed in the tents and said she was uncomfortable coming to the station. Connie was a very gracious and youthful woman of 50 or so. She still had a cute little figure and was highly polished, from her leather loafers to her well-styled auburn hair. She had what Tony thought of as the country club look. He imagined that she was not in her element being interviewed in an assault case so he tried to take it easy.

"Thanks for meeting me, Connie. It's hard to find anybody who knew Art Russo very well since this was his first year at the show. You've been visiting him in the hospital so I thought you might be close friends.

"Oh, I didn't really know him any longer than anyone else. In fact, we just met when the show started in January." Her eyes danced around the room. "You know, I've worked at the show for five years now. It's such fun being there. For ten weeks I get to meet the most interesting people. The artists are just great. They come from all over, so it's energizing, you know what I mean?" She lowered her eyes, then looked out the window, then over to the waitress standing in the corner. "And the customers...well, we have buyers who come back year after year, some very wealthy ones, too. Some of them fly in on their private jets, go to the Phoenix Open, maybe the Barrett Jackson car auction, and then come to the show and buy art. Of course, we also have busloads of seniors, too—they're so sweet—who come in from Sun City..."

"You were saying...you just met Art when the show started?" Tony wanted the conversation to go somewhere.

"I'm sorry. I'm rambling. I can't help it. It's just hard for me to deal with this." She finally looked directly at Tony. "It's much easier to talk about other things. The fact is, Art and I met and liked each other immediately. You're young, so you understand how that can happen. Love at first sight, I guess. Anyway, I didn't tell anyone in the office about our romance. I didn't want people watching us, talking about us, you know what I mean?"

Tony nodded. Once she got started she seemed to want to go on, and that was fine with him. Something she said might be of help.

"I'm really worried about him. I guess I don't think he's going to make it." She was trying hard to keep her composure and was taking nervous little sips of coffee. "And I feel so badly for his daughter. I don't think Art told her about us so I'm trying to be very careful. I'd like to get to know her, to help her, but I think I'll wait a little longer."

"That's probably wise," said Tony.

"Anyway, we fell in love right away. That's never happened to me before, and I've been divorced fifteen years. He's so much fun, so creative, and so kind. He isn't wealthy or well educated, not like other men I've dated, but we just clicked." She stopped talking and blinked back tears.

"I'm sorry," Tony said. "This is obviously very hard for you. But there's something I'm curious about. Were you and Art out earlier that evening?"

"Why, yes, we were. We went out to dinner. Then afterward he said he had to make some changes to a piece of sculpture, so he drove me home, oh, just before ten, and then he headed out to the tents."

"Was he upset? Worried? Anything different at all?

"No, he was relaxed and...content."

"Did you meet anyone, see anyone while you were out?"

"No, it was just the two of us. A romantic little dinner at Arrivederci's. We didn't see anyone we knew."

"What about this, Connie. His booth is right next to Peter Sterling's. Is there anything really valuable in that display case? Something valuable enough to...?"

"No, I don't think so. The jewelry sales I see go through the office are between a hundred and several hundred dollars. Of course, for some people that's a lot of money. But there's a lot of valuable stuff that gets left around, like cameras, even laptops, and all the artwork, of course."

"That's kind of what I thought. So now there's only one other thing I need to ask. Since you're aware of what's going on in the tents—you know, like friendships, jealousies, other gossip—can you think of anyone, anyone at all, who might have had a reason to do this to Art?"

"No, no one."

"What about Derrick?"

"There's certainly no love lost there, but everyone knows that."

"What about Jess? I've heard he didn't like Art. Do you know why?"

"Jess? Oh, he's just a kid with some problems. I don't think he means any harm. He's not vicious; just frightened, I think."

"A loner, maybe?"

"Yes, that's it, a loner."

"If you think of something later, will you let me know?" Tony asked, giving her his card.

"Of course. And will you please, please not tell anyone about Art and me. I really don't want anyone to know."

There was only one person who might be interested in Art's love life and Tony knew he wasn't going to be the one to tell her.

ELEVEN

Kate hopped out of bed and the brochures she had been studying late into the night fell to the floor. She piled them onto the night table and searched for her old fuzzy slippers. Anxious to get an early start on the day, she scooted into the kitchen to make coffee, stopping on the way to turn on her laptop. She had e-mailed Martin last night about her successful day at the show and was waiting for his response. She was sure he'd feel differently when he learned she had sold over $3,500 worth of sculpture for her father on her very first day.

She brought her coffee into the spare bedroom which her father used as a studio and perched herself on a stool to study the bronzes arranged on the shelves across the room. All but two of them were identical to those at the show, part of his backup inventory. One was a delightful depiction of a woman carrying a young girl on her hip, entitled *Mother and Child*, which reminded her of a Daumier painting she had once seen. The other was a much smaller, and probably older, sculpture of St. Francis of Assisi.

She didn't understand why her father had not replaced the last *Mother and Child* he had sold with this one. She decided to bring it with her this morning and place it on one of the two empty pedestals. It was about the same size as *Old Man Reading* and would look good over on the far side of the booth by the desk.

She debated about the St. Francis. It was so much smaller and more traditional than his other work that she wasn't sure if she should include it in his display. She finally decided to leave it for now. She could always bring it in later.

After she loaded the heavy bronze sculpture into the pickup, she caught herself stroking the door of the bright blue truck and laughed out loud, surprised at the affection she felt. For some reason she found herself remembering the illustrations of the brightly colored train in *The Little Engine That Could.* How silly, she thought.

When she returned to the house for her cell phone and purse before heading off to the hospital, she spotted her opened laptop and sure enough, there was the message she was expecting:

> Kate: glad you are having such a great vacation in Arizona. Of course you know the clinic may not hold your job. If you can't help your father it's time for you to come home. Martin

"Dang!" She stamped her foot, angry that he could be such...an ass. What had changed? Ever since her father had moved to Arizona last year Martin had been her support, her advocate, her cheerleader. He encouraged her in all her studies and introduced her to important people in the field. There were other things he had helped her with as well, his sense of style, for instance. The clean lines of her new dining room furniture and the elegant simplicity of the cocktail dress she had recently purchased—he had helped her select these things, carefully pointing out the important design elements. His love of jazz, of blown glass, of expensive wines, he had shared all this with her. And he had spent long hours explaining his political and religious views, conversations she truly valued.

But now, when she most needed his approval and encouragement, he seemed so distant and dismissive. What had she done wrong? Should she really go back home? Now? Was her job, the one she had so diligently pursued, really in jeopardy?

Well, what if it was? She shook her head. She would call the clinic tomorrow and talk to them. Maybe they could hold the job for her. Right now she would get into her father's bright blue truck and drive out to the hospital to see the man she loved more than anyone in the world.

She refused to move the napkin away from the front page of *The Arizona Republic*. It covered the caption and story that accompanied a photo of an attractive young woman. Kate had been enjoying a second cup of coffee in the hospital cafeteria and was determined to discover for herself the identity and circumstances of the young lady before she went up to see her father.

The woman seemed to be in her mid-20s. Her little smile reminded Kate of a client in one of the group sessions she had facilitated last semester. It was a smile that defiantly overlooked disappointment. There was a bravado and a determination in the expression, a forced optimism. Kate thought perhaps she was a single mom struggling against the odds...or maybe a bookkeeper who got caught stealing from her employer to pay for a few nice things...or even a wife escaping a pattern of spousal abuse. She finally gave up, removed the napkin and began to read:

Woman found dead along I-10

A 24-year-old Phoenix woman was found dead near Interstate 10 just north of Casa Grande. The body was discovered Tuesday morning. The cause of death has not been determined but foul play is suspected.

Lydia Lopez was found dead near a gravel pull-out at exit 190 and McCartney road, 45 miles south of Phoenix, at approximately 9:30 a.m. by a passing motorist who was experiencing car trouble and had pulled off the freeway. It appears that the death occurred several days earlier.

Department of Public Safety officials said that dispatchers received a call between 7 and 7:30 p.m. Saturday evening reporting a car parked at that location. A DPS spokesman

admitted that due to numerous accidents
and other emergencies caused by the storm,
they were unable to get to the location until
8:30 p.m. at which time no car was seen in
the vicinity.

Kate looked at the face again and wondered what had happened to the young woman. Perhaps whatever it was that Lydia Lopez had wanted in life was the cause of her untimely death. Even though it was only a strange coincidence that she had died the same night her father was attacked, Kate felt a bond with this unfortunate woman. She brushed her hand over the photo, and knew that she would never forget the face of Lydia Lopez.

A soft, familiar cough interrupted her thoughts. There he was again, at first smiling broadly, then raising his eyebrows with that "is it okay with you?" expression. She gave him a half smile, covered the paper with her elbow, and pointed to the extra chair.

"So what's new, Detective?"

"Not much, unfortunately. We just keep plugging along. But it's good your father's hanging in there, don't you think?" He set his coffee and bagel down on the table and then looked directly into her eyes, which made her so uncomfortable that she quickly looked down to study her coffee.

"Why do you bother to come here, Detective? Surely you know he can't talk to you."

He shrugged his shoulders. "You never know. What if he could? We'd love to hear what happened."

A moment of awkward silence followed. She didn't know why he made her feel so...what?...scrutinized? She hated feeling that way.

He coughed again. "We seem to have gotten off to a bad start, you and I," he began, stirring his coffee vigorously. "For you, it must seem like I just barged into your life, unwelcome, and under very bad circumstances. But in reality, you know, I'm one of the good guys." He smiled and raised his eyebrows all at the same time. "Honestly."

"Sure, I know that. But every time I see you I can't help thinking about what happened, Detective. That's all." She felt small-minded and knew her father would want her to be polite. Tony kept looking at her intently so she concentrated on a poster hanging on the wall behind him.

"And that's another thing. My name is Tony...Antonio, but everyone calls me Tony. I *hate* being called 'Detective.' Didn't you ever have a nickname or title you absolutely hated, and every time someone called you that..."

"Sister John Francis always called me Katherine Marie. 'Katherine Marie, pay attention! You'll never pass the test if you don't pay attention.' It used to drive me crazy." She could feel herself relax a little. It wasn't so awful having a conversation with him, after all, as long as they didn't talk about what happened to her father.

She was surprised to notice that he was squirming, adjusting his chair, even twirling his mug around in circles. He's nervous, she thought. Whatever for?

"Kate, there are a few things I wanted to talk with you about." He coughed again, and then sat up straight, professional and serious. "The first has to do with your safety. I heard you're going to be down at the show a lot. That's great. But please, please don't stay after dark and never go back after the show is closed. And be careful who you socialize with." He looked at her across the table, searching her face with his big brown eyes, and she wondered for a moment if he could really be that concerned about her.

"I promise, Detective...I mean, Tony. I won't hang around after dark. I'll be a good little girl, cross my heart." She said it sarcastically, in a singsong, but until then it never occurred to her that the show might not be a safe place for her. Of course, she'd be careful.

"The next thing I want to talk about is my mother." He was still looking at her carefully but a slight smile had crept across his face.

"Your *mother*?" She let out a little hoot.

"Yep, my mother."

"Do you know how weird that sounds? I mean..."

"Actually, you have no idea how weird. First I have to tell you that my mother has been praying for your father. And for you. And when she prays, by the way, she really prays." He leaned forward and whispered, "She's been known to move mountains!" He smiled one of his big broad smiles, raised his eyebrows and shrugged, like he couldn't help himself from telling her about his mother.

She let his words float around until they seemed to tumble crazily through the air and onto the table next to the coffee and bagel and the newspaper.

She leaned forward and whispered back, "You have a very pious mother." But she couldn't help smiling, the whole thing was so ridiculous. After a minute she added, politely, "I'm sure she's a very fine lady."

"That she is. But I'm not quite finished about my mother," said Tony, twirling his mug several more times before looking directly at her again, eyes twinkling mischievously.

Kate protested, "There's more?"

"Yep, there's more. I've gone this far and I'm not stopping now." He gulped some coffee. "She wants you to come for dinner tonight. Our whole family gets together each Wednesday, and well, she's a very good cook, and..."

"I'm sure she's an excellent cook, but I can't accept. I don't know you or your family. I mean, I'm sure you're all very nice..."

"She's making roast chicken, cheese enchiladas, refried beans and her famous caramel pudding."

Again he looked at her and shrugged his shoulders, smiling. "There aren't too many places you can go for a free Mexican dinner, even in Phoenix. Look, she's worried about you, thinks you're all alone, wants to feed you, that's just the way she is. And besides, if you don't come, she'll think I broke my promise and then I'll be in big trouble."

"Let me ask you something, Tony. Do you still *live* with your mother? Because, if you do..."

"Good Lord, no!" He threw his head back and laughed out loud.

"That's good, because I could tell you...oh, never mind." No time for psychoanalysis here.

This time she looked directly at him, trying to assert herself just a little. "You talk as if I'm not able to make friends out here. I'll make some new friends in no time and then I can go out with them, you know. I don't need strangers to feel sorry..."

"I know that, but my mother doesn't."

If only she could conjure up just one decent, airtight excuse to avoid this social disaster. In a desperate effort to sidetrack the conversation for a minute so she could think of something, anything, she lamely asked, "So your mother likes to cook Mexican?"

He laughed out loud, a big hearty laugh that made her smile. "My mother *is* Mexican."

"Oh?"

She saw him light up with a 'gotcha' look.

"Some people," he said with fake petulance, "think all Mexicans are lazy and shiftless. Of course those people are just stupid. They're like the people who think all Italians are in the Mafia, you know what I mean? I'm sure you don't think that about Mexicans, do you, Kate?"

"Of course not!"

"Good. Then I'll pick you up at six o'clock..."

"No, no that just won't work. I come to the hospital every night at six o'clock. I'm really sorry." She started to gather her things together, convinced her excuse would hold up and satisfy good manners at the same time. After all, he couldn't be insulted if she wanted to visit her father.

"That's okay," said Tony. "I'll pick you up at five-thirty, we'll go to the hospital so you can visit your father, and *then* we'll go to dinner."

With that he pushed away his mug, grabbed his bagel, bolted out of his chair, and exited the cafeteria before she could open her mouth.

Dang! How in the world did she let that happen?

TWELVE

"This is *not* a date!" Kate pointed an accusing finger at her reflection and kicked a skirt onto the pile of rejected apparel that was growing in the corner.

Jeans had been discarded as too casual, her dress as too proper, her skirt too flirty. And her pantsuit was, well, too dull. She had eliminated t-shirts, a sweatshirt, a turtleneck sweater and a silk blouse. She was left with one pair of navy blue slacks and a V-neck sweater, which she fervently hoped wasn't too revealing.

Flats or pumps? Jewelry, yes or no? Bracelet, necklace, earrings...which one, or all three? She slipped into her loafers and pushed her hair back to reveal the little half moon dangles, each sparkling with a tiny topaz, that Peter Sterling insisted she wear today.

"Every day you can model a different pair of earrings...then when people compliment you, you can just direct them over here. You make a wonderful model with that long neck and pretty pink ears and all that bouncy hair." Pretty ears, indeed.

She checked her watch. Five o'clock. Why had she left the show so early? Just to spend time getting ready? Actually, it was a slow day in the tents, with few customers—the mid-week slump, she was told. She had managed to get some help carrying *Mother and Child* all the way to her father's booth and when she put it on its stand, spot-lighted, she thought it looked especially beautiful. By comparison, *Old Man Reading* struck her as looking a little bulky, just as Mrs. Nielsen had mentioned.

Her reflection in the mirror made note of each agitated move as she finished getting ready. What in the world was she doing? Shouldn't she just call him and tell him she couldn't go? Where had she put his business card? Purse, pocket...which pocket? When she finally found it stuffed under a handful of old tissues in the pocket of her blazer she dialed the number, then hung up after the first ring.

A spritz of cologne and a brush of mascara...was that too much?...not enough? She checked herself again, front to back and head to toe, and added a scarf before stomping out of the bedroom and down the hall.

She glared at her laptop that seemed to be leering at her from the desk, its cover opened just a crack. Alright, that's it! She sat down and soon her fingers were stabbing at the keys.

> Martin honey; just in case you're interested, Daddy squeezed my hand this morning. So I'm not coming home. And the best way for me to help him is to work at the show, not sit in the hospital all day. I'll ask the clinic to hold my job. If they can't, that's just too bad. Kisses, Kate.

She quickly pressed 'send' and pushed the cover down just as the doorbell rang.

"Dang." Her heart was pumping quickly. She grabbed her blazer and mumbled under her breath, "This is *not* a date."

An hour and a half later she was seated at Inez Bannigan's dinner table, one of 11 guests who had gathered on this particular Wednesday night. Eyes lowered, she was peeking at the amazing platters of food and bowls of condiments that were arrayed along the entire length of the table.

They were saying grace. She found herself holding hands with Tony on her left and Angelina, Tony's niece, on her right. The one hand was big, sturdy and relaxed; the other feather-light and wiggly.

This was not the grace she remembered from her childhood, the standard "Bless us, O Lord, and these thy gifts..." That was a real prayer, straightforward and simple. This was, well, something else entirely.

Uncle Manny started it off. "Thank you, Lord, for allowing us to live in such a wonderful country, led by such a strong and God-fearing president."

Sophia, Tony's younger sister, a gorgeous raven-haired law student, immediately added, "And we pray for all those poor souls deprived of their rights who are detained *illegally* by our government in Cuba." Right on, thought Kate.

Apparently oblivious of the political banter, Louie, Tony's beer-bellied brother-in-law, followed with a prayer for the Phoenix Suns. That prayer was countermanded by a request from a tattooed teenager, whose relation to the family was unclear to Kate, who asked the Lord to assist the Los Angeles Lakers.

Angela, Tony's older sister, a prim and plump grade school teacher, prayed for peace in the Middle East, seconded by Uncle Manny's wife, whose name Kate couldn't remember.

The teenager's mother, a grim and unpleasant woman, prayed for the souls of those who were living in sin, sin of a sexual nature, if Kate could translate all the euphemisms accurately.

Father Miguel, the round and jolly pastor, quickly and cheerfully brought to God's attention all those who struggled to lead good and generous lives, mentioning Inez Bannigan by name, perhaps in an effort to be invited back to her table.

A sweet, short prayer by little Angelina for her best friend's mother's cousin's daughter, who was having a baby, was just the introduction Inez needed for her litany of names. The first half of the list were all those who were in trouble, or ill, including Art Russo, while thanksgiving was given for the second half, the people who were cured or otherwise relieved, thanks be to God.

Finally, Tony said, simply, "Lord, we ask you to bless all those gathered around this table." Silence followed. Tony squeezed her hand and Kate knew it was her turn. She felt herself flush and wondered if her nose was running. Quickly, desperately, she said the words of the old, familiar prayer. Then, in an effort to appear spontaneous, she added, "and thank you for such beautiful food."

Tony squeezed her hand again, then let it go. As if on cue everyone reached for the platter nearest them, murmuring sincere compliments to the cook and piling the beautiful food onto their plates.

Poised to enjoy her first bite of roast chicken, Kate heard the silly chiming of her cell phone from the next room. She almost knocked over her chair as she jumped up, excusing herself. The call could only be from Martin or the hospital and she really didn't want to hear from either of them.

"Hello? Martin?"

"I just got your e-mail." Martin's voice was taut and several notes higher than usual. "We need to talk."

"Not now, Martin, I'm having dinner."

"Well that's too bad. Just keep it warm and eat it after we've talked. This is important."

"I can't. I'm not home. I'm at...I'm out."

"So I can hear. Sounds like you're at a party. It doesn't take you long, does it, to throw everything aside..."

"I'm not throwing everything aside!"

"Look, just come home. If your father's in a coma he won't know if you visit him or not. You can fly back to Phoenix when..."

"He does too! He squeezed my hand again tonight. I felt it."

"Kate, you need to come home."

"No! No, I won't." She hung up and threw the phone back in her purse with a barely audible "shit!" If she could have turned the thing off, she would have, but there was always a chance that the hospital might call.

She stood for a moment in the center of Inez Bannigan's living room, trying to regain her composure and looking at the mismatched furniture, the untidy piles of books and magazines, the family photos arranged awkwardly on the wall. What in the world would Martin think of this place, this dinner? She knew exactly what he would think.

The black and white photographs over the sofa slowly came into her line of vision. They were very nice. She looked closer. How well composed they were! Direct, dramatic and heartfelt, they must have been taken by someone with a great deal of experience and insight.

"What lovely photographs you have over the sofa, Mrs. Bannigan," she said as she sat back down at the table. "Can you tell me about them?"

Inez opened her mouth to respond, but Sophia was quicker. She beamed from across the table and excitedly jabbed her fork in the direction of her brother.

"I told you, Tonio, I told you. You are really talented." Then she glanced at Kate and added, with a sly smile, "Don't you think he's talented?"

Before Kate could reply, Tony put down his knife and fork and held up his hands in protest.

"No, no. Look, I don't even know how to use a darkroom. I'm not really a photographer at all, just a computer guy with a good digital camera." He turned to Kate. "All you need is the right computer program...then you can turn a snapshot into black and white and manipulate the image till you get what you want. That's all I do. But what I really want is a Hasselblad. Saw a used one I could afford. The problem is that it would take a lot of time to learn how to use it, and I never seem to have any free time."

"But your pictures would be beautiful no matter what camera you used," Kate insisted. "You have a great sense of design and a real eye for interesting subjects."

"Told you so, Tonio. This girl knows what she's talking about, I can tell." Sophia beamed, first at Tony, then at Kate.

Inez finally chimed in. "And you're much better than Julio. He's a professional photographer, but he's not as good as you, Tonio."

"Oh, Ma."

She continued. "And Julio thinks he's so great. Big shot. Always on the low road with his high horse, you know what I mean?"

"Ma, low road doesn't go with high *horse*. Low *road* goes with high *road*. High *horse*..."

"...goes with low horse? That doesn't make any sense, Tonio. You're not so good with words, but with photography, very good."

Baffled and amused, Kate repeated, "Yes, very good."

Little Angelina leaned against Kate and whispered loudly, "Does that mean you like Uncle Tony?"

Everyone chuckled, except for Kate, who studied her plate, and Angela, who frowned at her daughter and shook her head as a warning. Inez passed another platter of food around and the conversation resumed on a different topic as quickly as if someone had changed channels. Kate, trying to appear unruffled, helped herself to one more enchilada, her third.

All things considered Kate had enjoyed the evening very much. The food, the margaritas, the lively conversation, all of it was so pleasant she almost hated to leave. But finally she was left alone once more with Tony for the ride home.

"That was nice. You have a wonderful family. A very healthy family, I might add. I'm used to dealing with a lot of dysfunctional families and relationships that aren't working very well at all."

"You and Sophia seemed to get along real well. What in the world were you two laughing about in the kitchen?"

"Oh, you wouldn't approve. Let's just say we share similar political views and we were roasting the opposition"

"Don't tell me you agree with *her*! With *Sophia*?"

"See, I knew you wouldn't approve!"

"But my sister's a *liberal* for heaven's sake! She doesn't believe in capital punishment or mandatory sentencing or..."

"Well, neither do I," said Kate.

"Oh god, I might have known." He laughed, and added, "Then you must have had a hard time listening to old Uncle Manny. He's more conservative than..."

"He's a sweet old man. He was telling me stories of the old days."

"Poor you. I've heard those stories so many times I know them by heart. You were kind to listen."

"Not at all. He was charming...and so was little Angelina."

"Who won the chess game?"

"She did...and handily. The whole time she was giggling and being silly and I was struggling just to avoid making a fool of myself."

She noticed his fingers start to drum the steering wheel as he took a deep breath. Nervous again, she thought.

"I'm glad you enjoyed yourself," he said, "but personally I think my family was way too distracting. Next time I'd like you all to myself. What about dinner Saturday night? Just you and me...at a restaurant. I know a great little Italian..." His eyebrows shot up hopefully.

"Look, Tony, tonight was not a date. I just can't go out with you."

"Because of the guy who keeps calling you from New Jersey? Is he...you know, is it all that serious?"

"Well, we're engaged."

"Engaged? Ouch!"

He continued tapping the wheel, but now he was frowning. "But I don't get it. Every time he calls you he seems to get you upset. Like tonight. I could tell. When you came back to the table. He had made you angry."

"He's just worried with me being so far away. That's all."

"Worried about you or worried about himself?" Tony made the question into a challenge, his fingers still drumming.

She was caught off guard and took her time to make her reply, which she enunciated very slowly and carefully. "Frankly, that's none of your business."

"I guess not." He gave the wheel a final, irritated thump with the palm of his hand.

She hadn't meant to be rude. After all, he had really been very kind. But all evening she had made it clear in every way she knew how that they were not on a date. It wasn't her fault if he couldn't see things the way they really were.

In the silence that followed she straightened her shoulders and concentrated on the view out her window. The tension between them was uncomfortable but she knew she couldn't break the silence without destroying the emotional distance she needed to maintain. Why was this so difficult?

At last the ride was over and he made the turn into her father's driveway. But before he could stop the car her cell phone rang again, startling them both and shredding the strained silence. Tony banged his fist on the wheel and growled, "Oh, for god's sake."

Kate yanked the phone out from under the mess in her purse and answered it as quickly as possible in a low and hushed voice. But this time it was not Martin. This time it was the hospital. They said they were so very sorry.

THIRTEEN

The Medical Examiner's report stared up at him from the confusion on his desk. He had been looking at the words for so long, not really concentrating, that the letters were beginning to dance up and down. There was 'evidence of traumatic energy.' In other words Art Russo had been killed by a blow to his head by an unidentified blunt object, irregular in shape. Well, where was the object? *What* was the object? His mind wandered, searching for possibilities.

His mind wandered a lot lately. Truth to tell, he was finding it difficult to concentrate on anything. He couldn't eat and he couldn't sleep. Tony Bannigan had fallen in love. And he had thought it could never happen again.

Of course, falling in love motivated him like nothing else could. He was aching to solve this crime, find the murderer, bring him to justice, see him behind bars...on death row. But first he had to catch him and that meant he had to concentrate.

For days now the memory of what happened Wednesday night washed over him whenever he looked up, even for a moment, from whatever he was doing, and especially when he climbed into his car where he could detect the faint lingering of her perfume. The scent was like a phantom, eluding him one minute and then wafting by discreetly the next. He could feel her hair against his cheek, her dark shiny hair, smooth and fragrant. He had embraced her and whispered into her hair, "I'm sorry...oh, I'm so sorry." And she had clung to him, briefly, sucking in her breath, trying not to cry. He had wanted to hold her longer, but when she drew away he quickly released her, not wanting to frighten her or impose on her or take advantage in any way.

He knew it was perverse to take delight in the memory, to nurture it, knowing that the very moment he treasured was the one that brought her so much sorrow. Her eyes, those beautiful eyes, had looked at him with pained surprise, as if she had never really considered that this might happen. She had said, in a small voice, "He died...I didn't think he would die."

But he had known that Art would die. He had known it all along.

J.D. breezed by. "So, when's the funeral?"

"Eleven o'clock."

"You really going?"

"Yes, I'm really going. I've told you that at least three times."

"But you've never done that before. Gone to a victim's funeral. Not since I've known you."

"Well, this time I am."

"Well, but you never..."

"Dammit, leave it alone, will you?" Tony threw his pencil on the desk so hard that it bounced over to the file cabinet before boomeranging back, just missing the desk and landing in the waste basket.

"Okay, sorry."

"Let's get some work done around here," said Tony, as he grabbed another pencil and began drumming the desk. "I want to review the cast of characters one more time."

"Okay. Where do you want to start?" J. D. sat up straight and frowned, trying to appear as serious as possible.

"At the beginning," Tony growled. He paused and brought his voice back to normal. "First of all we have Gary the Guard. I personally think he's told us everything he knows."

"I agree," said J.D. "Then there's the artists who signed in that night. Let's go over them one at a time. First, John Amory."

"Definitely not a suspect. Too frail. Cross him off...he's out."

"And Taylor McGrath?" J.D. knew the answer but felt better checking names off a list.

"Ditto. He was seen running in and out by two people and his wife confirms the story."

"What about the extra truck she saw?" asked J.D. "Have we learned anything there?"

"Nope."

"Couldn't the perp have just climbed over the fence?...walked, not parked? That's what I would have done."

"Sure, but he would have had to walk along Scottsdale Road for more than a mile, climb over an eight foot fence into the sculpture garden, and finally crawl under the canvas walls of the tents. It's just not likely. Then again, I suppose he could have walked all the way around to the back, through the parking lot and right in the entrance when the guard was away from his post." Tony frowned. Still, it would be worth it to check the fence. He wrote 'security fence' on a purple post-it and slammed it onto the side of his monitor.

"Okay, then what about Gretchen Schmidt? She was there that night. I wouldn't mind interviewing her this time." J.D. looked at Tony hopefully.

"I *bet* you wouldn't. No, she's got to be eliminated, too. She signed out just five minutes after Art Russo signed in. There's no way she could have hit him over the head, untied the flaps, dragged him out to the sculpture garden, come back in, retied the flaps—all in five minutes."

Tony couldn't help picturing Art Russo being pulled over the wet grass and left to die out in the wind and rain. He felt his blood pressure rise.

"But," said J.D., "it might be possible for *two* people, say Gretchen *and* the driver of the unknown vehicle, to do it together."

"Maybe. Hadn't thought of that. But it still seems too tight. Just to be safe, though, we won't eliminate Gretchen entirely. But she's way down on my list...that is if I had a list."

"Next, there's Jess. No, he's out, remember? He was at home with his mommy."

"Yeah, he's out."

"And then there's Derrick, the cowboy from hell."

Tony sighed. "God, isn't he a piece of work? What was his story? Oh, yeah, out drinking with Eldon. How did that check out?"

"It checked. Eldon *finally* got back in town. Said he was out barhopping with Derrick Saturday night till the wee hours. Then he drove up to Flagstaff for a day or so—to photograph something at the university, an inauguration, I think—and then some meeting in the town of Williams…politicians, Department of Interior, maybe some tree huggers. He hung around a few more days taking pictures up north. Said he hadn't read the paper so he didn't know anything about the murder."

"Were you able to confirm his story?" asked Tony.

"Not yet, although Eldon's girlfriend said that he came in very late Saturday night and then took right off again."

"Did you ask Eldon who drove when he and Derrick went out drinking?"

"Yep," said J.D., checking his notes. "He said Derrick did. Said Derrick picked him up and brought him back."

"I could have sworn Derrick was lying about that."

"Maybe they're both lying."

"Okay, then, let's check the bars," said Tony. "Dos Gringos and Martini Ranch, I think he said." Tony frowned, thumped the pencil on the desk and growled, "So what the hell are we missing? Or who?"

"You interviewed Connie. What did she have to say."?

"Only that she was in love with Art. No help at all."

"So now we're back to your theory about the jewelry."

"I wouldn't dignify it by calling it a theory. It's a hunch. A stupid schoolgirl hunch. I feel there's a whole lot of dots we should be connecting and we don't even have the dots."

"Well, here's a dot for you. Word just came in that there were seventeen large diamonds lifted from the Tucson Gem Show last weekend. Worth several hundred thousand."

Tony's pencil stopped tapping.

"Really? Well, well, well...and Peter Sterling was there."

"*Thousands* of people were there." J.D. protested.

"True, but still, I think we should take a better look at him."

"I've already checked out his booth. The jewelry is real gold and real silver and has semiprecious stones, but no diamonds other than little chips. Good stuff, but nothing really expensive."

"As if you could tell the difference."

"You think I don't know good jewelry? Just look at this here watch. Genuine Timex. Real classy."

Tony glared at him so he quickly sat up straight again and frowned.

"You're right, I'm no gem expert. But I got a pro to go by and look things over. Peter Sterling looks okay." J.D. sounded a bit defensive.

"Well, we need to do more than that. I want to know where he stayed in Tucson, and for how long. I want to know who he saw and who saw him and when. And what he bought, sold, if anything. Let's get the photo off his brochure and see who recognizes him."

"Good idea."

J.D. escaped down the corridor.

Tony was relieved to see him go. J.D. always managed to get on his nerves whenever his nerves were already shot. He put down his pencil and rubbed his forehead. Then he carefully laid out a series of photographs across the top of the desk. He studied how Art Russo' booth ran right into Peter Sterling's booth...and how the jewelry case was only a few feet away from where Art was hit. And then Tony noticed the empty pedestal right under the light switch where Art's head had been bashed in...a pedestal minus its sculpture...a heavy, blunt object with an irregular shape. Of course! He grabbed a pink post-it and wrote 'missing sculpture?' and smacked it onto the side of his monitor.

Then he stacked the photos on top of the medical examiner's report and got ready to leave. He had twenty minutes to get to the funeral.

FOURTEEN

The fact that there were already several rows of cars in the parking lot at St. Anthony's Church in south Phoenix did not surprise Tony in the least. It was simply a case of Inez Bannigan moving mountains. No one, it seemed, could resist his mother or the forces she put into play.

He put on his coat and tie, appropriate attire for a pallbearer, and checked his reflection in the car window. He had been recruited for this role, along with Uncle Manny, Louie, and his cousin, Emilio, who was told to cover his tattoos with a long sleeve shirt if he didn't own a jacket.

St. Anthony's had been the family's parish since his own baptism 38 years ago. Of course Inez knew most of the parishioners and had evidently called upon their friendship for today's service. She had probably rounded up some neighborhood book club members as well.

The organ music, sad and muffled, escaped into the parking lot from the tiny church in little staccato bursts each time the door opened to welcome another mourner. Tony gritted his teeth. He hated organ music...it always reminded him of his father's funeral and the black rage he had felt all through the service and whenever he went to church for many years afterward.

Kate was standing in the vestibule by the casket, her large eyes unfocused, absently holding a program with her father's photograph on the cover. Tony was offered a program but he was afraid to look at it, to see the face of the victim he now cared so much about, so he folded it and put it in his pocket. Father Miguel and the pallbearers took their places, and when the music swelled they brought the casket down the aisle into the half-filled church with Kate following, all alone. He hated that she had no family with her. And where was her damn fiance? For heaven's sake, you'd think he'd at least fly out for the funeral.

The service was simple. One large bouquet of flowers had been placed near the lectern and when beautiful Sophia got up to read from Scripture, Tony thought she had never looked so lovely and wished it had been another sort of occasion and that he had brought his camera. And later, when Angela and little Angelina brought the bread and wine to the altar, and Angelina broke away from her mother to sit beside Kate, he had to look away, because that little act of kindness brought tears to his eyes.

He noticed that the Morrows were there, and several of the staff. Connie stood to the side, wearing dark glasses. He could see her shoulders shake. Tony wondered if Kate had learned of their relationship and how she felt about it.

He recognized the elderly Nielsens, who were sitting very close together and holding hands. Beside them, tall and lovely, was the bombshell Gretchen Schmidt, dressed today in a sedate and modest black dress. Then there was Peter Sterling, attired in a beautifully tailored suit, sitting with a pretty Asian woman, probably his wife. They seemed to keep more than a respectable distance apart. There were a few other familiar faces from the art show, but he didn't know their names. He guessed that the young athletic-looking woman with the solemn-faced little boy was the artist who had the booth right next to Kate and Peter. Perhaps he should talk with her sometime.

When the Mass was over the pallbearers brought the casket out of the church and into the hearse. Although there was nothing he wanted more than to be near Kate, perhaps put his arm around her, he kept his distance. He watched as Sophia and Angelina gently hovered on either side of her and he knew she was in good hands. Now came the hard part, the final committal at Holy Redeemer Cemetery.

The three mariachis stood to one side waiting patiently for Father Miguel to conclude the short prayers and final blessing. At first Kate was astonished to see musicians waiting at the cemetery, but then, as with everything else she had experienced this day, she accepted their presence as an inevitable and charming gift from Inez Bannigan. The mariachis, old and dignified, stood at attention, their black and silver sombreros dramatically silhouetted against the vast and cloudless sky.

The grave site was on a slight rise, just high enough for Kate to take in the patchwork of red-tiled roofs which stretched all the way back to the pale blue mountains clustered along the horizon. She could see where the treelined road left the main thoroughfare and wandered lazily through the cemetery. A white car turned in at the gate just as the final blessing was said and the music began.

Bittersweet. That's how she would later describe the music. The cheerful, insistent strumming of the guitar was muted by the melancholy of the horn and the soulful strains of the violin. There was something comforting about the melodies, foreign and yet familiar, and she listened appreciatively, absentmindedly following the approach of the white car as it rounded the last curve and finally came to a stop beside the parked hearse.

A man in a three-piece suit emerged from the car and shaded his eyes to study the little group of mourners, now shrunk in size to the members of the Bannigan family. He hesitated briefly before starting up the path, craning his neck and scanning the group to find a familiar face.

Kate stood up and walked over to greet him, but he looked right past her, frowning at the priest and the musicians and the

Bannigans. He leaned in toward Kate, still eyeing the little group, and asked in a loud whisper, "What's going on here?"

"What do you mean?"

"Well, who are these people? What are they doing at your father's funeral?"

"They're friends...they've helped arrange..."

"But I told you! If you had only waited another day I could have helped you. Instead this..." his arm swept an arc across the scene, "*this* happened."

"I think it's beautiful."

"And the priest. I thought we agreed..."

"Hush!"

"And the musicians. Look at them in their ridiculous costumes."

"Please!"

"And these people, who are they? They look...I just don't understand, Kate. This isn't like you."

"Please be quiet. They'll hear you."

"Not over all that racket, they won't." But just then the music stopped, forcing him into silence. The service had ended.

It took only an instant—less time than to breathe in and out—for her to understand what her father had known all along.

So she said, very simply, and perhaps a little louder than she intended, "Excuse me, Martin," and turned her back to him.

Rejoining the group, she first thanked the priest, who kissed her and handed her the little crucifix that had rested on her father's casket. Then she embraced Inez, telling her how beautiful everything was and how she would always remember her kindness. Shaking hands with the musicians she complimented and thanked each of them, and they in turn bowed and smiled and politely murmured, "Gracias, gracias."

Tony was standing farther back so she mouthed a thank-you with a little wave and a smile. Finally, she reached out her hand to Angelina and said, "How would you like to drive back to your Grandma's house with me?" And off they went, hand in hand. They got into the bright blue truck and drove away.

PART 2

FIFTEEN

"This is exactly what I needed," said Kate, looking around the crowded bistro where she was enjoying lunch with Sophia. "But you've already done so much. Your whole family is just incredible."

"Incredible?" repeated Sophia. "Well, I don't know about that. Mom might be incredible. The rest of us? We're just ordinary folks." Sophia was delicately picking at her Cobb salad, totally ignoring the basket of warm, crusty bread. Kate wondered how she had so much self-control. No wonder she was so slim. And look at those lovely manicured nails. Kate doubted there would ever be a time when she would look so together, so flawless.

"Actually, this is just what I needed too," said Sophia. "Law school has been sucking the life out of me. It's nice to go out to lunch, and the art show will be fun."

Kate leaned back and sipped her iced tea, having completely devoured her grilled chicken Caesar salad and two pieces of buttered bread. "I was famished." she said, embarrassed by her appetite. "I've been living on Cheerios and peanut butter sandwiches for days."

"We've been worried about you. You've been holed up ever since the funeral, and when you wouldn't answer the phone..."

"I'm sorry. I didn't mean to worry anyone. I just needed to be alone and figure some things out."

"Do you want to talk? I'm a pretty good listener," said Sophia.

"Oh, I don't know. It's just that I miss Daddy," Kate began, blinking back tears. "He was a beautiful man and a wonderful father and all I did was take him for granted, thinking he'd be around forever." She paused. "But it's more complicated than that. It's about my mother, too. He was my connection to my mother. He would tell me stories, remind me of things she used to do. The older I got the more important the stories seemed to be. I wanted to hear all about her. What was she like as a young woman? Am I like her at all? That sort of thing. She seemed almost alive when he talked about her."

"That's got to be hard. It's like losing both parents at the same time."

"Yes, that's it exactly." Kate sighed. "And I'm losing Martin, too. Not that he's as important as my parents, but it's still hard to let him go. He was a big part of my life." She buttered another slice of bread and said, quietly, "It's like everyone important vanished from my life overnight and now I'm really on my own."

"Well, from what I saw of Martin, you're well rid of him."

"I guess. But I could always rely on him, Sophia. And maybe if I had followed his advice about the Mayo Clinic, Daddy wouldn't have died..."

Sophia sat up straight and pointed her fork at Kate. "Hey, don't ever think that! It wouldn't have made any difference, Kate, you know that."

"...and now he could be helping me with the will and the house and..."

"Hold it, girl. First of all, your father probably left everything in good order. Secondly, you're smart. You'll know what to do. And finally, if there's a legal problem I can help. You don't need Martin. And besides, is that all he's good for, *business*? I mean," she leaned in close, "was he any good in bed?"

"Sophia! You're one blunt woman."

Sophia smiled. "Well, that's what friends are for."

"Okay, so he wasn't the right guy for me, I admit it. Daddy knew it all along. Called him a prick, once. Not to his face, of course."

Sophia raised her glass and made a toast, "To the prick!" Then she looked at Kate and got serious again. "There's something else on your mind, isn't there?"

"Yeah. Actually, I've been trying to come to terms with a problem I have...with, uh, reality," Kate said, almost in a whisper. "I've never been good at dealing with things that are difficult or that make me sad or nervous...I just glide by and hope everything turns out all right, and if it doesn't, that no one will notice if I've made a mistake. In unprofessional terms, it's a denial kind of thing."

"We all do a little gliding now and then."

"But I do it big time, Sophia. Like with Daddy. I should have known from the beginning that he was probably going to die. I just couldn't face it. I got busy doing things that would help when he got better, like working at the show. And I never wanted to know what really happened that night...I *still* don't. I mean, I don't want to know how badly he was beaten up, things like that. As if by not knowing the details it makes things less horrible." She started to bite one of the nails that had begun to grow, but put her hand in her lap instead. "And even with Martin. Deep down I knew the relationship wasn't working, but I just went along because it was easier than breaking up."

Kate leaned a little closer, relieved to have a confidante. "And you know what else? I purposely ignored the fact that Daddy had a love life. He has photographs all over the house of this woman who works at the show. Connie. I saw her at the hospital a few times and she came to the funeral but I just couldn't make myself go over and talk to her. I'm ashamed of myself. After all, if Daddy loved her..."

"Oh, for heaven's sake, Kate. You're too hard on yourself. You've had a big shock and you're handling everything just fine. You'll find a way to talk to her, I know you will. Give yourself some time."

"That's what my analyst said."

"You found an analyst out here already?"

"No, no, I have one back home. You have to go into analysis when you're getting a masters in psychology and I had a really good one. I've been on the phone with her so often that I can't even imagine my phone bill."

"It's got to be worth it."

"It is. But I also need just plain common sense advice, for right here. For right now. I hoped you might have some words of wisdom, too. You seem so...so sure of yourself..."

"Only occasionally," Sophia laughed. "But I'll say this much. I think you need to keep busy. Not that you shouldn't think about all that serious stuff, and obviously you're going to have to go through a lot of pain. Grief is necessary, and who knows how long it will last, but I suppose you know all about things like that." She waved a fork vaguely. "I just think there's got to be a balance. Can't grieving be mixed with a little work, a little play?" Then she looked at Kate with a smile, her raised eyebrows causing little wavy lines across her forehead. "Maybe you could get a new guy. What about Tony?"

"Sophia!"

"Just kidding. Well, no, I'm actually not kidding. He's crazy about you."

"I know I have to get busy," said Kate, deliberately ignoring Sophia's last remark. "The first thing I have to do is go grocery shopping or I'll starve to death. Then, I guess, I have to sell as many of Daddy's sculptures as I can...and probably put his house on the market. But, the most important thing I want to do is—no, the most important thing I *need* to do is..." she paused and took a deep breath, "help find out who killed my father."

"What?" Sophia dropped her fork. "Find the killer? Good grief, girl, why can't you leave that to Tony? He's very good at his job, you know."

"I'm sure he is. But he thinks Daddy just got in the way of something else that was happening. You know, that he was in the wrong place at the wrong time. But how does he know that for sure? Maybe someone wanted him dead, someone from the art show." She lowered her voice. "Look, somebody killed my father and I need to know who and I need to know why. This time I'm not going to let things glide by. I've got to be involved. And since I'll be at the show, I'll *see* things. I'll *hear* things. I can even do some snooping. After all, I've got good insights into people...I can see patterns of behavior..."

"But what about your job in New Jersey?"

"When I told them how much more difficult it would be to settle Daddy's estate from a distance, especially with all his sculpture being committed to the art show, they said they'd hold the position for a month. Obviously, I didn't tell them that one of the reasons I wanted to stay was to help find the killer."

"Okay, okay. Go ahead and do your little sleuthing, Kate, but remember to always, always tell Tony what you've learned and let him handle it. And be careful." She waived for the bill. "Promise?"

"Sure, I promise."

An enormous bouquet of white roses had been placed on the empty pedestal in her father's booth. The flowers must have been there a day or so because they had already started to wilt under the overhead lights. The card read, 'Sympathy, Eldon Melrose.'

"Ah, a suitor!" teased Sophia.

"I've never even met the guy. He's a photographer at the show." She moved the flowers over to the desk, out of the spotlight. "But wasn't that nice of him?"

"Looks like you got some messages, too."

Kate picked up the first one. "Mr. Mark Von Steen would like you to call him regarding a commission," she read. "You'd think the office would have just told him that Daddy's died and can't do a commission. Why in the world did they leave me the message?" She picked up the next message. "But this is interesting. Somebody wants to order two of the *Girl with Dog* and would like to know if I would discount the second one. I wonder why anyone would want two? What do you think I should do about a discount?"

Sophia was walking around examining each piece of Art's sculpture, touching this one, then another, and without missing a beat she said, "Call the person first and see how badly he wants them.

Only give a discount if you have to, but don't make it easy." Then she looked up at Kate and shrugged. "I went to a seminar on negotiating once. Women tend to be doormats, so watch it."

"Well, I can't call now, anyway. My cell phone's dead. I've kept it turned off so Martin couldn't reach me."

"Kate, you're going to need your phone here or you'll lose sales. If you don't want Martin calling you, then you're going to have to call him first and get it over with." She looked up from a sculpture just long enough to hand Kate her own phone. "Go ahead. Use mine. Make the sale, girl."

Kate took the phone out into the sculpture garden, sat down on the bench beside the two bronze children and made the call. Following Sophia's advice, she held back any offer to discount and found she could make the sale without it. The buyer said he would immediately call the office with his credit card number so Kate could consider the sale final.

Wow. That was easy...and just the shot in the arm she needed. She sat quietly for a minute, soaking up the sun and admiring the many large sculptures: the lion and the horse and the alligator, the rotund nudes with their silly gold fig leaves, the Christ figure in the center—even the immense steel shapes which rotated in the breeze and looked to Kate like bad imitations of Calder. Her favorite of them all, though, was the dignified Indian scout who seemed to be carefully observing her and the children.

She heard Sophia call out, "Kate? Kate? Where'd you go, Kate? Oh, *there* you are. You were sitting so still I thought you were one of the statues. Did you make the sale?"

Kate marched back to the booth and with a flourish added the buyer's name to the next two lines of the pre-cast list. "Ta-da! Now, there are eight."

Then she glanced over at the *Old Man Reading* and noticed that it had two names on its list, not one. One of the sales staff must have made a sale for her while she was gone. Altogether, a very good day.

Kate picked up the message from Mr. Von Steen, stuffed it in her pocket, and led Sophia over to see Peter Sterling's jewelry.

Peter immediately put his tools down and removed his visor, winking at Kate and letting his eyes rest a while on Sophia. He automatically thrust his hands into the display case and extracted several pairs of earrings, which he lined up on the counter. He selected a pair for Kate, reminding her that she agreed to model a different pair every day. Then he turned his attention back to Sophia, who was leaning over to examine the earrings. He delicately brushed a loose strand of hair away from her face with the back of his fingers.

Sophia stiffened and backed away.

He ignored her reaction and selected a particularly beautiful pair, sliding the mirror in front of her. "Try these on. They're you, absolutely you."

"Sorry. They're beautiful, but no thanks."

Peter seemed eager to push ahead with another pair of earrings but was interrupted by a hearty "Hey, Peter."

"Eldon! Good to see you, man. But tell me, why the hell do you always appear when I've got beautiful women looking at my jewelry? It never fails. Do you know these young ladies? This is Kate Russo and her friend..."

Eldon was tall and slightly gray at the temples. He looked like a businessman, dressed in a jacket and tie, and he carried himself with the confident and positive manner of an entrepreneur. He stepped forward and took the hand Kate offered, holding it firmly in his own and looking directly into her eyes.

"It's good to finally meet you," Kate said. "And thanks for the flowers. They're beautiful."

"I'm glad you like them. I wanted something to cheer you up." He held on to her hand as he turned to Sophia. "And you're Kate's friend...?"

"I'm Sophia."

"Let me guess, Sophia...Peter's been trying to sell you some jewelry." Eldon was still holding on to Kate's hand.

Peter grinned and shrugged his shoulders. "Of course I am. Why not? The fact is, Eldon, you're just jealous of my sales technique. Said so yourself."

"True, but I see your technique didn't work this time." Eldon laughed and looked back at Kate. "How are you doing, really?"

"Fine, just fine," she said, gently extricating her hand. "But you'll have to excuse us. We're off to tour the show. Sophia wants to see everything...and so do I." She led Sophia across the aisle to Vicki's booth.

Peter called after them. "There's wine and cheese tonight. Just hang around right before the show closes. It's a good time to socialize and get in on the gossip."

"Sounds great." said Kate. She nudged Sophia and whispered, "Just think. I get to snoop and drink wine at the same time. What a deal!"

"Better watch out for Eldon, girl. He seems to like you."

"No, you read him wrong. He's just a really cool, take-charge kind of guy. Body language says it all. I almost didn't get my hand back. But from what I saw, Peter was making a play for *you*."

Sophia rolled her eyes. "Lord, deliver me from men like that. They think they're charming and they always turn out to be such bastards."

"Oh, Sophia, Peter's harmless."

SIXTEEN

It was a half-hour to closing when Kate noticed that a group of artists had dragged a table out into the middle of the aisle. Immediately wine and beer appeared, along with chips and salsa, brie and crackers, plastic cups and paper napkins. One artist took a bowl of shrimp out of a cooler and placed it in the center of the table. Another brought a platter of raw vegetables and dip. Kate could smell popcorn, and apparently every one else could, too, because a crowd of starving artists converged all at once from the booths in the south tent. Some unceremoniously reached over shoulders, grabbed a glass of wine, and returned to work. Others dragged one of the ubiquitous white plastic chairs from someone's booth or from the sculpture garden and settled in to party.

There was still a sprinkling of customers strolling through the show and a few paused to have a glass of wine with artists they knew. Kate was enjoying the festivities, all the while observing the individual artists and the group dynamics. Who wouldn't make eye contact with her? Who was avoiding her all together? Frankly, she was grateful that Derrick had not appeared. When she and Sophia passed his booth on their little tour, he had crossed the aisle when he saw them approach and remained with his back to them as they passed by.

On the other hand, Kate was surprised that Eldon didn't join the party. Twice he walked right through it, carrying an enormous painting down to his studio and back, but he never stopped. She had admired the photograph that he had on display of her father's *Nude Bather*, but Sophia wasn't impressed with his work and they had quickly walked on. After they completed their tour Sophia had left, and now, Kate realized, Vicki was staying by her side, almost protectively, leaving every once in a while to check on Zach, who preferred to stay in his fort. Kate had brought him popcorn, hoping to make friends with the little boy, but he stayed well hidden under the table.

"Hey, Jess," shouted Peter, "be careful, will you? You almost knocked over the wine."

"Then move the goddam table out of the way!" The words were spit out by a sullen looking young man with an unshaven face and a dingy t-shirt who stood in the narrow space between the table and the tent opening waiting for someone, anyone, to move the table to one side.

"Can't you close the other flaps first? Then come back here later? Use your head. Can't you see we're having a party?"

Jess didn't bother to look up at the speaker. He simply leaned over and began pushing the table out of his way and mumbling "fuck you" just loud enough to be heard. Two of the artists grabbed the table and lifted it over to one side, causing wine bottles to jiggle and napkins to fall to the floor. Conversation stopped, and they all watched Jess as he let the flaps down and began lacing the loops of rope through the eyelets from top to bottom. He turned his head once to glare back at the silent spectators and Kate caught his eye. He locked onto her face, then blinked and turned back to his job. So this was the creep who had given her father a bad time.

Kate felt unnerved as the closed tent shut out the fresh air and the high ceilings lost their glow after the sun had set. The interior lights, with no daylight to moderate them, focused only on the artwork, leaving great patches of darkness in the far corners and in between the booths. Conversation from the party, with no way to escape, bounced from wall to wall down the whole length of the aisle and then echoed back. The setting now seemed somehow ominous and lent a surreal quality to the gathering, and when the temperature dropped suddenly, Kate remembered what Tony had said about staying after dark.

But then the party was over just as suddenly as it began. Food was taken away, some saved, some thrown out, and half-empty bottles of wine were snapped up by their owners. The table was returned to its original location and one by one the artists picked up their back-packs and paint boxes, their unfinished canvasses, extra frames, cameras and laptops, and turned off their lights and headed out.

Kate watched Jess as he lashed the last of the flaps together. She saw Connie walk over to him and heard the argument that ensued, but she couldn't make out the words that ricocheted off the walls in angry bursts. Then Connie reached into her purse and handed Jess some bills which he snatched up, jamming them deep into his pocket before turning away. What astonished Kate was what Connie did next. She reached out and gently patted Jess on the shoulder. It was an exquisitely tender gesture. What was *that* all about, Kate wondered. She picked up her purse and walked out past the guard into the darkened parking lot, determined to discover the meaning behind the encounter she had just witnessed.

~~~~~~~~~~~~~~~~~~~~~~~~~~~~~~~~~

Zach watched the party from one of his fort windows and nibbled on the popcorn the new lady brought to him in a paper cup. She had reached inside the opening and set the cup down, saying, "Hi, Zach! Here you go!" and walked back to the party. She was nice, he decided. He was too tired and hungry to use the popcorn for cannon balls, and besides, his soldiers were already lined up for the night and didn't want to go to battle.

Outside the other window he watched the man remove his robot goggles, stand up and stretch. Then the man squirted blue stuff all over his glass cabinet and rubbed it down with a paper towel until it squeaked. He locked the cabinet, put the key in his pocket, and bent down. When Zach saw him reach into his fort, he held his breath like he always did when that happened. Would he find out that the King was missing? Would he find out that Zach took it? But very quickly the man stood up again, grinning and holding a bottle in each hand. He walked over in the direction of the party and out of Zach's line of vision, so Zach scooted back to the first window and watched the man put the bottles on the party table.

So many people were crowded around the table that he couldn't see his mother. What if she had gone home and forgotten him? He liked his fort but he sure didn't want to stay in it all night. That would be really scary, he thought, and the more he thought about the possibility, the more frightened he became. It was already getting dark outside, which made the Indian and the galloping horse look more dangerous than before. He started to cry and reached for his stuffed owl, whispering in its ear, "Where's Mommy? Look for Mommy!"

And then he saw her, standing near the table talking to the new lady, and he felt silly for crying. But she quickly disappeared again behind the man who was carrying a large painting right through the party. When the man moved on, his mother reappeared, standing exactly where she was before. She looked over at his fort and smiled, so he was sure she had not forgotten him.

Suddenly, the party got quiet and everyone watched the sad guy sew the tent together. The sad guy confused Zach. He looked so angry but one day Zach had seen him get a bird out of the tent by cooing and whispering and standing very still, with his arm out to his side like a scarecrow. When the bird finally flew onto his finger, the sad guy walked slowly out to the grass, raised his arm and the bird flew away. Zach liked that.

While everyone was quiet, Zach heard voices behind him, so he scrambled over to the third window, careful not to spill the popcorn, and saw two of his favorite people. One was the pretty lady with the silvery hair who looked like the Christmas angel, with bright blue eyes and pink cheeks. Only this angel lady had big boobies and looked really soft. She had no shoes on, only long white stockings that went all the way up. The other was the cowboy. Zach thought he looked much better that Woody in *Toy Story* except he didn't wear a holster like Woody did. The only thing Zach couldn't understand was why the cowboy hadn't gotten rid of the Indian or roped the big galloping horse.

The cowboy turned off some of the lights, but Zach could still see him. He was kissing the angel lady and touching her all over. The angel was kissing him back and saying things so softly that Zach couldn't hear. He knew he shouldn't watch, because once his mother had turned off the TV when people were kissing like that. She had said, "That's not for children." Ever since then he had wondered what all the fuss was about, so he pushed a pillow over to his window, sat down with his popcorn and his owl, and pretended he was watching TV.

He heard the cowboy say, "Tonight," and the angel say, "Oh, no we can't." Then the cowboy said, louder, down in his throat, "I said *tonight!*" Then she said, in a little voice, "Please, no, I don't want to," and he said, like he was really mad, "Don't tell me *no*." Zach could hear her cry and then he saw the cowboy grab both her arms and hold them over her head and push her hard against the back wall. He could hear the wall thump and he could hear her say, "Oh, no. Please!" and he wished he wasn't watching but he couldn't stop. She cried out softly and this time the cowboy said "Shut up" and smacked her back up against the wall again. Then the cowboy twisted her arm and pushed her through an opening in the wall into the dark space where Zach was sure spiders crawled around among the ladders and brooms and boxes.

He shut his eyes, trying to squeeze the TV picture out of his head, and didn't open them until he had crawled back to the other side of his fort, spilling his popcorn all over his soldiers. People were leaving the party and his mother was saying good-bye to the new lady, so he grabbed the King, wrapped him in his blankie, and put him under the pillow. Then he climbed out of his fort and said, "I want to go home. Now!"

SEVENTEEN

"Hey, take a look at this!" said J.D., pushing the newspaper across the plastic tabletop. Lydia Lopez stared up at them right above the headline:

Dead woman identified as jewel thief

"This the same gal they found on I-10?" asked Tony, gulping down his Egg McMuffin and scanning the article. "She was involved in the Tucson robbery?"

He slowed down to sip his coffee, frowning in concentration as he finished reading the article. Apparently several jewelry reps saw her photo and identified her as the female accomplice who switched stones at the show.

"Says here the Tucson police are looking for the male partner and the Pinal County Sheriff's office is looking for her car." Tony looked over at J.D. and said, "There's gotta be a connection. The two murders happened the same night."

"You're stretching," said J.D. "Besides, she was strangled and Russo was bashed over the head. Doesn't seem like the same perp to me. The fact that both occurred on the same night is just a coincidence." He got up and walked over to the counter and grabbed another packet of ketchup for his fries. "And we still don't have any evidence that Russo's murder had anything to do with jewelry."

"Yeah, I know," Tony agreed. "But the fact is that Peter Sterling lied to us. He said he stayed at the Marriott in Tucson but they never saw him after he registered. He just walked in and then walked out again. No suitcase. No evidence he slept there or used the shower or anything. Had the room two nights and never even used it."

"Yeah, well he paid for the room so he didn't do anything illegal." J.D. sighed and added, "I'm kinda jealous of the guy. I'd like to take off for a weekend and do just what I damn well pleased and have nobody know what I'm doing, who I'm with, where I am. I'd sure like that." He sighed again and stared out the window.

"But he lied to us, J.D. He looked right at us, cool as a cucumber, with that self-satisfied grin. He's too smooth. And he's got too much money. The way he dresses, with his Rolex watch and Italian loafers. How can he afford a BMW? He's selling jewelry in a tent show for heaven's sake. I don't trust him."

J.D. finished his fries. "Look, he was registered at the gem show. He had the proper credentials. People who know him saw him there Friday afternoon, but not Saturday, and they don't connect him with the robbery. I mean, people saw the photo of what's her name... Lydia Lopez, and recognized her immediately as one of the thieves. But no one made that association with Peter."

"We need to contact Tucson, though. And let's stay in touch with the Sheriff's office. If they find the car there may be finger-prints. And they could have found a shoe print near the car...we've got that partial, remember? Why haven't we gotten the report back on that yet? And I want to talk to Peter again and maybe his wife. Shake him up a little."

"Maybe we should shake Eldon and Derrick up, too. No one saw them that night at any of the bars Derrick mentioned. Showed the bartenders pictures, everything. Why aren't you concerned about them?"

"We'll get to them later. But right now I'm more interested in Peter."

They were just about to leave when Tony's phone rang. It was Kate, so he shooed J.D. away and sat back down at the booth farthest in the corner, putting his back to the aisle, and hunching over for privacy. It was not a personal call, however. She had some information for him. Apparently she had promised Sophia she would tell him anything she found out.

He met her at a little donut shop not far from the show. He didn't want more coffee, so he had a juice and donut. If he wasn't careful, he was going to spread out like his Dad did.

She looked thinner and her demeanor was more pleasant, less frazzled. She even greeted him with a smile. Her eyes were as amazing as he remembered.

"I'm sorry to bother you, but I think this may be important," she began.

"Okay, I'm listening."

"Did you know my father was dating a woman at the show? Connie?"

"Yes. Actually, I wondered if *you* knew. She seemed very nice." He wasn't sure where this was going.

"You met her?"

"Yeah, we had a little talk."

"What did she tell you?"

"Kate, I'm sorry. I can't tell you that. I hope you understand..."

"Oh, yes, of course. I didn't mean to...well, anyway, I'm sure you also heard about Jess, the maintenance guy, the one who gave my father lots of trouble?" She looked at him expectantly, waiting for his response. Tony nodded but didn't say anything.

"Did you talk to him, too?"

"Yeah. We talked."

"Did you know they're related, Jess and Connie?"

"No, I sure didn't. But..."

"Well, they are. I could tell there was something between them, so I asked around. Not too many people knew this, but Jess is her son. He's Jess Whitcomb, and she's..."

"She's Connie Cunningham. Well, that's very interesting," Tony said, wondering how he had let that get by him. He tried to remember the details of his interview with Connie, but all he could recall was how upset she was about Art. And hadn't J.D. said he'd spoken to "Jess' mother"...something about watching videos? What was going on?

"The important thing is that Daddy apparently put a crimp in Jess' lifestyle. Whenever Jess got into trouble, Connie would bail him out. Whenever he needed money, Connie would give him some..."

And whenever he needed an alibi, Connie would provide that as well, thought Tony. The parts still didn't fit together, but he'd wait for Kate to leave before he tried to make sense of it all.

"Apparently Daddy tried to get Connie to stop being such an easy target. He thought Jess was taking advantage of her. When she stopped giving him what he wanted, Jess got furious with Daddy."

"That certainly explains the animosity," Tony admitted. "But you know, even if that's true, Jess is just a loner...a loser, really. In my experience those guys just thrash around when they get mad and then slink away. They're usually not..."

"I know. But if you'd like to hear my professional opinion, I think this guy is truly antisocial. He's aggressive and irritable. His posture, his vocabulary, his whole appearance...he doesn't consider other people's feelings. No apologies, no remorse. He treats his mom like shit one minute and gets her to give him money the next. Sometimes those people are just misfits, like you say. But some of them are criminals, too. I'm sorry, I don't mean to lecture you on the disorder..." She shook her head in frustration. "Look, Tony, I don't know if you have any other leads, but I really think Jess could have done this. And if he did, I would expect that Connie would cover for him. Did she?"

"I told you, Kate, I can't..."

"Yes, I know." She sipped her coffee and made a face. "Nothing worse than cold coffee."

She started to bite a nail, frowned, and moved her hand down to her lap. She looked so vulnerable that he said exactly what he knew she wanted him to say. "Kate, I think you found something important, and believe me, I'll follow up on it right away. I promise." He reached out to touch her hand. She pulled it back, but not too quickly, he noticed. He decided to get back to the subject at hand.

"But how did you find all this out?"

She smiled at him and put her finger to her lips. "So sorry, Tony. I have to keep my sources confidential."

He smiled back. "Speaking of confidentiality, don't talk to anyone about your suspicions, or what you're thinking, or what you're telling me. In fact, I wish you wouldn't get involved in this at all. That's what I'm here for."

"Oh, I'm not, not really. It's just that I'm pretty good at reading body language, that's all. I'm looking for...what you'd call non-verbal clues." She pushed her hair behind her ears and he saw she was wearing Peter Sterling's distinctive gold and silver dangles. Were those garnets or rubies, he wondered?

"You've got on another pair of Peter Sterling's earrings. Very nice on you, by the way." He added, as casually as he could, "Have you bought a lot of stuff from him? Sophia mentioned..."

"That he made a little play for her? Well, she shot him down real fast. Actually, he was only trying to sell her some jewelry, but she thought his approach was really irritating."

"Has he made a play for you, too?"

"Peter? Oh, no. Actually he's been very nice."

"Well, do you agree with Sophia? That his approach is irritating? Or even intimidating?"

"Well, yes and no. He can be a little overbearing. But harmless, I think. And his jewelry is gorgeous." She touched the earrings and said, "I haven't bought these, you know...I just model them for him. If any one compliments me, I'm supposed to direct them to his booth. I've only had to do it once, so I'm probably not a very good model."

"You look wonderful; you're a great model." He felt foolish as soon as he said it, and immediately added, "Be careful, Kate. Please be careful."

"Why? With Peter?"

"Yes. No. With everyone. Just take care."

There was an awkward moment. She picked up her things and said, "Please let me know what you find out about Jess. As soon as you can. He frightens me, he really does." When she stood up she added, "If Jess did this..." She couldn't finish the sentence. "I just need to know."

He watched through the window as she walked to her truck. She still took long strides and her hair swung back and forth, but somehow she was different. He was still wondering what it was about her that had changed when she pulled out into the traffic and disappeared around the corner.

He immediately reached for his phone and called J.D. He tried not to raise his voice.

"I thought you interviewed Jess' mother."

"I did. What's the matter?"

"Did you meet her?"

"No. Just talked to her on the phone. Real nice lady."

"What was her name?"

"Hold on." He could hear J.D. fumbling around, probably flipping the pages of his notebook.

"Here it is. Mary Whitcomb."

"Mary? You sure?"

"Well, if you want to be formal, Mary Constance Whitcomb."

"Mary Constance? That's Connie!"

"Constance. Connie. I don't get it. What're you saying?"

"You spoke to Mary Constance Whitcomb on the phone and she gave Jess an alibi—something about watching videos. I met with Connie Cunningham at the Cheesecake Factory and we had a different conversation altogether. She said she and Art went out for dinner that night. Point is, Mary Constance and Connie are one and the same."

"Holy shit!"

"How the hell did we let that happen?" Tony knew his voice was getting louder, so he hung up before he yelled at J.D. The fault belonged to both of them.

Tony bounded up the short set of stairs into the office, greeted Mrs. Morrow, and asked to see Connie. If she was surprised by the request she didn't show it. She merely picked up a microphone and paged her. "Connie, please come to the office." She repeated the message twice and Tony walked back down the steps so their conversation couldn't be overheard by the staff.

He watched her approach. Today she was wearing a long wool skirt and boots, with some kind of quilted jacket. Everything, including her jewelry, was classy and understated. He could see her pleasant expression change when she saw him, but then it returned, this time like one of those generic smiles, the kind that looked pasted on.

He greeted her first. "Hello, Connie. Can you take a break? Perhaps we could go outside and walk around?" Before she could reply, Tony cupped her elbow with his left hand and extended his right arm, pointing her toward the entrance. It was a polite gesture and one she was not likely to resist.

They walked past the parked cars until they came to the path that circled the lot and separated it from the surrounding desert.

"Okay, Connie. You did a little song and dance for us. Now why don't you set us straight."

"I didn't mean to...Oh Lord! I knew you'd find out. I don't know what to say." She was nearly in tears, but she held her head up as if she had often faced setbacks and had always forged ahead.

"Let's start with you and Art. You were at Arrivederci's for dinner that night. True or not?"

"Yes, we were. That's all true."

"So you weren't home watching videos with Jess, like you told Detective Harris?"

"No, well, not exactly."

"Why did you lie?"

"Lie? That's such an ugly word."

"True. Nevertheless, why'd you lie?"

"Jess asked me to," she said quietly.

"Did he say why he wanted you to lie?"

"Yes. But it didn't have anything to do with Art. He was out with his friend, Lewis. They were probably drunk. They usually are. Things got out of hand and they broke a store window. The alarm went off, and they ran."

"What store? I can check, you know."

"Ralston's. I already checked. And paid for the repairs." She sounded weary. "Look, he has a record and this would really be a big problem."

"You're right, it would."

"He got home right after I did, around ten o'clock, and stayed home, so you see he didn't have anything to do with what happened to Art. He didn't like Art, but he could never hurt anyone, not like that. It's just that the two things happened the same night and it seemed simpler to...and then...oh, I don't know."

"But surely you knew someone would find out. You can't be two people for long."

"I know, I know." She was silent for a minute and then added, "You'd be amazed at what you do when you've got a son like Jess. Are you going to have to report him?"

"Let's get to that later." They had rounded the parking lot and were within a hundred feet of the entrance to the show. Tony asked, "If you lied to me before, why should I believe you now?"

Connie stopped and turned to look at him. "You know, Detective, no one has ever doubted my word before. I don't like not being trusted." She resumed walking. "But I guess I can only blame myself. All I can say is that I'm not lying. Please believe me. I was under a lot of stress, what with Art in the hospital..." She gulped in a breath and straightened her shoulders defiantly. "I'm really sorry I lied. And I'm sorry Jess keeps getting into trouble. But most of all," her voice cracked a bit, "I'm sorry Art is dead." With that she turned away and walked back into the tent. Tony knew that if there had been a door she would have slammed it in his face.

Did he believe her? Yeah. He never thought it was Jess, anyway. Still, he'd have to check it all out before he told Kate.

EIGHTEEN

The tent flaps remained laced up as a protection against the cold wet weather that had slipped into Arizona in the middle of the night. The forecast was for several days of drizzle with daytime temperatures in the 50s and near freezing at night. The tents were drafty, the asphalt floor was cold as ice, and the only heat was whatever radiated from the halogen spotlights installed by the artists.

Kate had rummaged through her father's closet and found an old brown windbreaker that was large enough to go over her sweatshirt, which in turn went over a turtleneck sweater. She remembered the jacket from years ago. It was worn and soft on the elbows and under the arms, but the zip-in alpaca lining was as good as new. She smiled at the evidence of her father's thrift—a 25-year-old windbreaker, for goodness sake.

This morning she was sitting in the café with Vicki, trying to warm herself in the steam that rose from her coffee cup. The plastic chair seemed to draw every bit of warmth from her body and she realized that what she needed most of all were thermal underwear, mittens, and thick-soled boots.

Zach was under the table br-br-brum-ming a miniature tank in a complicated pattern on the asphalt floor, occasionally ramming it into Kate's new tote bag or over her cold feet. She knew the ramming was accidental because it was always followed by a gentle, apologetic pat on her shins.

Vicki poked at a photo in the newspaper. "I really, really want to go to the ArtWalk this week. If I get Mom to babysit Zach, will you come with me?"

"Art walk? You lost me. What's an art walk?"

"It's every Thursday night. Downtown Scottsdale. All the galleries. You just walk from one gallery to the next. Look at art. Drink wine. Meet artists. Schmooze with lots of artsy-fartsy types—collectors, wannabes. I guess I'm a wannabe myself," she laughed, adding, "Seriously, I don't want to miss Brad Brenner's opening.

Vickie pushed the paper across the table for Kate to see. There was a photo of the artist, tall and handsome, posing in front of a large, distorted portrait of a young woman.

"Sure, sounds like fun. But I don't know beans about contemporary art." She squinted at the photo again. "Frankly, I like your work better than his."

"Well, then you're absolutely right: you *don't* know beans about modern art. Not if you like my stuff better than his. Just wait till you see it in person. It's totally amazing. Ouch. Zach!"

A little voice under the table said a soft "sorry" and Zach scampered out, nudged close to his mother, and whispered in her ear, all the while eyeing Kate.

"Potty break," Vicki mouthed to Kate, getting up quickly. "Keep the newspaper."

Kate turned to the local news section and glanced briefly at the photo of a young woman in a cap and gown, but before she could even wonder about the girl's story, her eyes moved over to an article about the Lydia Lopez murder. There was no picture this time, only more information about the gem theft in Tucson and the fact that the Lopez car had been located, hidden behind some scrub brush out in the desert, a mile northeast of where the body had been found. The medical examiner determined she had been strangled. Kate got another cup of hot coffee and read the article through a second time. She remembered Lydia Lopez' brave little smile and couldn't stop shivering.

The ladies' room, which was part of an unheated trailer attached to the tents, was not very appealing, and Kate had avoided it as much as possible. Today the room was absolutely freezing, and Kate was trying to untangle her layers of clothing as expeditiously as possible when she heard a cry—or was it a moan?—from the next stall. The sound so startled her that she froze, curious and cautious. Another moan, soft and childlike, escaped into the cold air. Kate quickly reassembled her clothing and asked, "Are you all right in there? Can I help?"

"No. I'm okay."

Kate emerged from her stall and tapped lightly on the other door. "Do you need some help? May I come in?"

"No. I said I'm okay."

Kate paused. "I'll wait then."

"No. Don't wait. Just leave. I won't come out unless you leave. I don't want... don't want to see anyone."

Kate couldn't place the voice, although it was familiar. "I can go get some help. Do you need any help?"

"No. No help. Please, please leave."

Kate paused again. "Okay, then. I'm leaving."

She walked out of the restroom, closed the door behind her, and leaned against it. Whoever it was couldn't stay in there forever. She wished she had thought to look under the partition, if only to see whether the person was young or old. Should she wait or should she go to the office? Would they even care if someone was crying in the ladies' room? What if someone else came by? Should she keep everyone out? The door finally nudged open and Gretchen Schmidt emerged. Her head was down and silvery hair veiled her face. No beautiful hairdo with wraparound braids this morning.

Kate moved close, put her arm through hers, and said quietly,

"You okay? Would you like a cup of coffee...or maybe some hot chocolate?"

Gretchen turned her head away and mumbled, "No, no. I just want to go home."

"That's probably a good idea. I'll walk you out to your car."

Gretchen didn't protest, so they went out, arm in arm, past a few customers at the ticket table, through the gray, drizzly parking lot to where her Camry was parked. While Gretchen fumbled to get in the driver's seat, Kate slipped in on the passenger side.

"Gretchen, are you sure you're okay to drive? Let me take a look at you." She reached over and touched her on the chin. Gretchen winced and turned her face away. Then she turned back, and Kate had to stifle a gasp as she took in the cut lip and purple bruises and swollen eyes.

"Oh, Gretchen, who did this to you? And how in the world did you even drive here this morning? You can barely open your eyes!"

"I'm okay. Please, please don't say anything." Tears flowed down her cheeks and when she tried to wipe them away she made the same moaning sound Kate had heard in the rest room.

"You didn't drive here this morning, did you? You were here all night! Who were you with? Who did this to you?"

Gretchen looked down, letting her hair cascade over her face. She was crying softly. Kate was almost in tears herself. She struggled to put herself in a more professional frame of mind, to remember what she had learned over the last several years. But all those classes seemed so long ago and so foreign to the here-and-now. Besides, she had never had very much practical experience, and what she did have was in a controlled environment, not suddenly, emotionally, out of nowhere, to be handled in a cold damp car with someone she knew.

"Gretchen, listen to me. You need to see a doctor. You may need some stitches. And you need to tell someone who did this to you. Do you want me to call the police?"

"Oh, no, please, please, no! That would just make it worse. Besides, he didn't mean to hurt me. He really didn't. It's just that

115

he…that I made him mad." She tugged at her short skirt and then pushed her hair back from her face. "I want to go home now."

She was clutching her keys tightly, her knuckles white. But when she tried to insert the key into the ignition, her arm shook so violently that Kate reached over to steady it. "Is there someone at home to take care of you? Can I come with you and make sure you'll be all right? I could drive you home or follow you in my car. Just to make sure you're okay?"

"No. I don't want anyone coming home with me. I'll be fine." She took a deep breath, put the key in the ignition, and said, in a soft, low growl, "Now please get out and leave me alone."

The new tone of voice surprised Kate, so she patted Gretchen's hand and reluctantly got out of the car. Gretchen backed out of the space slowly, and Kate found herself standing in a shallow puddle next to a black Silverado. A gun rack caught her eye, and the violence it suggested, added to what she had just witnessed, made her shiver. As she turned back to the entrance she noticed some of Gretchen's drawings on the front seat of the truck. If she were a betting woman, she'd bet this was the guy. Well, it shouldn't be too hard to find out who owned the dang truck.

When she approached the office and saw Connie walking down the steps, she stepped back out of sight and waited for her to disappear down the aisle into the south tent. All morning she had been waiting to hear what Tony had found out about Jess, whether he could have been the one, whether Connie might have known something. Yesterday she was sure it was Jess. Today she didn't want it to be him, because she didn't want Connie to be involved. She had looked at Connie's pictures last night, especially the one on her father's dresser, and knew that he would not have been pleased with what she had done yesterday. He would have wanted her to protect Connie. Instead, look what she had done—squealed to the cops. She was beginning to make a mess of things, as usual.

Once in the office she was greeted by one of the staff, an overwrought young woman with spiked red hair and black eyeliner.

"Oh, Kate, there you are. I was just going to page you. Mr. Von Steen is on the phone for you." She was waving the phone from across the room.

"Would you just take his number? Tell him I'll call him right back." Kate was trying to focus. On Gretchen. On the truck.

"But this is the third time he's tried to reach you. You really should take the call." She walked toward her with the phone, still waving it, blue fingernails flashing.

"Who's got a black Silverado with Idaho plates?" Kate blurted out, accepting the phone.

"The one with the gun rack? Derrick. Derrick Hughes. Why?"

"Derrick?" Kate repeated, lifting the phone to her ear.

"No, this isn't Derrick. This is Mark. Mark Von Steen. Am I speaking with Kate Russo?"

"Yes. This is Kate. Sorry, I was talking to someone else. I'll call you right back." Without waiting for a response she hung up and repeated, "Derrick? You said Derrick owns the Silverado?"

"Yeah. It's Derrick's. Is it blocking someone? His lights on? Something the matter?"

"No. No, nothing's the matter." She handed back the phone and turned to leave, trying to put Derrick in focus, too, along with Gretchen.

She was all the way down the steps before she realized she had not gotten Mr. Von Steen's phone number. But before she could go back up, the phone rang from inside her purse. She watched at least three people nearby check their pockets to see if the call was for them, but when the tinny little tune continued, they all resumed what they were doing.

It was Tony. Yes, he had checked on Jess' alibi. And yes, Connie had tried to protect her son. But no, Jess didn't do it. Yes, he was sure.

At first, Kate was relieved. But then, she thought: if Jess didn't do it, her father's killer was still out there somewhere. *Derrick* could be the killer! He was certainly violent enough. She was about to tell

Tony what Derrick had done to Gretchen, but before she had a chance, he said he had to go, he would call her tomorrow.

She shivered again and pulled up the collar of the old jacket. She smelled the familiar after-shave and felt like crying. She should never have gotten involved. She should just let it be, let it alone. Let Tony do it all. She should go back to the house. Go pee in a nice warm bathroom. Take a hot shower. Light the fire. Curl up like a cat and take a nap. That way she couldn't mess anything up.

So that's exactly what she did, pushing visions of Gretchen's bruised and swollen face to the outer edge of her mind's eye. In her dreams she glided in circles around and around a large cold rink, nervously skating on the thin ice, past Gretchen and Derrick and Connie and a blur of people sitting along the perimeter. Perhaps they wouldn't notice if she fell.

NINETEEN

"You should have invited Kate," said Sophia, pointing her fork across the table at Tony.

"Sophia. Put your fork down. The dinner table is no place for the duel." Inez passed her daughter a platter of tamales.

"Sorry, Ma. But Tonio, you're really such a schmuck..."

"Sophia. No name calling." She passed her a bowl of green chili sauce.

"Sorry, Ma. But don't you think he should have invited Kate?"

There were only the three of them tonight. Angela and her family had gone to Los Angeles for a visit and Uncle Manny was in bed with the flu. Inez apparently had chosen not to extend any other invitations. Tony thought she looked a little tired.

"I think it's up to Tonio," Inez said, shrugging. Her tone of voice suggested that she agreed with her daughter and was secretly insulted that Tony had ignored her invitation to include Kate for dinner this evening.

"The next time I invite Kate anywhere it will be a real date. Just the two of us. And she's not ready for that."

"I wouldn't be so sure, brother dear. I think she likes you. And besides, she needs to have some fun. What's wrong with that? You don't want her to get back with old what's-his-name in New Jersey, do you?"

119

"She won't. She's changed somehow. She's a little more...I don't know...serene. Still, she needs more time."

"Has she found out anything yet? You know, like clues? Wouldn't it be great if she helped find the killer?"

"Sophia! No detective-talk at the dinner table. What's the matter with you tonight? And why poor Kate has to do detective work, anyway? It's not safe. Why should she have to skate on hot water?"

Tony grinned, but a chuckle bubbled up from Sophia's throat. "Oh, Ma, you skate on *thin ice*, not *hot water*."

"Sophia!" Inez turned red. "You are excused from the table. You do not laugh at your mother."

But instead, Inez herself got up from the table in a huff and stomped into the kitchen to make the coffee.

Tony looked over at Sophia and shook his head. "She'll forgive you by the time the coffee's made, you know that. But you hurt her feelings. You need to apologize."

"I will, but *skating on hot water*. Can you picture it?" Sophia leaned over and whispered, "Seriously, have you got a suspect yet?"

"I'm not sure. We may know in the morning."

J.D. and Tony sat on the matching wingback chairs that flanked the large stone fireplace in Peter Sterling's vast living room. J.D. was acutely aware that the matching chairs emphasized the difference in their stature, so he sat up straight and planted an elbow on each of the upholstered arms, determined not to be gobbled up in the cushions.

Debra Sterling, small, delicate and reserved, had insisted on lighting a fire and serving them tea, more to avoid conversation than to be hospitable, Tony thought. Peter was upstairs in the shower and had no idea they were there.

"So, Mrs. Sterling, you didn't go to the Tucson Gem Show with your husband?" asked Tony.

"No. I stayed here. At home." She appeared to examine an imaginary spot on the carpet.

"May I ask why?"

"I don't like the gem shows. I only like to design."

"*You're* the designer?"

"Yes. I design. Then Peter makes the jewelry."

"I had no idea you worked at this together."

"I didn't say we worked together. I said I design. Then he adds what he wants later. He likes gemstones." Her chin went up. "We do not design together."

Tony noticed the pendant at her throat. The style was by now familiar to him, but there were no stones on the pendant. There were no stones on her ring, either. Tony rather liked the look. Clean, uncluttered, but richly textured.

Peter entered the room, his soft leather loafers quiet on the carpet, and Tony caught the flush of confusion on his face when he saw who was there. A broad and friendly smile quickly followed.

"Captain Berrigan, right?"

"*Detective*. Detective *Bannigan*," Tony corrected. "And this is Detective Harris. We'd like to ask you a few questions."

"Certainly." Peter looked around the room quickly. "Debra, sweet, could you get me a cup of tea, too? I'm rather chilly, even with the fire."

As soon as she left the room Peter sat down on the sofa nearest Tony and whispered, "My god, man, why'd you have to come here? What's this got to do with my wife, anyway?"

Tony responded without lowering his voice. "You weren't honest with us, Peter. We wanted to help refresh your memory. We thought your wife might assist..."

"Okay, okay. You're right. But, for heaven's sake, let's not do this here." He stood up and called to his wife. "Debra, sweet, never mind the tea. The gentlemen would like to see the putting green out back."

Peter walked over to the row of French doors and said, "Please, it's right out here."

Tony and J.D. followed him out to a broad, covered patio paved with handsome saltillo tiles. Crimson-tipped bougainvilleae grew out of gigantic clay pots in the far corners and climbed up the thick columns before flaring out from the red-tiled roof. The desert foothills were so close to the property that they seemed to break up into huge boulders just inches from the low stucco wall that surrounded the property. Inside the wall were a pool, a spa and a beautifully manicured putting green.

"It's cold out here, Peter, so make it quick," said Tony, purposely ignoring the surrounding luxury.

But J.D. smiled and turned his head very slowly, as if to enjoy every square inch of the scene before him. "You got a really nice place here." He turned his head some more and paused. "Real nice place. Real nice car. Real nice clothes." Then he turned to Peter, still smiling, and added, "You must sell an awful lot of real nice jewelry."

"Look, I don't know what you guys think I did, but whatever it is, I didn't do it." He turned and glanced back through the French doors, lowering his voice. "I cheated on my wife, that's all. Honest. I went to Tucson and met someone. We had a fling and then I lied about it. Naturally. I lied to my wife. Then I lied to you. That's it." He put his hands in his pockets, looked down at his perfectly shined Italian loafers, and said, "Look, we're all men of the world..."

"We don't all live in the same world, though, do we?" asked Tony, glancing around the property. Then he shifted his gaze to Peter's boyish face and jabbed his finger into his chest. "We'll give you a break this time. We won't embarrass you in front of your wife if it's not necessary, but we want to see you down at our place in two hours. Expect to stay a while. And we don't serve tea."

J.D. looked at the report, shook his head in amazement, and said, "Just lookee here. We got a shoe print from the Pinal County Sheriff's office and you'll never believe it: it's a woman's size 12W Made by Naturalizer. Style's called *Napoli*. Ugly shoe. Just look at this picture." He handed Tony the report.

"Wait a minute! I've seen shoes like that." Tony squinted at the photo. "Yeah, when I was talking to Gretchen Schmidt. She was in her stocking feet, and she had kicked her shoes in the corner. They were just like that, plain black loafers with fat, chunky heels—and I wouldn't be surprised if gorgeous Gretchen wears a size 12W, would you?"

"No, but I *would* be surprised if she had anything to do with the Lydia Lopez murder. Fact is, she was in the tents that night, remember?"

"Sure, she was there, J.D., but not until after nine. What time did the Lopez murder happen?"

"Who knows? They didn't find the body for a few days, so they're probably not going to know the exact time." J.D. frowned. "But this is just crazy..."

"Yeah. It's crazy, all right. Too crazy. It's probably not Gretchen's shoe at all." Tony glanced at his watch. "Peter Sterling will be here any minute now. I'll take him on and you go find out what size shoe Gretchen wears. And where she was earlier that night." Then he winked at J.D. "Just don't get too close—she might be dangerous."

J.D. smiled. "I sure hope so."

Tony finished the interview with Peter, returned to his desk, looked at his computer monitor and groaned. Colorful reminders of questions still unanswered were stuck to the sides. He impatiently peeled off a few old ones that belonged to other cases, crumbled them into a brightly colored ball, and shot it in the direction of the wastebasket. He stuck the remaining notes in a neat row across the top of the screen.

A bright yellow post-it screamed 'extra vehicle.' Tony still didn't know who else had driven to the show the night of the murder, and although there seemed no way to find out, he left the post-it in place.

The one in the middle was purple, noting 'security system.' Well, at least they had checked that out and found the fencing intact and the security light in good working order. Nothing had been tampered with. He peeled off the post-it, folded it in half, and sent it flying into the air.

Then there was the hot pink 'missing sculpture?' reminder. Although he had inquired of both the staff and other artists, no one seemed to remember if there had been another sculpture on display in Art Russo's booth before the murder. The photo he had found of the mother and child sculpture was no help because he knew it couldn't have been the weapon. It would have been impossible to hold up something that heavy with one hand and strike someone over the head with it, and if held with two hands, the impact would have killed Russo instantly, leaving blood and skull and brain splattered all over the place. No, what he was looking for was smaller, perhaps six, maybe eight inches high, and lighter weight.

He scratched his head, pulled out a blue post-it and wrote 'is Peter gay?' Next, on a lime green one, he wrote 'Gretchen's shoe.' He hated the lime-green color, but he knew that it would probably be peeled off as soon as J.D. got back. Finally he added 'Derrick's alibi: Eldon?' on luminous orange. He smacked all three across the top next to the other two, looked at the collection, and groaned again.

The interview with Peter Sterling had irritated him almost beyond endurance. The more the guy talked the more Tony found that he actually liked him. Worse yet, the more he talked the more innocent he looked, and the more convinced Tony became that the guy was gay and was just doing his best to hide the details of his little outing to Tucson. Tony had nothing against gays. There were several in the department, and one of his cousins was gay, and it just didn't seem to matter in real life. But it was different with a suspect. Then everything mattered. Absolutely everything.

Apparently Peter's wife had inherited a good deal of money, which explained their lavish lifestyle. As for the weekend, Peter maintained that he had registered at the Marriott only to fool his wife. He claimed to have no recollection of whom he had been with or where they had gone. Just one blur of booze and fun and sex, he said. Tony didn't believe he was the booze and fun and sex kind of guy. A straight guy, out on the town, would have been willing and able to describe *something* of his adventures. Too much detail—or too little—was a sure giveaway that a story was fabricated. When asked directly if he was with a man or woman, Peter lost his unflappable charm, uttered a string of obscenities, and reeled off a list of topless bars where he was sure someone must have seen him.

What troubled Tony was why, if Peter was gay as he suspected, had he come on to his sister. Was he flirting just to cover up? To make a sale? Perhaps Sophia had misunderstood. She was usually a pretty keen observer. And so was Kate, he realized. God, he missed her. Then he remembered how it felt to hold her close that night in the car. He groaned again, and threw his pencil against the wall.

TWENTY

Kate wanted to exchange one pair of earrings for another, her usual morning ritual with Peter, but he hadn't come in yet. She had been looking forward to hearing him tell her what pretty ears she had and what a wonderful model she made. She knew it was vain and child-ish, but today she simply wanted to feel she was good at something.

What a wimp she had been yesterday. She had slept poorly and awakened with feelings of dread, but during the two hours she had taken this morning to shower, dress and read the paper, she had managed to pull herself together.

The weather had warmed considerably. During the drive to the tents, in her now-beloved blue truck, she saw that the sun was occa-sionally popping out from behind the fast-drifting clouds. Maybe by tonight, for the ArtWalk, the weather would be clear. She was sorry she had agreed to go, but it was too late to change plans now that Vicki had arranged for a baby-sitter.

The first thing on her agenda today was to decide whether to report Derrick to Tony. If Gretchen didn't want to bring charges against him, was there anything she could do? She should have called Tony back yesterday. He would know how to handle it. She wouldn't mind seeing him again, anyway.

She shoved her tote bag under the desk and dusted off the

sculptures. Then she reached for her cell phone, only to be interrupted by Eldon.

"You have a minute, Kate? I've been wanting to talk to you about this piece, the *Girl with Dog*." He was looking handsome in his usual tweed jacket, but weighed down by two large cameras strapped to his shoulder. Dangling from his other hand was a small digital camera. "I have a niece who has a dog just like that. Her mother would absolutely love that sculpture in her living room."

"It really is nice, isn't it? I get more comments on that one than on any of the others, except *The Cook*. I sold two of those this week."

"Kate, when someone says they really like one of the sculptures, you're supposed to try and sell it to them. Don't you want me to buy it?"

"I didn't think you were really...of course, I'd love to sell it to you, but isn't it a little expensive...?"

"Hey, don't insult me, too! You're never supposed to suggest that a customer can't afford to buy what he wants. And yes, I can afford it, so put my name down on the list and I'll settle with you tomorrow." He smiled at her surprise. How did he manage to look appreciative and patronizing at the same time, she wondered.

"You're kidding! Well, sure..."

"No, wait, put my sister's name on the list instead. She'll be visiting in a few days and I can surprise her by showing her the list. A good birthday present, don't you think?"

"I'd say. Here, why don't you write her name down, next to number nine."

"Well, well, number nine. Business must be good if you've only got one more to go. By the way, what happens if you don't sell one more before the show's over? Will you have it cast anyway?"

"Goodness, I don't know. Hadn't thought about it. But I'm sure I can sell one more. After all, I've got two weeks left."

"True enough. Hey, looks like you've got another customer, so I'll see you later."

He no sooner walked off than Kate heard a familiar voice behind her.

"Kate? Kate Russo?"

"Yes?"

"Good morning. I'm Mark Von Steen."

"Oh dang, I forgot to call you back! I'm so sorry, really I am."

Mr. Von Steen was at least 80. He had a full head of white hair and tiny blue eyes and smelled of after-shave. He smiled and shook her hand. "Actually, you've forgotten three times, young lady, and if you were my daughter—or granddaughter—you'd get a severe talking to." He walked over to the chair, asked "May I?" and sat right down.

"Certainly. Let me just...let me borrow someone's chair...hold on, and then we can talk...yes, now what did you want to see me about, Mr. Von Steen?"

He didn't reply right away so she continued. "You wanted to talk to me about a commission? Perhaps you don't know, but my father died recently, and so a commission is impossible."

"Oh dear, no, no, that's not it at all." He frowned, a little confused. "It's about the competition your father won, for the Northern Arizona Insurance Company."

"I'm afraid I don't know what you're talking about."

"Well, well," he said, obviously surprised at her response. "Just let me think a minute." His blue eyes darted over toward the sculpture garden and he sighed. "Oh my. Things do get me a little confused sometimes." He let his eyes wander around the booth, from sculpture to sculpture. His gaze finally rested on *Old Man Reading*. "I don't suppose you saw me at the funeral, my dear, but I was there and I wanted to talk to you, but then I realized it wasn't the right time. You see, I knew your father and thought very highly of him. I'm so sorry for your loss, my dear, I really am." He turned his head and looked at Kate. "Do you miss him?"

"Yes, I do." She fought back the tears that came unbidden and looked away. "A lot. I miss him a lot."

"Yes, well that's a good thing. It really is." He paused. "He told me a little about you."

Kate squirmed. "I'm sorry, Mr. Von Steen, but who are you, exactly?"

"Me? Oh, I'm sorry. I'm chairman of the board of Northern Arizona Insurance Company. You see, we had a competition for a sculpture to be placed in front of our corporate headquarters and your father won the competition. He did a small study, you know, in clay, a rough version of what the piece would look like. It's about, oh, twenty inches high. Of course, the finished bronze was to be life-size and would stand on a magnificent pedestal." He looked off into the sculpture garden again, as if he might find it there.

Kate was about to ask what the sculpture looked like, when he continued. "His subject was a father and daughter. The girl appears to be about nine or ten. Looks a little like you, I think. It's just lovely. The father is comforting his daughter as they stand near a headstone. The gestures are so simple, so true. They show how much the father cares for his daughter, and how he will protect her, and since we're an insurance company, it seemed..."

"I never knew any of this!"

"You never knew about the eighty thousand?"

"Eighty thousand? Dollars? You're kidding!"

"When you're my age, you don't waste much time kidding, my dear."

"Eighty thousand. Dang, that's a lot of money! Daddy must have been thrilled, not only about the money, just the honor..."

"Now, of course, the commission will have to go to the second place winner. That was in the rules, you know. But I wanted to see you because I would like to buy the sketch. I'd like to have it cast in bronze, and have just two copies made, one for you and one for me. I'd pay you five thousand and pay the foundry costs, of course. If that's not enough..."

"Five thousand? For a study? And you'd pay the foundry cost and then give me one? You've got a deal, Mr. Von Steen! But why?"

"Oh, it's really for my daughter. She loved it, too, and she'll inherit it, of course. You see, I lost her mother back..." His eyes wandered around, as if looking for something he had misplaced, and then he turned back to Kate and shrugged his shoulders.

She felt like kissing the old gentleman but instead said a simple

"Thanks so much. You're very kind."

"Well, that's that, then," he said, standing up unsteadily. "I'll have my secretary send you the check." He placed her hand in his and gave it a squeeze. "But next time don't keep an old man waiting so long. It's not nice." He smiled at her and then looked at his watch. "Now I guess I'll go find Derrick Hughes and tell him he's got the commission."

"*Derrick?*"

"Yes, my dear, Derrick. Frankly, I don't like his work very much at all, but I wasn't the only one judging, so there you have it."

Tony pulled into the driveway and remembered the last time he had been there, the soft and sad embrace and the smell of her hair. He shook his head to chase away the memory and make room for the issue at hand. Kate's urgent call had gotten him out of the station and over to her father's house in less than 10 minutes.

They sat across from each other at the breakfast room table, drinking coffee. The nearby window looked out to the back patio, still wet from the rain. The potted plants were thriving, bright spots of color cheering the still-gray day.

Her eyes were opened wide and they stared directly into his. She leaned forward so far that Tony caught a whiff of the phantom fragrance.

"Don't you see? Eighty thousand dollars! And now it's all his." She stared right into him, demanding that he agree with her.

She sat back again, but the fragrance lingered over the table between them, and he tried to memorize it, like he would a flavor, or a color.

"Don't you agree?" she insisted, "that it's a motive? I mean, eighty thousand dollars is a lot of money."

"Granted. But there would be simpler ways..."

"And he's violent. He could easily have..."

"How do you know he's violent?" Tony was alert now.

Kate looked down at her hands, frowned, and lowered them to her lap. She closed her eyes and Tony saw her long lashes flutter as she searched for what to say.

"I was going to talk to you about that yesterday, when you called to tell me Jess wasn't the murderer, but you got off the phone so quickly. I should have called you back." She looked up at him and said softly, "I saw what he did."

"What Derrick did? What he did to whom? When?"

"Two nights ago. I saw…"

"Nights? You saw him at night?"

"No, no, you don't understand…"

"For heaven's sake, Kate, how could you be so stupid…"

Her chin came up and he saw her face change from thoughtful to furious in a split second.

"Don't yell at me. And I wasn't out with him. He did it to Gretchen. In the tents. At night. I found out the next morning." She glared at him and spit out the rest. "He beat the shit out of her." Tears flowed, and she looked away as she wiped her face.

He let the moment pass in silence, absorbing the information, estimating its importance, calculating its relevance. He wished he had heard back from J.D. about the damn shoe so he'd know how to put Gretchen into the picture.

The old Kate was looking back at him, the one from the first night in the hospital—prickly, defensive, temperamental. She sounded the same, too. "And how dare you call me stupid. I'm giving you important information and you're treating me like a child. Look, I know I was wrong about Jess. And I'm sorry about that. But this time it's different."

"Oh, Kate, for heaven's sake. Forget what I just said. I worry about you, that's all."

His phone rang, jangling his already taut nerves. He pulled it out of its case and barked into it, "Bannigan here," ready to hang up at the slightest provocation. Instead, he heard Sophia say, "Well, brother dear, I see you're in a cheerful mood today."

"What do you want?"

"Wow, Tonio, what's wrong with you? I think you need a date...a little..."

"Don't even go there, Sophia."

"Oops, sorry! Why don't you just call Kate? Take her out and get to know her, you know, in the biblical..."

"What's the hell's the matter with you?"

"Well, it would do you both good. Beside, she likes you..."

"You said that before. But you were wrong then and you're wrong now. What do you want, anyway?"

"Oh, just to tell you somebody called me, trying to get in touch with Kate. He wouldn't leave his name though. I thought that was strange, that's all."

"Yeah, that's weird, all right. Now go back to class or whatever it is you do and stop bothering me. I'll call you later." And he hung up.

Tony put his head in his hands, irritated at his own testiness. "I'm sure making a lot of enemies today. First I yell at you. Then I yell at Sophia. But you need to stay out of this, Kate, you really do."

"Look, Tony, you've got to understand something. I can't stay out of it. I mean, this is about my father, after all. So you're just going to have to put up with me. Besides, not doing anything is the worse thing of all. Like yesterday, when I saw Gretchen, I should have called you right away. I should have taken her to the hospital, I should..."

"The old shoulda, coulda, woulda. You can't solve her problems for her, Kate. And of course you're right to tell me about Derrick and the eighty grand and what he did to Gretchen. But finding the killer is not your job. It's mine. I want you safe, that's all."

The phone rang again. Again he barked, "Bannigan here." He was hoping it was J.D. And it was.

"The shoe print in the tents is also a Naturalizer 12W, slightly different style though, called *Cadet*. And you're right, Gretchen does wear a 12W. She said she was at the mall earlier in the evening and even has the receipt for something she bought there." One thing Tony appreciated about J.D. was how quickly he could get to the point.

He tried to digest the news, but nothing added up, so he replied, "This is screwy. I'll be back there in a few minutes and we can think this through."

He stood up. "Gotta go. But first, tell me more about Gretchen. How badly was she hurt?"

"She was a mess. Probably should have gotten stitches on her lip and eyebrow. Why?"

"Did she tell you, actually confirm that it was Derrick?"

"No. She wouldn't say who it was. She was afraid to. I just noticed when I walked her out to her car that it was parked next to Derrick's truck, and some of her artwork was on the seat. I assumed...well, don't you think...?"

From what he knew about Derrick, her conclusion was right on. But Tony was in a quandary; he wanted to sound appreciative—after all, Kate had given him some really valuable information—but he sure didn't want to encourage her to snoop around and perhaps put herself in danger. Better to nip this sleuthing in the bud.

"We'll look into it, Kate" He pointed his finger at her. "Did you hear what I just said? We'll look into it. We will. Not you. And you stay clear of Derrick, all right? Promise?" He pushed his chair back under the table. "By the way, Sophia says someone's been trying to get in touch with you or something. You might want to call her."

They picked up their mugs and brought them over to the sink—a comfortable moment of domesticity. He liked the way that felt, how she moved, how her stride matched his, how her hair brushed her shoulders.

He set the things on the counter by the sink. They were standing close together, arms touching briefly as she reached for a towel. Without planning to, he reached over and pulled her into his arms. She didn't push away, so he held her close, his cheek against her hair. For a moment neither of them moved. Then, slowly, he felt her head lean against his and her arms begin an embrace. He was aware of her hands, her hair, her breasts. He could feel her heart beat. Or was it his? He brushed her cheek with his and said, "You know I've fallen in love with you." She didn't reply, so he let her go

133

and stepped back, trying to take the measure of what she was feeling. But she was silent, and her face told him nothing.

He took another step back and put his hands in his pockets. "I was married once," he heard himself say. "I have a son. He's six. Name's Tony, like me. Lives in California. I worry about your safety. I love your eyes. And the way your hair smells. I think about making love to you all the time." He knew he sounded stupid, but he couldn't seem to shut up.

She tilted her head, crossed her arms, and seemed to study his face. Finally, she smiled and said, "If you're thinking about making love to me, perhaps you should first think about asking me out. Dinner would be nice."

"Yes, of course! How about tonight?"

"Can't."

"Can't?"

"Promised to go to the ArtWalk."

"Oh."

"How about tomorrow?" she asked.

"Can't."

"Can't?"

"Meetings."

"Oh."

"Saturday?" he asked

"Saturday's good."

"Wonderful. Italian?"

"Italian's good."

"Great. Six?"

"Yeah, sex is good. I mean six is good."

There was a moment of surprised silence as they looked at each other. When she scrunched up her face in embarrassment he let out a big laugh and gave her another hug, this one more friendly, comfortable. "I sure hope that was a Freudian slip."

"Don't get your hopes up," she laughed. "Freud is overrated."

TWENTY-ONE

Derrick sighed and took the seat offered to him.

Tony stood by the door, leaning against the wall.

"Why don't you start by telling me where you were two nights ago," Tony began.

Derrick raised his eyebrows, folded his arms across his chest, and leaned back in the chair. "Why do you want to know? Someone else get murdered?"

"No, just beat up pretty bad."

"Lots of people get beat up pretty bad, or haven't you noticed?"

"True, but this was a real pretty lady, real pretty. And with your history…"

"Who says I had anything to do with some lady getting beat up? You have any witnesses?"

"You'd be surprised what we have, Derrick. But if you don't want to talk about that, why don't you tell us about Northern Arizona Insurance Company?"

"What about it?"

"You can start with the eighty grand you're going to get now that Art Russo's dead. He came in first, I hear, and you, well you came in second. How did it feel to come in second, Derrick? Did it piss you off?"

135

"Getting pissed off is not a crime, last I heard." Derrick shifted his weight and examined his boots. "Sure, I was pissed off. My work's better than Russo's. But the old man—Von Steen—he wanted Russo to win. He's a sentimental old fart, but he's the chairman of the board. So, hell, he got his way. Sure, I was pissed off."

"You told us you might have lost a couple of grand competing with Art Russo. Eighty thousand is not a couple of grand."

"You asked me about sales. Not commissions."

"Sales, commissions, whatever. Competition is competition. And we think that you did something about it. That you beat up Russo just like you beat up Gretchen."

"Who said I beat up Gretchen?"

"Who do you think?"

"Well, she's lying. Her word against mine. I wasn't even in the tents two nights ago."

"Who said anything about the tents?" J.D. asked from the back of the room, where he had managed to sit, ignored.

Derrick swung around and glared at him. J.D. smiled back, shaking his head from side to side. "Derrick, what's the matter with you, beating up pretty ladies and old men?"

"I never beat up any old man," Derrick hissed.

"Oh, but you do beat up pretty ladies?" J.D. asked the question as if he was expecting an answer, eyebrows raised and attentive.

Derrick swung back to Tony. "If you want to arrest me for something, fine. Otherwise I'm out of here."

Tony took two steps and stood close to Derrick's knees, confining him to his chair without touching him. "Hold on just a minute," said Tony. "Gretchen said you're lovers. I take that to mean you have sex now and then, which isn't the same thing at all, but maybe you don't know that. She said that you enjoyed getting rough with her. And that you often did the deed in the tents after hours. And..." he paused and enunciated each word clearly, "she said you were in the tents the night Russo was killed."

There was silence in the room, interrupted only by the muted sound of footsteps walking down the hall and a phone

136

ringing in a distant office.

"You want to tell us about it, Derrick?" J.D. asked sweetly.

"I had nothing to do with Russo's murder. Nothing. Period. I was out with Eldon. I already told you that." Derrick was talking to Tony's belt buckle.

"Good, then there shouldn't be a problem," said Tony. "Thing is, that alibi doesn't hold up. No one saw you and Eldon out drinking that night. And Gretchen puts you in the tents. So that's two strikes against you. One more, and uh oh, we got you where you belong."

Derrick pushed back his chair and stood up. "You better watch it, Detective. One wrong step, one illegal move, and you won't forget making my acquaintance." He sauntered out, cowboy boots clicking on the linoleum floor, and slammed the door behind him.

Tony figured he wore a size 11, but it was hard to tell with cowboy boots.

Tony sighed. "At least now we know who parked the 'extra vehicle' that night, don't you think?"

"Yeah. Gretchen wasn't lying. I'd swear to that. Derrick was with her that night."

"Okay then, but that raises a lot of other questions. Why did Eldon lie for Derrick, confirm his alibi? And then there's Gretchen's shoes. You sure they were stolen, like she said?

J.D. frowned, choosing his words carefully. "Gretchen looked absolutely convincing to me. Not that that's proof. But she was so humiliated and, kind of...*damaged*...over everything that's happened." He looked up at Tony, perplexed, and shrugged his shoulders.

"A beautiful girl like that. Go figure. When was her stuff stolen?" Tony asked.

"A month or so ago, right out of her booth. Who was she going to report it to? The Morrows? And tell them she was robbed while she and Derrick were going at it in their little love nest behind the back walls?" He paused. "I believe her. It's as simple as that."

"There aren't many reasons someone would steal a pair of shoes. A purse, yes, a jacket, okay, but shoes?"

"Unless you're just plain mean."

"And then, once you had them, it might occur to you to use them for a cover up," Tony said. "A woman's size 12W would fit a man who wears a 10 ½ N and that might confuse an investigation."

"Which brings us back to the folks who used to roam around the tent at night and might know who was grunting and groaning behind the walls. There's Eldon and Jess."

"Jess is out. I trust what his mother said. In fact, I trust Connie the way you trust Gretchen. That leaves Eldon. Maybe Eldon and Derrick are in this together, whatever this is. Or then, again, it could be someone we haven't even thought about."

"You're giving up on Peter Sterling?"

Tony ignored the question. "Let's go see Eldon. We need to follow up on that drinking-with-Derrick alibi. And his trip to Flagstaff and the Grand Canyon. And I want to question the guard again. What's his name? Oh, yeah, Gary the Guard. How could Gretchen get beat up so bad and the guard not hear a damn thing? And while we're at it, why don't we persuade the Morrows to close up at six o'clock. They might even want to stay and close it up themselves each night, shoo everyone out. The more this thing stretches out, the more likely someone else is going to get hurt."

"Like Kate?" J.D. asked, but without his usual smirk.

Main Street glittered in the cold air, warmed only by thousands of tiny lights that were strung merrily back and forth across the street and wrapped around the palm trees that edged the sidewalk. They were even hung from the awnings of the outdoor cafes, while larger, brighter swaths of lights spilled out from every gallery and antique shop along the three-block art district. Street musicians added to the festive atmosphere. And, of course, wine flowed lavishly in each of the galleries, allowing artists and buyers and winter visitors to mingle together for the sake of art, to say nothing of fame and fortune and acquisition.

Vicki and Kate wended their way through the crowds, popping into one gallery after another. Western art, Russian, contemporary, traditional, it was all there. Kate's favorite was the Long Gallery, with its rich red walls laden with smallish, impressionistic paintings. When she stopped to look at some paintings by an M. Stapley, Vicki hurried her out, impatient to see Brenner's opening.

Progress was slow. Every few minutes they bumped into someone they knew from the tent show. They shared a glass of wine with the Morrows, who tonight seemed unusually solemn, at the Meyer Gallery; they chatted with Jan McLaughlin and Dorothy Ray, two of Kate's favorite painters, on the sidewalk in front of Trailside Gallery; Kate spotted Eldon and a friend crossing the street, but when she tried to get their attention, the men turned into a tiny, bustling bistro and were soon lost in the crowd—surprisingly, since Eldon's friend must have weighed at least 300 pounds. Finally, Vicki ushered her into Wilde-Meyer's, where they joined several other artists from the show who had come to see Brenner's latest work.

Kate was surprised to find the work appealing after all. When seen in person, the female faces were more emotional than the newspaper photograph suggested, distorted, but somehow engaging. They stayed for almost an hour, Vicki entranced, Kate anxious to move on, especially after Connie arrived. That was still unfinished business and now was not the time to take care of it.

When they finally left, Vicki checked her watch and announced, "We have to start home pretty soon. Mom hates staying up late."

"That's okay. I'm beginning to suffer from sensory overload, any-way," Kate said, but at the end of the block, she stopped short. "Oh, wait, can we go in here for just a minute?"

"They're only photographs, Kate."

"Only? C'mon, Vicki, photography's art, too, don't you think?"

"Never thought much about it, to tell the truth. But sure, we can go in. A few more minutes won't hurt."

"Just look at this stuff. They're really nice, don't you think? And these over here...the way the background is faded so you can only see the shapes of things, not the things themselves...and how the objects in the front are so much stronger in contrast, darker and crisper against the light..."

"Wow, Kate, for a non-artist, you sure talk the talk."

"Really? I don't know a thing about it, honestly. It's just that I saw someone's photographs recently and I really loved them. His work would be good enough to hang here, I know it would. And the things he photographs, his subject matter, is different, kind of edgy, streetwise, you know what I mean?"

She picked up a business card from the gallery owner and slipped it into her pocket, smiling at the thought of giving it to Tony Saturday night. She would present it to him over cocktails and describe the nice little gallery and convince him that his work would look great hanging there. That way, their conversation would start off without any reference to the awful things that had been happening. It would be the start of a wonderful evening.

By Friday morning, the clouds and drizzle had disappeared and the sky was bright blue. But the air was still crisp and the tent flaps had not yet been tied back when Kate arrived a few minutes before the show opened. She was better prepared now for the chilly weather, having enhanced her wardrobe with silk undies, a fleece vest, wool gloves and a pair of crepe-soled shoes. Her most valuable new possession was a thermos, which she had filled with hot cider.

She had discovered that on days like these, uncomfortably cold or rainy, the attendance at the show actually increased. On the beautiful days, people were out playing golf or sunning by the pool, especially winter visitors who had come to Arizona to escape the snow of Minnesota or Connecticut or Canada.

This morning Peter didn't greet her with his usual charming smile. Instead she got a rather flat, "Morning, Kate," and then, a little later, "Before I forget, I'm supposed to remind you that there's another wine and cheese party tonight."

"Wonderful. Can I bring something? I could run out to the store..."

"Sure. That would be nice. But the party's going to start earlier tonight, probably around five. The Morrows want to close the place at six sharp from now on. I can't imagine why they're being so careful now, can you?"

"Maybe they know something we don't." Like people getting beat up. She walked over to the counter and put on the earrings that were waiting for her. She moved over to the mirror.

"Sorry about the lights, Kate. Something's gone wrong and I don't know how to fix them. I asked Jess to do it, but he's taking his sweet time, naturally."

"Oh, I don't need any more light than this to know that these look terrific!" They were little geometric dangles—a circle, a square, and, at the bottom, an elongated diamond. "I just might have to buy these, Peter. How much are they?"

"Three hundred. But for you, two fifty."

"Why should I get a discount?"

"Why not? You're my model."

"But I haven't really..."

"Oh, yes you have. And besides, I like to see you wearing my jewelry. My wife makes a good model, too, but she doesn't like the selling part. She won't come here and work in the booth. Likes her privacy, I guess."

"Well, the show would be hard on someone like that, someone more private, maybe even a little introverted. Not everyone likes sales, you know."

Peter reached over and swept her hair back behind her ear, cocking his head to admire his model. "You really do make a good model, Kate. And you're right about these. They look terrific on you. Actually, I'd even let you have them for half price if..." he hesitated, "but, well, I have a little favor to ask you."

"Sure, anything."

"Can you, uh, keep me posted on how things are going with

141

the investigation?"

She straightened up, unsure of how to answer the question. "What do you want to know?"

"Well, the detective was asking me all sorts of questions yesterday. He seemed to think I had something to do with it, can you imagine? You know me better than that, don't you? Could you tell him to just back off? He's making things difficult at home. My wife's..."

Making things difficult for *Peter*? It's *Derrick* he should be making miserable—Derrick with the eighty thousand dollars and the vicious temper.

"I really don't know anything, Peter. I think he's questioning lots of people." She turned to leave, then turned back. "Tell your wife I'm sorry. I'm sure it'll be over soon."

She turned again and caught a glimpse of Derrick as he walked past them toward the office from the direction of Gretchen's booth. Gretchen would not be in condition to return to work this quickly, she was sure of that. Curious, she waited a moment and walked down the aisle in the opposite direction. She was right. There was no one in Gretchen's booth, or the two booths on either side. There were no customers, either, as the show had barely opened. There was only silence and stillness and the cold air. But something made her stop, alert and curious, in the middle of the aisle.

First she smelled the acetone. It took her a minute to find its source. Then they came into focus. Ugly black Xs were spray-painted on the glass over each of Gretchen's paintings. The scene looked almost sacrilegious, a kind of desecration, or like some surreal government prohibition: No! It is forbidden to enjoy the flowers.

Enraged, she set out to confront Derrick, but quickly decided that was a pretty stupid idea. Better to call Tony, tell him about the vandalism, and then report to the Morrows. Then she would go back to the booth and mind her own business.

Customers came and went. She made several sales, and even came close to selling *Mother and Child*. But the buyer decided, after almost two hours of consideration, to order *Old Man Reading* instead. Now there were three orders on the pre-cast list. She remembered what Eldon had asked: what would happen if she didn't get enough orders by the time the show closes? She wasn't worried about *Girl with Dog*, with nine orders. But the other, with only three, how should she handle that? She should probably have it cast anyway, otherwise she have to return the deposits.

It was four o'clock before she remembered the party. She asked Vicki to keep an eye on her booth and drove out to a grocery store a few blocks away where she selected several good cheeses: a wedge of brie, one of cheddar and a small gorgonzola, her favorite. She bought a breadboard to use as a platter and a small knife, both of which she could use at home, and a box of crackers. A bottle of wine completed her purchase.

The checkout line was long and everyone was irritated by the delay caused by the man in front who was shouting at the cashier. He suddenly slammed his fist on the conveyor belt and threw a can in the direction of the produce department. Intermittent explosive disorder. The words came to her in a flash. She smiled. Such a fancy name for unchecked rage. But the words made her think of her recent degree...of all that knowledge that was temporarily parked somewhere else, unused. Perhaps it was parked back in New Jersey alongside her Honda, waiting for her return.

Her phone rang from the depths of her tote bag. She pulled out her wallet, her sunglasses, her still-filled thermos of cider, her gloves. By the time she got to the bottom of the bag where the phone had sunk, it had stopped ringing.

TWENTY-TWO

The apartment was masculine and austere, all gray and black and oversized. Diagonal shafts of light spilled out from between the slats of the vertical blinds that covered a sliding door. Tony walked over to the door, disturbing the parallel streaks of light on the deep red carpet, and noticed that the balcony was empty of furniture or plants.

Except for three cameras on the desk top, there was not a hint of the personal life of its resident—not a picture, not a souvenir from some adventure or travel, not a sign of a hobby, not even a half-read book. A few magazines were stacked in a neat pile on the coffee table, next to a sculpture of a cowboy on a bucking bronco. The sculpture was especially noteworthy because it alone had curved lines and a sense of movement, energy, or life. How can anyone live in such a soulless place, Tony wondered.

"You're going to need to explain again where you were the night Russo was killed, and this time, Eldon, try telling the truth." Tony was looking out the balcony door to the traffic lined up below on Scottsdale Road. He could see the tops of the white tents a mile to the north. "You told Detective Harris here that you were out drinking with Derrick that night, and then you drove up north. We know the first part's not true, so let's start over." He walked across the room and joined J.D., who was sitting on the black leather sofa, busily looking around and writing in his notebook. He didn't miss much, J.D. didn't.

Eldon looked from Tony to J.D. and back again. Then he settled comfortably into a huge easy chair as if he had just made up his mind about something and was content with his decision. He wore a button-down shirt, opened at the neck, and a tweed sports coat.

"You're right. I wasn't with Derrick. I was in Flagstaff." He crossed his legs, pulled at the fabric over his knee and kept his eyes on Tony, his mouth smiling, but not his eyes.

"Really? Then why confirm Derrick's alibi?"

"He asked me to."

"Asked you? Don't you know you risk being an accomplice..."

"Accomplice? Come on, don't make me laugh. Derrick didn't commit a crime. Unless you think having sex with Gretchen is a crime. He just didn't want anyone to know he was in the tents that night. It would look bad, he said." Eldon shrugged and opened the palms of his hands in a gesture of reasonableness.

"That's what he told you?"

"Yeah, that's exactly what he told me. It would look bad because everyone knew how much he hated Russo."

"That might explain Derrick's motive, but it hardly explains yours. Why'd you agree to lie for him?"

"The reason is sitting right in front of you, on the coffee table." He gestured with his arm in the direction of the sculpture, as if that explained everything.

"You mean the sculpture? Is that one of Derrick's?"

"Yeah, it's a beauty, don't you think?"

J.D. put one foot up on the massive coffee table, nudged the sculpture about an inch with his toe and then smiled across the room at Eldon. "It sure is all balls and brawn and brass," he said.

"Balls and brawn, sure, but it's *bronze*, not brass," corrected Eldon, smiling back, still affable, relaxed.

Tony leaned forward and twirled the piece around, examining it with a frown. "I'm looking real hard here, but I don't see anything that explains your lying to us."

He raised his head and stared at Eldon. "Start talking."

"Sure, happy to, Detective. But where to start?" Eldon rubbed his chin and looked off into an imaginary distance as if to begin a great and complicated story. "I like sculpture, you see. Always have. Even when I was a kid. I like that you can see all around it." His arm swept a large slow circle in the air. "And I like that it's big." He paused. "And strong." He paused again. "And dark." He smiled, daring Tony to order him to get on with it. After a moment of silence, he continued. "But of all the stuff at the show, this piece of Derrick's was my favorite. Liked it from the very first day. But I decided not to buy it when Derrick wouldn't budge on the price. He's an arrogant s.o.b. so I told him to go to hell." He turned his attention to the sculpture and smiled. "Then, when Derrick found himself at the scene of a crime he claims he didn't commit, he needed an alibi. He offered me the sculpture in return for saying I was with him. So I agreed. That's it."

"You lied to the police for a piece of sculpture?" Tony's brows shot up.

"Yep. That's it."

J.D. shook his head slowly. "But that's not it, Eldon."

"What do you mean?"

"Now you need an alibi for yourself. Where the hell were you? And where's your girlfriend, the one I talked to, the one who supported your story?"

"Jeannette?"

J.D. flipped through his notebook. "Yeah, Jeannette Spinelli."

"Well, Jeannette just got up and left a week or so ago."

"Where'd she go?"

"I don't keep track of my ex-girlfriends, do you? They're here one day, gone the next. Anyway, she just told you exactly what I told her to tell you. Did me a favor. That's what friends are for…to do favors."

Tony said, "Favors? I bet your girlfriends are especially prone to do favors after you've photographed them in the nude and perhaps threaten…"

"You accusing me of extortion, Detective? Get serious. A nude photograph doesn't shock anyone anymore, believe me."

J.D. looked confused. Tony coughed, his signal for J.D. to keep quiet. Then he pointed a finger at Eldon and said, "Now let's get serious. We want to know two things. Did Derrick tell you in so many words that he was in the tents that night? And where were you if you weren't with Derrick?"

Eldon stood up and walked over to the massive desk that took up most of the wall at the end of the room. There was nothing on its surface but a lamp, an answering machine, and the cameras: an old Nikon, a Canon with a large telephoto lens, and a Kodak digital. He reached into the top drawer and pulled out a folder.

"Tax records," he said by way of explanation. "Here's the hotel receipt for two nights in Flagstaff. As you can see, I was there Friday and Saturday nights. I photographed the installation of Dr. Haeger as the new university president. Then I drove up to Williams for a conference on the Grand Canyon. I have those receipts as well." He handed the papers to Tony.

"Anything else?"

"Photographs. I have the photographs that I took up there, and depending on the camera, some of prints have the date printed on them."

"Dates can be reset in a camera," Tony replied.

Eldon paused. "Sure, but the dates for Haeger's installation at Northern Arizona University can't be reset."

Tony noticed a bit of annoyance had crept into Eldon's voice, so he redirected the conversation to relieve the tension. "I'm an amateur photographer myself, Eldon, so perhaps you could help me out. I'm trying to decide what kind of camera to buy. What would you recommend? I've had my eye on a used Hasselblad..."

"No, don't go that route. I used to have a Bronica. Sold it. Stick to a 35 mm, a Pentax or a Canon, something like that. Easier to control."

Eldon walked back to his desk, slower than necessary, Tony thought, probably trying to maintain control of the situation. This time he opened a file drawer and pulled out a manila envelope. "Everything's in here, Detective. Photographs, programs with dates, times, and people's names. If you want to check my story, it's all in here." He handed it to Tony. "Go ahead, take it."

"Thanks. We'll look it over." As Tony reached for the envelope he looked down at Eldon's feet. He had decided not to ask his shoe size. That was one bit of evidence he wanted to keep a secret for now. But he saw that Eldon's feet, in brown brogues that went with his tweed jacket, were large, definitely too big to fit into Gretchen's shoes.

Eldon moved toward the door. "I have a question for *you*, Detective. What motive do you think I could possibly have for killing Art Russo?"

Tony had been wondering the same thing and had pretty much concluded that they were probably wasting their time. Rather than answering, he posed a question of his own. "By the way, Eldon, where do you do your processing?"

"Down in the garage."

"We may want to take a look later."

"Sure, Detective, any time." He sauntered over to the door and held it open for them. "But I better warn you. The darkroom is full of naked ladies. I wouldn't want you to be shocked."

J.D. opened his mouth and Tony coughed.

It wasn't until they had walked all the way down the steps to the parking lot that J.D. finally asked, "What's all this naked ladies stuff?"

"I guess you never looked very carefully at his booth. He has an Arizona sunset made up entirely of tiny photos of nude models. Stupidest thing you ever saw."

"Sounds beautiful." J.D. replied.

~~~~~~~~~~~~~~~~~~~~~~~~~~~~~~~~~~

The party began at five. The chief topic of conversation was why the show was going to be closed at six o'clock sharp from now on.

"Damn inconvenient, especially if you're from out of town and have no other place to work," someone grumbled.

"Maybe something spooked them and they're just being careful," someone else opined.

"Well, we all better be careful ourselves," another artist laughed, "or maybe we'll find ourselves beaten to a pulp and laid out on the grass by Jesus..."

A few of the artists glanced over at Kate, eyebrows raised and looking embarrassed. Less inhibited, Vicki jammed her elbow hard into the speaker's ribs. "Shut up, you moron," she hissed.

The group went silent, all now painfully aware of Kate's presence.

"Well," said Kate, "about the Jesus thing. He told us to feed the hungry, didn't he, so I'm going to do just that and pass the cheese." It took a second, but the tension was broken by a few forced chuckles, and soon the party was back to normal.

He was found out in the sculpture garden? By the statue of Jesus? Why hadn't anyone told her? You'd think someone would have...no, of course they wouldn't. She hadn't allowed anyone to talk about the details of that night.

She took a large swallow of wine, then a few more quick sips, imagining her father, all 'bashed and bloody,' lying at the feet of Jesus. She sipped more wine, all the while chatting pleasantly about the weather, the food, the week's sales. Then she poured herself another glass, filled a paper cup with popcorn and brought it over to Zach's fort. She noticed that Peter was still in his booth, putting away his jewelry and locking the display case. My, how sullen he had been today. Was he really that upset about the investigation? About his wife? Or was he just irritated that Jess hadn't fixed his lights?

Suddenly, the party was over. The table was cleared, people trotted off in different directions, and Kate returned to her booth, holding her breadboard, the knife, and an almost untouched hunk of gorgonzola. She should have known she'd be the only one to eat it. She wrapped the cheese in a paper towel and threw everything in her tote bag.

It was 10 minutes to six. Mr. Morrow ambled down the aisle, glanced over at Kate, and pointed to his watch. Not a man of many words, she thought. In fact, he had never actually spoken to her. She sat down at her desk, quickly put away the copies of the day's sales slips, and wrote down the names of new customers in her father's notebook.

A man's voice, low and raspy, spoke from behind the wall. It was unintelligible at first. Then she heard "*take care of Gretchen* something, something, *finish the job.*"

Kate put her pen down and leaned to one side, her ear up against the wall. Whose booth was back there? Oh yeah, Beth Page, the artist who painted the delicious still lifes. But she had seen Beth leave almost fifteen minutes earlier.

Then she heard the man say "something *threatened* something," and more mumbling. It was a one-sided conversation, perhaps on a cell phone because there was no response, not even a whisper. Then she was startled to hear "*No, Russo's booth, that's where it* something," and a mumbled, "*tonight.*"

She wished she hadn't had so much wine. It was hard to concentrate. Her head hurt and she could feel her heart beating. But she heard the next words very clearly: "*I said tonight*"...and then something more. There was no doubt at all that the words were said as a threat.

She pushed her chair back and stood up, ready to tiptoe around the wall to discover the speaker's identity. Instead she came face to face with Vicki and little Zach.

"I thought you had left!" said Kate, startled.

"We did. Zach forgot something," replied Vicki, shrugging her shoulders. "He refused to leave unless I brought him back here first."

Zach dropped his mother's hand and trotted over to his fort, turning around every few steps to see if his mother was watching him.

Kate was aware that Mr. Morrow was now turning off the artists' lights, one by one, starting at the far end of the aisle and working his way toward where they were standing. She saw Zach disappear into his fort and emerge a few seconds later, smiling.

"Well, what did you forget?" his mother demanded.

"I just forgot to *do* something," he replied in his quiet voice.

"Ugh!" Vicki groaned. "I thought you had left something behind that you needed. Okay, now let's go home. You too, Kate. It's almost six."

She looked at her watch. It was two minutes to six. Mr. Morrow went into another booth and turned off the lights, while Vicki and Zach walked away in the opposite direction toward the entrance. There was no one else around, except perhaps the mysterious person on the cell phone.

Something was going to happen tonight, that much she knew. And it had something to do with her booth and something to do with Gretchen. She saw Mr. Morrow head into the next booth. As soon as he was out of sight, she grabbed her tote bag, scooted over to Vicki's worktable, and crawled into Zach's fort.

TWENTY-THREE

The rush hour traffic on Scottsdale Road was thick and slow, but since the commuters were accustomed by now to the big white tents, they probably didn't notice that the lights had gone out earlier this Friday evening.

At seven o'clock, Mr. Morrow drove his red Mercedes convertible out the long driveway and merged into the northbound traffic, leaving the security of the tents to Gary the Guard, who was instructed never again to wear headphones during his watch. When Mr. Morrow left the parking lot, it appeared that only Gary's truck remained. Someone more observant might have noticed the outline of a pickup glimmering softly beneath the huge mesquite tree that stood at the far end of the lot at the very edge of the dark and silent desert.

Not everything was in darkness, of course. The security light was on in the sculpture garden, which was the only thing anyone driving by at night ever noticed anyway. Children in particular enjoyed the way the galloping horses gleamed in the spotlight, although some preferred the dancing nudes and giggled at the gold fig leaves and the naughtiness of it all.

The light from the sculpture garden seeped ever so delicately through the laced canvas walls and illuminated the chilly interior just enough for the shapes of things to appear, if not the things themselves—like the distant objects in a black and white photograph, thought Kate, everything in shades of gray with soft and smudgy edges.

Of course, that was not the first thought that came to Kate's mind as she crouched under Vicki's worktable. For ten minutes she had remained on her hands and knees, hunched over her tote bag, waiting for Mr. Morrow to finish turning off the lights, afraid to move into a more comfortable position for fear of being discovered. She cursed herself for being so stupid, angry tears rolling off her face onto the floor. Even worse than her stupidity was her fear of the humiliation she would face should anyone find out what she was doing. The thought of crawling out and making some joke to Mr. Morrow crossed her mind, but only briefly. Whenever she did something this stupid, she simply hoped no one would notice. Lord only knew what she would tell Tony.

Eventually all was silent, although she thought she heard the distant hum of people speaking. But it didn't sound like a real conversation. More likely it was the TV she had seen the guard watch when she left each evening. Occasionally there was a creak of the steel beams or the snap of the canvas wall when a gust of air pushed it a few inches over the asphalt flooring and then sucked it back out again.

It wasn't until she righted herself that she realized that the fort was really quite roomy. In fact, if she had been a child, she would have loved it. The table was fairly high—probably counter height —and at least six feet long. She sat forward, hugging her legs and resting her chin on her knees, grateful there was carpet on the floor beneath her.

She noticed the little windows right away. The one to her side gave her a murky view of Peter Sterling's booth. The glass of his display case shimmered where it caught the soft light and she could make out the mirror, a silver oval, which stood on top of the case where he always left it. She twisted around, leaning back on one hand, and peered out the opening behind her and saw that the corner of her father's booth was visible, as well as several of his sculptures. But the little window in front of her was too far away to peer through, her long legs taking up the intervening distance. It faced the aisle where the security light shone through, so it was quite bright. In the corner between the front and side of the fort was the opening, a narrow slit where the fabric didn't quite meet.

Her right leg cramped, so she rolled over on her left hip, toward the side of the fort that had no window, stretched her leg out as far as she could, and shook out the cramp. She found herself face to face with all the little soldiers in Zach's army. They stood in a neat row on either side of a pile of boxes and aimed their rifles right at her. Tanks and jeeps and motorcycles were lined up in front of them. Careful not to disturb the army, she used her fingertips to explore along the edge of the table skirt and into the corners, where she discovered a few pieces of popcorn, several stuffed animals and some pillows.

Having examined the one side, she rolled carefully onto her other hip, stretched out her left leg and investigated the opposite side of the fort. But there was nothing, only the tiny square window. She stared at the canvas cloth, wondered what the hell she was doing there, and rolled onto her back. The tents were silent, except for the muted hum of the TV.

What exactly had she heard that had caused her imagination to run wild? Nothing all that mysterious, now that she thought about it. So why not just crawl out, walk down the aisle, and say good night to the guard? What could he do, arrest her? Actually, maybe he could. Was she trespassing? Well, then, she could try to sneak out. If the guard fell asleep, she might be able to slip right past him. But then the thought of the long dark walk on the noisy gravel to where she had parked the truck made her shiver. The lot had been full when she returned from the grocery store, so she had been forced to park all the way at the end, under the tree at the edge of the desert.

Suddenly the overhead lights came on, startling her with their brightness. She peered through the narrow opening and waited to see what would happen.

Footsteps headed toward her, but the slow, rhythmic shuffling assured her that there was not a hint of hurry or alarm or danger in the approach. The guard walked down the aisle, staring stupidly ahead, not even bothering to look into the booths as he passed. A minute later she heard him stop at the end of the aisle and turn around. His footsteps got louder as he returned, but as soon as he passed, the shuffling became quieter until all was silent again. The lights remained on a few minutes longer, enough time for him to cross the lobby and head down the north tent and back. And then, just as suddenly as the lights had come on, everything was thrown into darkness again.

It soon became evident that the guard patrolled the place every hour on the hour, so it would be possible for her to walk out undetected while he was over in the north tent. But what if someone else was waiting in the shadows, behind a display wall or outside in the parking lot? She had to admit she felt more secure right where she was. If she remained in the fort nothing could happen to her, so she decided to stay put, and when the lights went out she fished in her tote bag for the cheese and apple cider, grateful she didn't need the rest room, and wondered how she was going to keep all this from Tony.

At half past nine, and much to her surprise, since the timing seemed off, the overhead lights went on, and voices—normal voices, not electronic—accompanied the footsteps heading in her direction. First she saw the guard walk by, and then Jess. They stopped a little farther down the aisle, near Gretchen's booth, she guessed. There were sounds of objects being moved, and then "Hey, hold on!" and "Watch it!" and "Here, grab this corner."

That's when it dawned on Kate that what she had heard from behind the wall were probably instructions to Jess, instructions to take down Gretchen's paintings and finish removing the Xs from the glass. She could smell the varnish remover. How stupid she had been! She was not in any danger after all. And now, if she were quick, she could get out and no one would even know she had been there.

She pushed everything back in her bag and started out the opening. Her head and shoulders were emerging when she heard a noise behind her, a soft thump against a wall. At the same moment the guard walked up the aisle in front of her. If he had turned his head, even slightly, he would have noticed Kate, an improbable vision, hair in her face, crawling out of Zach's fort. Perhaps he also would have noticed whatever had caused the noise behind her. Kate immediately pulled back in, like a turtle shrinking into its shell.

The slight clatter and scraping and mumbling continued to come from Gretchen's booth, so try as she might, Kate couldn't identify any other sound. She sat absolutely still for ten or fifteen minutes, occasionally turning her head so she could look from one opening to another and watch for...what?

Jess eventually finished his work. She peered through one of the windows and watched him trudge by, shoulders hunched, head thrust forward. He hesitated right by the fort and looked over at Peter's display case. His expression changed from glum to sneering. His fist rose, middle finger raised, and he spat out a quiet "fuck you" before he went off again.

A few minutes later the lights went out, but this time it was noticeably different. Total darkness surrounded her. There were no shades of gray. There was nothing at all. It was as if everything, even the air, had turned into a void. The security light had evidently gone out in the sculpture garden, and although she could see headlights occasionally float by in the distance, they were too weak to penetrate the darkness.

She had never been afraid of the dark, not even as a child, but this was different. She reached for a pillow to hug, and her hand felt a hard object, wrapped in a soft cloth, resting under it. She picked it up and loosened the cloth. A piece of sculpture? Her fingers glided over the shape, identifying the wolf, the bird on the shoulder, the halo on the head. She wrapped it back in the cloth and held it to her chest. Had Zach stolen it? Whatever for?

It took a moment for the footfall to register in her mind as a distinct and dangerous sound. Barely audible and coming from behind, it was hesitant and cautious. She gripped the sculpture in her right hand and stopped breathing. She was afraid even to blink.

The intruder moved the air as he passed the fort in the direction of Peter's booth—no, perhaps her father's—it was hard to tell. She heard other sounds, too, but they were indistinct and unrecognizable. She squinted hard, but in the blackness she couldn't even locate the little window just inches from her face.

When the overhead lights blared back on it so startled her that she gasped with surprise, but the sound of her gasp was not as loud as the scuffling that came from the direction of the intruder. She quickly put her eye to the window, but it was already too late. All she saw was a dark shape melt around the back of the fort, to the side where there was no little window, where Zach's army was lined up. She heard something scrape over the carpet, and was aware that a body was squatting or kneeling on the other side of the canvas cover. A tiny soldier fell to the floor, but made no noise on the carpet. A knee, or perhaps an elbow, bumped into her shoulder and she had to fight the instinct to cry out or to move away. She could hear him breathing. Could he hear her?

Then good footsteps approached, the kind that announced they had a right to be there, and Jess reappeared, this time with a toolbox and a small stepladder. He opened the box on the floor, removed some tools, and shoved the stepladder with his knee against her father's wall. Then he climbed up and reached for the electrical junction box that rested on top of the freestanding wall. In a few minutes he climbed back down and flipped the light switch on and off in Peter's booth. The lights responded, on, then off. So *that's* why her father's booth had been mentioned during the mysterious conversation.

Jess picked up his equipment. She thought, oh, Jess, please don't leave me! Should she cry out to him? If she did, would he know what to do, or would he just turn and run? What would the intruder do? Before she had time to answer her own questions, Jess trudged back toward the lobby. She felt the intruder crawl around the corner of the fort behind her, but she was afraid to turn her head, afraid that she might see his eye looking through the little window into hers.

It seemed an eternity that the two of them, crouched in silence in the lighted tents, no more than two feet distant, remained invisible to one another. But soon the lights were extinguished. The figure immediately stood up, turned on a penlight, and walked right beside the little window to her side. Kate leaned over, accidentally brushing her cheek against the canvas, and peered out. All she could see were pant legs and shoes. Strange looking shoes, similar to Gretchen's, she thought. But she knew this was not Gretchen.

Back in the lobby, voices rose as Jess and the guard started arguing. The intruder stood still beside her. She could feel him tense with indecision, his weight first on one foot, then the other, as if he couldn't decide whether to stay or to leave. Then a single light went on diagonally across the sculpture garden, probably in the café. Like the headlights, it glowed cheerfully but shed no light into the darkness that surrounded her. The argument continued, something slammed shut, more yelling.

The penlight and the strange shoes moved away silently. The figure was momentarily silhouetted against the light from the café, but immediately disappeared into the blackness. She felt a draft and finally all was still.

She reached into her purse and pulled out the knife. She lay back, clutching the knife with one hand and St. Francis with the other. "Jesus, oh, sweet Jesus," she prayed, tears falling back into her ears.

She woke at dawn, stiff with cold, her icy hands still resting on her chest, clutching St. Francis and the knife. She didn't move until the guard came by at six. When she was sure he had gone over to the north tent, she crawled out of the fort, dragging her bag behind her, and hurried towards the lobby. The TV was on, the only sign of life. She rushed past the ticket table toward the entrance, but just as she was about to walk out into the crisp morning air, a bright red convertible pulled into the parking space near the entrance. Kate turned on her heels and bolted toward the restroom. Just as she was closing the door, she saw Mrs. Morrow walk up the steps to the office.

Michèle Stapley

TWENTY-FOUR

It took only a few seconds to get from the front door of her father's house to the bathroom at the end of the hall. She let her tote bag drop to the tile floor and placed the St. Francis on the vanity next to the hair spray and body lotion. Then she drew her bath, stripping off her clothes and leaving them in messy piles on the floor.

It had been years since she had soaked in a tub. She got in when it was only half-full and let the hot water continue in a fine stream so the temperature would remain just this side of scalding. She leaned back, placed a wet washcloth over her face and tried to go blank. She reached her toes up to the faucet to fine-tune the water flow, but as soon as they touched the chrome she jerked her foot back in panic, afraid that it was sticking out too far, that the intruder might trip over it with his strange shoes. Oh, get a grip, she told herself, and lowered her leg into the water, ordering it to go limp. She could feel her feet bob up and down in the little waves created by the running water.

The hot water worked its magic, soothing her sore muscles and warming her bones. Her back and shoulders curved into position against the tub, and her arms free-floated at her sides. She wiggled her stiff fingers along the water's surface.

The phone rang. She refused to answer it. Not now. It stopped.

But right away it rang again, so she reluctantly reached a dripping arm over the side of the tub and retrieved it.

"That you Kate?"

"Sophia?"

"How're you doing, girl?"

"Fine. Could I, you know, call you back? This isn't a good time."

"Sure thing. But first I just wanted to tell you I finally figured out who tried to call you on my phone. I feel stupid it took me so long. It had to be whoever it was you called on my cell phone that day—at the show—remember? The..."

"Sophia, I'm sorry, but I really can't talk now." This could wait, Kate was sure.

"No problem. But hey, wait a minute. I hear you and Tony got a date tonight. It's about time."

"Tonight? Oh, my god, you're right, it *is* tonight! I'd forgotten."

"Forgotten? What's the matter with you? Am I the only one who knows you two are made for each other?"

"Please, Sophia, I really have to go. I'll call you tomorrow, I promise." And with that, Kate hung up and threw the phone back into her bag.

The water had become uncomfortably hot, so she got another toe grip and turned off the faucet. She pinched her nose and slid backwards, letting her head go under. How many minutes could she hold her breath? She had practiced just that way as a child, all one winter, so that when summer came she would impress her Daddy when they went to the lake. He'd let her climb up his back and stand on his shoulders, and then she'd dive off and swim under water, making figure eights through his legs while he counted the seconds. No matter how long she stayed under, he always looked amazed and delighted.

When she came up for air, the phone was ringing again. Damn.

"Kate? Hi, this is Gretchen."

Kate sat up straight, squeaking the tub bottom and causing a wave to lap forward and back and spill over the edge. "Gretchen! Are you okay? Anything wrong?"

"No, no, I'm fine. Really. I'm all better now. I'm coming to the show tomorrow." Kate pushed wet hair off her face. "I just called to thank you. It's hard to say thanks when people are standing around."

"You don't have to thank me, Gretchen. I didn't do anything."

"Yes you did. You were very kind and I wasn't very nice to you. I was embarrassed for anyone to find out, and I hurt like hell." Kate heard the catch in her voice and waited for her to continue. "But, it wasn't all his fault, you know. I made him mad. And Kate? I also wanted to tell you that me and Derrick, we didn't have anything to do with what happened to your father. Honest, Kate. The detective, I think maybe he thinks Derrick did it. Derrick is, well, you know how he is, but I know it wasn't him. Will you tell the detective that?"

"Don't worry about Derrick. Sooner or later the police will find out who did it, and no one's going to accuse anyone of anything until then...so don't worry, okay? Just take care of yourself. And don't be alone with Derrick. He's probably furious with you for telling on him, so you need to stay away. Promise?" Kate wondered if Gretchen knew about the spray-painted Xs.

"Yeah, I promise. And Kate? There's one more thing I wanted to ask you. In the beginning of the show your father had a beautiful statue of St. Francis. I loved it because it didn't look all stiff and, you know, holy, like others I've seen. But, when I went to look for it the morning...the morning they found him, it wasn't there. Do you still have it or did it get sold?"

Kate looked over at St. Francis standing in a cloud of steam by the hair spray and agreed that St. Francis certainly didn't look very holy at the moment.

"Yeah, I still have it." And two more in the studio.

"Oh, good. I used to love the stories about St. Francis. When I was a kid we memorized the St. Francis prayer. Do you know it?"

"Now that you mention it, I remember there was a prayer, something about being an instrument of peace..."

"That's it! *Make me an instrument of Your peace, where there is hatred let me sow Your love…"*

Kate didn't remember the prayer, but the words of the hymn came to mind. "…*And where there's injury, Your pardon, Lord, and where there's* something, something, I forget the rest."

"I've gotten it written down somewhere. I'll give it to you if you'd like."

"Why yes, Gretchen, I'd like that."

"Your dad must have liked St. Francis, too, don't you think? Or he wouldn't have bothered to…Anyway, I'd like to buy it. How much is it?"

"I have no idea. I'll have to look it up." Based on his other work, it would probably be about five, six hundred dollars. But that seemed awfully high, especially when you're sitting in a tub talking to someone as sweet and beaten up as Gretchen who says she wants to buy it.

"The reason I want to have it is that I've been injured pretty bad —well, you know all about that—and now I guess I have to learn to pardon, too, like the prayer says…"

"Hold on, Gretchen! You need to look after yourself first. You can worry about Derrick later, if ever. And forget about the pardoning…"

"No, Kate, I need to…And maybe you should think about it, too. After all, it'll be important for you, the pardoning thing, when they find out who killed your father. Don't you think?"

Kate opened her mouth to reply, but had no idea what to say. "Gretchen, you're way ahead of me here. I haven't thought that far in advance. To be honest, I sure don't feel like pardoning anyone just now. In fact, I want whoever did it caught and dead." Her words surprised her and she shivered. The water was cooling off and her hair felt like cold plaster on her head. "What about a trade? You get St. Francis and I get one of your paintings. How would that be?"

"Really? You really want one of my paintings? Which one?"

"I'll pick one out tomorrow, okay?"

"Or I could do one specially for you."

"That would be nice, too. We'll talk about it later, Gretchen, but right now I've got to go."

"Oh, and Kate?"

"Yeah."

"One more thing. Watch out for Eldon."

"Eldon? Why Eldon?" she asked.

But Gretchen had hung up.

Kate threw the phone into her bag and slipped under the water again. What was that comment all about? Why would she have to watch out for Eldon? He was one of the most professional and personable people in the show. She had certainly felt the need to watch out for Jess, and also for Derrick, and maybe even Peter, with his wily charm. But Eldon? That just didn't make sense.

When Kate came up for air the water had cooled down considerably. She could get out, or heat it up once more. She opted for the latter, for another five minutes in the tub. As the hot water gushed over her feet, she thought of all the movies she had seen where some naked actress posed provocatively in a huge bathtub, covered discreetly in bubbles and glowing in candlelight. None of them, she was sure, could have enjoyed a bath more than the one she was enjoying now.

So when the phone rang the third time, she let out a groan. She turned the water off, stood up and grabbed a towel, wrapping it around her now shivering body. She sat on the commode and answered the phone.

"Hi, it's Vicki. Where *are* you? You okay? It's Saturday. Why aren't you here?"

"I'm not coming in today...I've got a cold," she lied.

"Oh, that's good. No, no, I mean, that's too bad. But at least you're okay. I was worried. I need to talk to you."

"What's the matter?"

"It's about Zach. He said someone was in his fort last night. That it smelled funny. Like throw-up, he said. He also said something was missing. He won't tell me what it is, though. And then, when I went in to see for myself, I found one of Peter's earrings. Can you imagine? What would an earring be doing in Zach's fort? I got to worrying about you because I thought it might be one you were wearing and that something might have happened to you. I was going to take it over to Peter but Zach just screamed and carried on and begged me not to. He made so much noise that Mrs. Morrow rushed over and told me I'd better get him under control or we'd have to leave. So I promised Zach I wouldn't tell Peter about the earring— ever— and he finally stopped crying. What do you think I should do? Do you think this is something the detective should know? Should I call him? I mean, how stupid would I sound, saying there's this awful smell and an earring in my son's fort, and he's petrified of the jeweler...so I'm calling the cops."

Kate smiled. What would Tony think if he got such a call? It certainly sounded pretty silly. That is, if you didn't know about the intruder. And if you didn't think the intruder might be the murderer.

"You're right, Vicki, the cops would find the story pretty silly. It might be different if some kind of crime had been committed last night—you know, someone getting hurt, or something valuable being stolen. But you know what? I did lose an earring yesterday. It probably fell off and somehow got kicked under the table, maybe when I brought Zach popcorn during the party. Anyway, just hold on to it for me. I'll return the pair to Peter when I trade them for new ones and he'll never know the difference. How's that sound?"

"Okay, I guess, but what about what's missing from the fort? And the funny smell?"

"Maybe the smell's from some rotten food that Zach forgot about. An apple core, or carrot sticks or even part of a hamburger." Did gorgonzola really smell like throw-up to a 4-year-old? Poor kid.

"I suppose."

"And heaven's knows what's missing, Vicki. You know all of Zach's toys, don't you? Are they all still there?"

"Yeah, I think so."

Kate had stopped dripping on the floor. Goose bumps were forming on her arms and her teeth were beginning to chatter.

"Look, Vicki, I'll see you tomorrow. But right now I need to hop in the shower."

She got up and wiped a clear circle in the foggy mirror. Under her wet and matted hair, one earring glistened. She pulled it off, got into the shower, and washed her hair. Tony liked her hair and the way it smelled. But he didn't like her wearing Peter's earrings, she knew that. So tonight she would wear her simple gold hoops and spritz some cologne on the back of her neck. He'd like that. She smiled at the thought of him kissing her neck, which she fervently hoped he would do. For starters. But first she would turn off her phone, hop into bed, and catch some Zs.

TWENTY-FIVE

J.D. stacked the contents of the manila envelope on one corner of the long conference table and flipped open his notebook. Tony thought J.D. was obsessive about his notebook, but since it had occasionally yielded an investigative gem, Tony refrained from teasing him about it.

"The reception for the new president of NAU was in Flagstaff on Saturday evening, ending just about the time Art Russo was getting his head bashed in. Since Flagstaff is two, two-and-a-half hours away, Eldon couldn't have had anything to do with the murder. See here? These are the photos from the reception."

J.D. spread out a dozen photos across the table. Celebrities and professors and the new university president were gathered in small groups around dining tables or in front of the university banner or behind the podium at the center of the head table. J.D. added the dinner program to the line of photos and pointed to a few names, including the chairman of the dinner committee.

"I called several of these folks. And I not only spoke to the chairman of the dinner committee, but I e-mailed her the photographs, which she confirmed were from that evening. Some of them were taken at the very end of the celebration, she said, so Eldon had to have been there the whole time. Everything checks out. I also sent her a photo of Eldon and she remembers seeing him over the weekend, along with several other photographers."

Then J.D. tossed a small envelope on top of the photos.

"The negatives are in the envelope. They match the photos exactly. I checked them all."

Next, J.D. lined up the photos of the actual ceremony, which had taken place on the campus grounds the day before, on Friday afternoon. There were many more prints of this event, probably 30 or 40, so J.D. arranged them in several neat stacks. Then he added another envelope of negatives and a printed program to the collection.

Tony looked at the photos and frowned. "I wonder who hired him for the job. We never thought to ask him that." He picked up one photo from each of the events and studied them side by side. "He does better indoors. Outdoors he seems to lose his sense of purpose. His composition gets a little sloppy. See here? Of course, it's distracting when you're outside. And outdoor light's always a challenge." He put the photos down. "Anything else?"

"Here's another group of shots. These are from the meeting up in Williams the following day. Sunday. Here's a workshop. A lecture. A dinner with a speaker at the podium. All about forestry research. And here's the program and the negatives for this group."

Tony picked up one of the prints and examined it closely. Then he picked up one from the dinner at NAU and compared the two. "You know, it's amazing how some people make a living. Look at this one from up in Williams. See how much better it would have been if he had put the guest speaker right about here, not so far over to the edge?"

J.D. studied the photo. "The speaker looks fine to me. Ugly guy, though. Typical tree-hugger type. But that's not Eldon's fault."

"That's not what I meant, J.D. Just think how much better it would look...oh, never mind. You've got no eye at all."

"Now wait a minute. I appreciate beautiful things. Look here. There are more pictures. See the imprinted dates? It looks like he used this particular camera all weekend long, taking pictures in between the different events and on his way back to town. Took them just for himself, I guess. They're real nice, don't you think? Must have gone up to the Grand Canyon, and then over to the Rim country. Here's Four Peaks. And look at that sunset!"

"For heaven's sake, J.D., they're just ordinary snapshots. Taken with his digital. They're okay, I guess, but you could do just as well."

"Me? No way. I took a picture of a sunset once and it was upside down."

"Only because you were too dumb to turn the print right side up."

"Oh, so that was the problem..."

Tony looked over the collection and asked, "That all?"

"Yep. Oh, except for the newspaper clippings. Here's one from *The Arizona Republic* and another from *The Arizona Daily Star*."

J.D. began gathering up the photographs to stuff them back in the envelope. "So, whaddya think?"

"I think you're right. Everything looks fine, and besides, why the hell would Eldon want to kill Art Russo? There's no motive, and now we know there's no opportunity, either. I think we can cross him off our nonexistent list."

"This clears Eldon, but we still don't know where Derrick was."

Tony rubbed his forehead and sighed. "Gretchen signed out at 10:20 p.m. and said Derrick left a few minutes later. Said she called him when she got home. I don't think it's Derrick."

J.D. stopped stuffing the photos into the envelope and turned to Tony. "You don't think...? Well, dammit, it's got to be Derrick! He had opportunity...he was *there* that night! He had motive...*eighty thousand dollars* worth. And he had the means...that guy could crack open a skull with no effort at all. Plus—and you gotta admit this is important—he had easy access to Gretchen's shoes, to say nothing of easy access to Gretchen..."

"But think a minute, J.D. Derrick was in the tents early that evening, while Gretchen was at the mall. Then Gretchen comes, they make whoopie, and they leave. Later she calls him at his apartment. That pretty much takes care of the whole evening—that is, if we can verify the phone calls. Derrick was way too busy to have anything to do with the Lopez murder, and

I'm still convinced the two murders are connected."

"Well, I'm not. Maybe that night Gretchen and Derrick *weren't* whooping it up. Maybe that night Derrick came in to meet up with Gretchen, but when he saw that Art Russo was there he told Gretchen to get lost and then he murdered the poor guy. It wouldn't surprise me any if Gretchen lied about when Derrick left to protect him. Victims do that sometimes, you know."

"Then, all we have to do is check the phone records. That ought to settle it."

J.D. finished jamming the last of the photographs in the envelope and looked up at Tony. "You keep saying the two murders are connected. If you really believe that then we need to go and spend some time down in Casa Grande with the sheriff. We could drive down tomorrow."

"You're right, J.D. Why don't you call them. Tell them we're coming down tomorrow and why."

"Tomorrow's Sunday."

"I know."

"You don't mind?"

"It's my job, why should I mind? You?"

"No, I don't mind. Want to go out tonight and get sloshed?"

"No. I got other plans."

"Thought so."

"What makes you so smart?"

"I'm just lucky that way."

La Locanda's was a tiny out-of-the-way Italian restaurant where the food was excellent and the service unobtrusive. Even though Tony had asked Jerry, the maitre d' and an old high school buddy, to save him the table at the back of the room, he got there a half-hour early just to be on the safe side and sat down facing the entrance.

He straightened his tie, checked the wine list, and looked around the room. Only a few of the tables were occupied. Soft chatter and the tinkle of glassware blended with the magic of Pavorotti's tenor, kept at such a low volume as to be an insult to the singer. But the mood was perfect, enhanced by the small candles and simple bouquets of flowers that graced the tables. It would be nice to see Kate in candlelight.

The only disappointment was that she had insisted on meeting him at the restaurant. He would have preferred to pick her up, simply because he would have preferred to drive her home. Driving her home would have allowed for all sorts of possibilities.

He ordered a drink and thought about the trip to Casa Grande in the morning. He probably should have done it sooner. He was eager to see for himself exactly what they had on the Lopez murder. He was more convinced than ever that the two murders were related.

He did a quick review. There had been three suspects to start with, but then Jess had been eliminated, leaving Peter and Derrick. Then Eldon had been added, but now he seemed the least likely. J.D. was right: there was only one, Derrick, who had motive and opportunity, but Tony couldn't see any connection between Derrick and Lydia Lopez. Peter, on the other hand, had some sort of connection to Lopez because he was in the jewelry business and had been to Tucson that weekend. But Peter had no apparent motive to kill Art. Of course, there was always the possibility that it was someone else entirely, a complete stranger. Maybe the Sheriff had a suspect.

Tony sipped his drink slowly. He thought how hard this must be on Kate and how patient she had been, anxious maybe, but never demanding. He wondered if he would have been so understanding. There were others who were beginning to lose patience, though. Lieutenant Holmes, for one. His mother, for another. Of the two, it was easier to deal with Holmes, who understood how a case could have an abundance of leads one minute and hit a stone wall the next. But his mother, that was something else. She told him sternly to "Leave no stone unturned" and "Get down to brass tacks"—those were last week's phrases. This week's was "If the mountain won't come to Mohammed, Mohammed must go to the mountain." "What's that got to do with anything, Ma?" he had asked. "You'll see," she had replied, smiling her mother-knows-best smile. The strangest part of all was that he kept repeating the expression, hoping it might shed some light on the investigation.

The door opened and he sprang up, only to see a young couple enter and head for the bar, laughing. A few minutes later a mother and daughter arrived, and he saw Jerry escort them to the table over by the window.

The next time the door opened he saw Kate. She looked around, embarrassed as people often are when they're looking for a friend in a restaurant, not sure if they're the first to arrive or if they'll fail to identify the person they're meeting, or even what they should do if their dinner partner fails to show up at all. Jerry spotted her immediately. Tony saw him greet her with a smile and a little bow and lead her back to the table. On the way he gave Tony a discreet grin and a thumbs up. She looked wonderful. He could spend the rest of his life looking at her. But for now he would try to memorize the way she looked when she skirted the tables, smiling briefly at one of the waiters and finally, smiling at him. He stood up, leaned toward her and kissed her cheek. This was going to be a perfect evening.

TWENTY-SIX

What was she thinking? She should never have agreed to have him come back to the house for coffee. Actually, she hadn't agreed to anything; she had suggested it herself.

But how could she resist? The evening had been perfect, magical, the conversation flowing so easily back and forth, their fingers touching across the table, the suggestive looks and teasing remarks, to say nothing of the unbelievably delicious meal, the perfectly prepared veal scaloppini, the excellent wine, the exquisite tiramisu.

She was in the kitchen pouring the coffee. He had excused himself to use the rest room. Did he think they were going to make love tonight? She hoped not, because, much as she wanted to—her whole body seemed to be demanding it—she was going with her intuition that told her, no, not now, not this time, not so soon. She had gone through too much lately and there was simply no room for another heightened experience. Her very being had been stretched in too many new directions. She needed to get further away from all that was going on, all the other things that had gotten her adrenaline going and her emotions whirling about. Would he understand that? Or would he think she had been leading him on?

Her phone rang. The stupid tune came from the hall table and she almost didn't answer it. It was a little after ten o'clock, for heaven's sake. Who would be calling at this hour?

"Kate, how are you?"

"*Martin?*"

"I've missed you. I hoped you might be missing me, too, and that we could..."

"Martin, no. I should have called you and settled things, but..."

"I thought you might be coming home soon, and we could get together..."

"I don't know when I'm coming home, Martin..."

Just then Tony approached, holding something in his fist, wrapped in Kleenex. He just stood there looking at her curiously, eyebrows raised, his forehead in horizontal pleats, his free hand extended palm up as if he was waiting for an explanation.

"Martin, I can't talk now, I'm sorry." She hung up the phone and looked at what was in Tony's hand. Under the tissues she could see that it was St. Francis.

"I know this is your house, Kate, and this is your statue, but what the hell is St. Francis doing in your bathroom?" He sounded tense.

"I just put him there," she responded, and told herself it was the truth, after all.

"Kate, please, tell me about the statue. It's one of your father's, isn't it?"

"As a matter of fact it is, and there are two more of them. Come on, I'll show you his studio."

She led him down the hall, too embarrassed to tell him about her adventure last night, and watched him place the statue next to the other two, slowly unwrap it, and step back.

"It's different, isn't it?" he said, frowning.

It certainly was. It was darker, a strange color that did not resemble the patina her father used on all his sculpture.

"How long have you had this in the bathroom, Kate? Did it get wet recently, sprayed with something, perhaps?"

"No."

"Kate, for heaven's sake, help me out here. No woman who went to Catholic school would ever put a saint's statue in a bathroom, especially a male saint who could see her undress, even watch her pee! I'm not a prude, and it wouldn't bother me at all, but it doesn't *fit* you."

"Why are you yelling at me? Why should you care what I put in the bathroom?" Her voice rose.

"Because I've been looking for a missing sculpture just this size for the last two weeks! This is it, I'm sure of it." His voice rose even louder.

"This is *what?*" she shouted, stamping her foot.

"The goddam *murder weapon!*" he shouted back.

She felt her jaw go slack. She looked at the statue and then she looked at Tony. It was difficult to put it all together. St. Francis had been used to bludgeon her father? What irony—an instrument *of peace* was the instrument of her father's death! And the murderer hid it in Zach's fort? Why would he do such a thing? Was the intruder trying to get it back last night? Would he have killed her, too? And then she pictured the scene Vickie described with little Zach: Zach knew the statue was missing and was petrified of...Peter!

"Well?" Tony boomed.

"Well *what?*" she asked, her voice trembling. She sat on one of the stools and stared at the statue.

"Kate, please. I know you know something. I need to know it too. Just tell me." He moved over and tried to put his arm around her, but she shrugged him off.

"I wish you wouldn't shout at me," she said.

"I wish you wouldn't shout back," he replied, his voice tight, his temper barely in check.

"I found the statue in Zach's fort." That was all she would tell him.

"In Zach's what? Oh yeah, under that big table. Where the kid plays. What was it doing there?"

"How the hell should I know?"

"Well, then, what were you doing there?"

"I brought Zach some popcorn during the party." That also was the truth. She could add that much to the story. No more.

"So, you brought him popcorn and saw it in the fort? That's it? You just took it and brought it home?"

"Something like that."

"*Something* like that?"

"Well, I found it and brought it home, just like I said."

"Kate, you're hiding something here and it's beginning to piss me off. You seem to forget I'm investigating a crime and the crime is that your father was murdered. Why can't you help me out?"

"Frankly, because you yell at me whenever I get involved in this. You act as if whatever I do is stupid...."

"I have never, for one minute, thought you were stupid," he said, rubbing his forehead. "Let's start over again. I won't raise my voice at all, okay?"

Kate didn't look at him. She didn't move.

"I believe this is the murder weapon. We have several suspects. I need the weapon as evidence. If you want your father's murderer found, you need to tell me how you came upon this statue." He said it all in monotone and waited patiently for her response.

So she told him. About what she heard behind the wall, about hiding in the fort, about finding St. Francis, about the intruder. Then she told him what Vicki had told her this morning, about Zach being afraid of Peter.

Tony listened to it all, his eyes never leaving her face, his head shaking back and forth. He finally said, "You actually stayed there all night?"

She nodded, but didn't say anything.

"But why...?"

"Like I said, to find out what was going to happen. The voice said..."

"But didn't it occur to you that hiding there was a dangerous thing to do?"

"It wasn't dangerous. I was... safe."

"*Safe*? I take it back, Kate. All of it. You *are* stupid!" Then he strode over to the shelf, wrapped St. Francis up again and stormed out of the room.

When he got to the front door, she heard him yell, "And if you ever do anything this stupid again, I'll have you locked up!" Then he slammed the door.

"Go to hell!" she yelled back.

Once again the phone rang, but this time she didn't answer it.

~~~~~~~~~~~~~~~~~~~~~~~~~~~~~~~

How in the name of heaven could any woman be so brainless? So boneheaded? So stupidly irresponsible?

Tony opened the back door of his car, pawed through a box on the floor, extracted a plastic bag, and shoved St. Francis in it. Then he got in the car, slammed the door, and peeled out of the driveway.

He got no further than a hundred feet before he slowed down and pulled over to the side of the road. He couldn't drive like a madman. He wouldn't allow himself to lose control like that. Just because she was headstrong and ill-tempered didn't mean he should behave the same way.

It's a good thing he found out what she was really like before things got too serious. Funny thing, he never remembered getting so angry with Darlene. She had never inspired rage. Hadn't inspired much of anything, as it turned out, except for those first few dates, certainly passionate in their own way, which led inevitably to the pregnancy and then to the wedding and then to nothing at all. But at least Darlene wasn't exasperating or headstrong or prone to flirting with danger.

He decided to drive to the art show, to see what it was like out there in the middle of the night. He should have done that before.

As soon as he pulled off Scottsdale Road into the long drive, he heard the crackle of his tires on the gravel and remembered what Gary said, that it was impossible to approach the place silently. The parking lot was empty except for one truck, parked right near the entrance, presumably Gary's.

He walked in and Gary jumped up, face flushed, looking somehow guilty. He smiled at Tony and croaked "Hi." Tony felt sorry for him but was in no mood to be gracious.

"Gary, why the hell is the gate opened?"

"The gate?"

"The gate. Right here. I walked right in."

"Well, the gate's always stayed open...for the artists."

"But the artists aren't allowed in here at night anymore."

"Yeah, you're right. It's not as interesting being here at night as it used to be..."

"I don't give a damn whether it's interesting or not, Gary. Only whether it's safe. So, why didn't you close the gate?"

"I dunno. I never did before and nobody told me to do it now."

"Well, I'm telling you to. Every night when the show closes, I want that gate closed. Understand? See the lock?"

"I'll have to check with the Morrows..."

"No, you don't have to check with the Morrows. I'm telling you to lock the gate and that's that."

Gary's face had turned bright red. His eyes were glued to Tony's and sweat was collecting on his forehead. Tony felt sorry for him all over again.

"You do a really good job out here, Gary, but any cop would tell you that the *better* way to do your job is to lock the gate. Okay? It's professional advice, you might say." It took an effort, but he smiled his most friendly smile.

Gary tried to smile back but he failed and nodded his head instead. "Sure, if that's what you think. But no one comes out here anymore. No one at all."

"Anyone here last night?"

"Nope."

"No one? You sure?"

Gary took his eyes off Tony's face for the first time and looked around the lobby, as if searching his memory.

"Oh, yeah. Jess was here. He had work to do down at Gretchen's booth. Then he had to fix some lights. What a creep. Pulled a real hissy fit. Wanted to get into the refrigerator. Wanted a free Coke. Thought I had the key. Hell, I don't have the key..."

"Any one else here?"

"Nope, not a soul. Not a creature was stirring, not even..."

"I'm going to take a look around now, Gary. You stay right here."

Gary looked doubtful. But he shrugged his shoulders, turned on the up-lights, and returned to his television program.

Tony began in the restrooms. Not a bad place to hide if you wanted to stay after the show closed. Then he looked around Derrick's booth, which had no hiding places at all. He wandered into the cafe. There was a long counter where food was served, but it was unsuitable as a hiding place because it was perpendicular to the lobby and visible to the guard. Of course, this guard probably wouldn't see a suspect if he stood by the entrance with a revolver in his hand.

Tony walked slowly down the aisle into the south tent, peering behind walls and under worktables. He examined the laced tent flaps, tied down from the inside. Russo's booth held no surprises; neither did Peter Sterling's. There was a skirted card table, but it was crammed with plastic boxes and a few wine bottles. The jewelry display case was glass and you could see right through it. Then, of course, there was Zach's fort. When he peered into the opening, he could see how Kate could have stayed there unobserved and fairly comfortable.

There was something strange about the configuration of the back walls at this point, so he walked through a narrow opening and found himself in a space between the back of the display walls and the outside canvas wall, a kind of narrow storage area where artists kept stepladders, brooms, extra frames, boxes of this and that. In one corner there was a pile of blankets, and it took Tony less than a second to realize this was probably Derrick and Gretchen's hideout. Worse than a cheap motel, he thought. Why would a beautiful woman like Gretchen, a sweet and talented woman, succumb to the brutality of the likes of Derrick Hughes?

He continued down the aisle, all the way to the end, to Eldon's booth, where there was a counter that could indeed be used as a hiding place. That made how many places to hide? The restrooms,

Zach's fort, the storage space, Eldon's booth. There were probably as many places down the north tent. In fact, if he remembered correctly, another artist, Robin Branham, had made a child's fort out of her worktable.

Tomorrow he would recommend to the Morrows that they search the tents before they closed at night, and that Gary keep the entrance gate locked. In the morning he would have someone check out the security fence again. Not too complicated. Not too inconvenient. Thing was, why the hell was someone wandering around the tents at night, making all this precaution necessary?

TWENTY-SEVEN

It was Sunday morning. Kate had not been to church in years and she wasn't going to start now. But this morning she passed up her morning coffee, walked right through the café and out to the middle of the sculpture garden. She stood in the shadow of Jesus Christ and studied his face. It was a kind face, and she was glad for that. She walked around the statue and then sat down on the pedestal, which was the perfect height for sitting, and looked at the grass, wondering if there were some indication of where her father had lain, a blade of grass or a little stone that would magically reveal part of the secret, or perhaps there was a faint impression in the earth, or even—she hoped not—some drops of blood. But all the grass looked the same, fresh and green and recently mowed.

Had her father been conscious? Had he seen Jesus? Had he said his fervent, "Jesus, oh, sweet Jesus," that he had always, respectfully, prayed when he was troubled?

Across the bright green lawn she saw Connie leave the café and walk toward her with two cups of coffee. That's okay, she thought. It was about time they talked, and this was a better place than most.

Connie gave her a cup and said "Cream, no sugar. That's what he told me." She nodded her head in the direction of the café.

"Thanks."

Connie apparently didn't feel the need to fill in the silence and took her time getting settled on the pedestal beside Kate.

Finally Kate asked, "Did you see him lying here?"

"Yes, but only from a distance. By the time I learned about it, they wouldn't let any one near. And then they took him away."

"Do you think he knew? Do you think he suffered?"

"I don't know, Kate. But I keep telling myself that if he were conscious at all it would have been a comfort to him, lying here, at the feet of Christ. He was a religious man, as you know."

"A lot of good it did him."

"Oh, Kate. Sometimes life is tough. Sometimes people do awful things. That's got nothing to do with God."

"I know. I just want to be angry today."

There was another stretch of silence. Then Kate asked, "Did you two really love each other? I mean, really?"

"I think so. The time we had was too short to be certain, but I think we would have been happy together."

Kate pondered that for a minute. "You didn't know him very long, but it's almost worse for you. You might have had a future together. With me, well, he was my father, and everything was in the past."

"Oh, but love doesn't live in the past, or in the future. It lives in the heart, and the heart is right now." Connie spoke softly and paused before adding, "Your father told me you were in love with someone. Engaged to be married. Do you love him very much?"

"Martin? No, that's all off. Daddy didn't like him. He probably told you that."

"Yes, but you don't make those decisions based on what your father thinks, do you?"

"But in this case he was right. There's someone else now, but I don't know whether I love him or hate him." Why was she telling Connie this?

Connie chuckled. "Oh, one of those relationships—they're always painful but so exciting."

This time it was Kate who kept the silence. She watched the

tents slowly come to life in the morning sun. The flaps were unlaced and tied back, chairs were moved out onto the grass where artists gathered for coffee and gossip, paintings were propped up on easels ready to be worked on. A few customers wandered leisurely from one booth to the next.

Kate finally said, "I want to apologize for avoiding you all this time. It was childish and selfish. I've been wanting to say something to you for so long..."

"It's okay, Kate."

"And I'm sorry about Jess. I didn't mean to make things worse for you..."

"It's okay, Kate, really."

They settled in to another comfortable silence. Then Connie stood up and said, "C'mon, let's go back to your booth. I've got something to show you."

There were no customers in the booth, and Connie paused for a moment before moving from one sculpture to the next, touching each one affectionately. She finally stopped in front of *Mother and Child*. "I've wanted to tell to you about this piece. It was your father's favorite, and you should never sell it because it's the very last one. See where it's marked down here at the base, AP? That means it's the 'artist's print'. Besides, look closer."

Both the mother and the child were looking down, as if admiring shells on a beach or flowers in a garden. When Kate moved in closer she noticed the details of the child's dress, the smocking beneath the collar. Didn't she once have a dress like that? She remembered an old photograph...and the woman, why her hair was pulled back just like her mother's. Of course! Why hadn't she seen it earlier?

"You're right, Connie, I could never sell it. I'll take it back home with me today."

"You don't have to do that, Kate. Keep it here and let people enjoy it. You could put a note on it that it's not for sale."

Kate turned to Connie and impulsively gave her a hug. "How can I thank you?"

"Well, you actually need to thank me for one other thing. Look over here." Connie pointed to the pre-cast list for *Girl with Dog*. "I sold number ten for you yesterday. Nicest lady. She just fell in love with it."

"Oh my heavens, thank you!" Kate said. "I'll take it to the foundry tomorrow. Do you want to come? Could you get the day off? We could..."

"No, I can't. But let me at least get Jess to help you put it in the truck this afternoon."

Kate's phone rang, so Connie waved goodbye and headed back to the office. The caller identified himself as the customer who had purchased the two sculptures of *Girl with Dog* at the same time. He was delighted to hear that Kate would be taking the piece to the foundry tomorrow because he was looking forward to having them soon, one for Mother's Day and the other for Father's Day. He was trying to placate his parents who were hatefully divorced and agreed on only one thing: they both loved their granddaughter who had an Irish setter. What interesting family dynamics, thought Kate. Three generations and a dog, connected to each other by little more than her father's art and a several pounds of clay.

Kate got herself some coffee and walked down to see how Gretchen was doing. She found her hard at work, absolutely radiant and evidently fully recovered. Her tunic was new, robin's egg blue, and just as short and revealing as all her others. She was in her stocking feet and her hair was beautifully done up in tiny braids. If there were any bruises remaining, they were well hidden by makeup.

"Did you hear about the Xs someone sprayed on my paintings?" Gretchen wanted to know.

"Yes, I did, but everything looks cleaned up now. It's hard to believe that Derrick could be so mean."

"Oh, I don't think it was Derrick."

"Gretchen! Of course it was Derrick. Who else would do such a thing?"

"Oh, there are people. Mean people. Derrick isn't mean. Actually, he's very kind. He's angry, and that's different."

"Gretchen, I'm sure it was Derrick..."

"No, you're wrong, and I don't want to talk about it anymore."

She went back to painting, but then looked up, smiled, and seemed somewhat surprised at her own absentmindedness. "We have to talk about which painting you want. Do you like any of these? Or do you want me to do one just for you?"

"I like the irises. They're my favorite flowers. But I'd like it smaller. Could you do one half that size?"

"Half? You don't like...?"

Gretchen seemed insulted, so Kate said, "No, you're right. That's the right size. But maybe the background could be deep green, instead of black. Could you paint one like that?"

"Sure. It'll take me a day or two. And when it's done you can bring me St. Francis. Oh, Kate, I really feel guilty about this. I know I'm getting the better end of the deal. I really owe you."

"Gretchen, no ... don't be silly." As she turned to leave she suddenly remembered to ask, "What did you mean when you said to be careful about Eldon?"

"Just be careful, that's all."

"But why do you say that?"

"He's not who you think. I don't want to say anymore. You're telling me to be careful of Derrick, and I'm telling you to be careful of Eldon."

Later in the day Kate got another order for *Old Man Reading*. The woman who bought it asked if Kate had a photo of it so she could mail it to her husband who was out of the country on a long business trip. Kate happily gave her one and then, while flipping through the file box of photos, decided to find a picture of *Mother and Child* to take home with her. But there were none. It was hard to believe that her father had overlooked having this particular piece photographed. She would have to check with Eldon. Perhaps he had taken them but then forgot to give them to her after her father died. When she walked down to Eldon's booth, however, there were at least three other artists in line to place orders with him, so she decided to wait until tomorrow.

What Kate really wanted to do was to call Tony. She wanted to tell him he had been rude and insufferable and patronizing. She wanted to tell him she despised him. That she was not stupid. But in the end, no matter how much she brooded, she knew she had done a stupid thing, maybe even a dangerous thing. How could she explain that she was actually kind of proud of that stupid thing? At least she wasn't letting life glide by.

Two hours of brooding was enough, so in the middle of the afternoon she gathered her things and prepared to go home. Jess arrived, awkward and silent, to help her with the sculpture. He was surprisingly careful transferring the work from the turntable into a large box, making sure the armature didn't get jostled or the clay touched or scraped. He rolled it on a cart out to the lobby and waited for Kate to drive the truck up to the entrance. Then he lifted it onto the bed of the truck and secured it with bungee cords.

When she turned to thank him, he had already turned around and was heading back through the entrance.

~~~~~~~~~~~~~~~~~~~~~~~~~~~~~~~~~~

His mother peered in his fort and said, "C'mon, Zach, we have to go to the office."

Zach didn't want to go to the office. He was in the middle of a complicated movement of troops and equipment from one side of the battlefield to the other.

"And after that we'll go get some ice cream."

Ice cream meant a Klondike bar. He'd like that. Zach never quite understood the exact relationship between ice cream and everything else in his world, but he did know that ice cream often came before he was supposed to do something nice or right after he did something nice. It didn't matter. He really loved Klondike bars, so he crawled out of the fort.

This time his mother wasn't carrying one of her paintings or walking with a stranger, which is what usually happened when they went to the office.

They climbed up the steps, but instead of staying in the room where people were standing in lines with artwork, and others were sitting behind desks using computers and counting money, they turned into a small room with a very big desk and lots of boxes on the floor. A big man with a big smile was waiting for them.

"Thanks for coming," said the big man to his mother. Then he turned to Zach and held out his hand to shake it. Zach forgot which hand he was supposed to use, so he put them both in his pockets.

"Shake hands with the nice man, Zach. His name is Detect...his name is Tony. Say hello to Tony."

Zach said 'hello' but kept his hands in his pocket.

The big man sat down behind the desk and his mother sat in the other chair. Zach looked around to find a place to sit. He wanted to crawl up on his mother's lap but was too embarrassed to do that in front of the man. But then the man said, "Hey Zach, why don't you sit right here, on the box. Looks just about your size." He pointed to a box between the desk and his mother.

Zach sat on the box and looked at his mother. Is it okay to sit on the box? But she was talking to the man and didn't seem to care one way or the other.

Then his mother looked at him with one of those serious right-in-your-eyes looks and said, "Zach, I want you to answer Tony's questions. Can you do that for me? And tell the truth. We've talked about the truth and how it's different from pretend. Remember? So tell the truth. It's very important."

Zach turned and looked at the big man and noticed that wavy lines had appeared on his forehead.

"Okay, Zach," the man said, "let's talk about your fort. I bet you've got the best fort in the tents."

Zach didn't think that was a question, but he nodded yes anyway.

"Your mother tells me you have an army and trucks and animals in the fort. Is that right?"

Zach nodded again, still looking at Tony's forehead.

"Do you like playing in your fort?"

Zach wasn't sure how to answer that. Yes, he liked his fort. He nodded yes. He also liked watching television, but there was no television in his fort. And the King was missing. So he shook his head no. Then he thought of the popcorn and the blue stars and his owl, and nodded yes again. The man smiled and his forehead smoothed out.

Then the man put his hand into a large brown bag and pulled out the King! The King was in a plastic baggie. How did the man get the King? Did he come in the middle of the night and take it? Was he the one who made his fort smell so bad? He wanted to sniff, but thought he better not.

The man said, "Zach, someone found this in your fort. We need to know how it got there."

That wasn't a question, was it?

"Did someone put it there?"

Yes, he put it there himself. Did that count? Should he say yes? He looked over at his mother, but she was waiting for the answer, too. He decided not to say anything.

"Or did you find it somewhere else and bring it back to the fort yourself?"

He couldn't say no, that wasn't the truth. So he nodded yes.

This time his mother asked, "Where did you find it, honey?"

Zach didn't know whether to look at the man or his mother, so he looked at his feet. He didn't like this question. He couldn't say yes or no. He had to give a real answer with words. He watched his feet wiggle back and forth.

"Zach, where did you find it?"

He said, as quietly as he could, "In the little fort."

He saw the big man look across at his mother. "The little fort?" the man asked.

So Zach turned his head and looked at his mother, too. She was frowning. She looked at him and asked, "Zach, honey, what's the little fort?"

Zach thought everyone knew about the little fort, so he shrugged his shoulders and looked back at his feet.

"Oh! The little fort!" he heard his mother say. "He must mean the table in Peter's booth. There's a card table with a skirt over it. That must be where he found it."

His mother didn't sound mad that he had taken the King from the little fort. The big man didn't look mad either.

Then the big man asked him, "Is that where you found it? Under the small table that looks like a fort?" Zach saw that his forehead was all wrinkly again. He nodded yes and hoped this would be over soon. He wanted his ice cream. He also wanted the King back.

"Thank you, Zach, thank you very much," the big man said, smiling at him.

His mother smiled at him, too, and stood up. But Zach didn't move.

"Can I have the King back now?" he asked the man. His voice sounded funny to him.

"The king? Oh, I see, the *king*! No, I'm really sorry, Zach, but I have to bring the king to a safe place. Maybe your mother could buy you another...king. Would you like that?"

Zach looked at his feet again. He wanted his old King, not something new.

His mother walked to the door and held out her hand. "I'm very proud of you, Zach. You told the truth. And you did a very good job taking care of...the king. You must have known he was important. But he's so important that Tony has to take him to a special place, okay? Now let's go get some ice cream. On the way home tonight we'll go to the store and buy something you like. How about the Incredible Hulk?"

The green guy? Zach wasn't so sure. Spiderman might be better.

TWENTY-EIGHT

Kate had looked forward to this day ever since she began working in her father's booth: she was taking *Girl with Dog* to the foundry. She would miss having it around, would miss the compliments it generated, would miss having little girls smile as they rotated the turntable.

But she wished she had done a little research. She knew nothing about the casting process, not even how long it would take.

The address led her to the less glamorous outskirts of the neighboring city of Tempe, where the houses, low-slung ranchettes from the 50s, were scattered on half-desert, half-suburban acreage. There was a messiness about the neighborhood, aged and weary. It didn't seem to matter that a pickup was parked under a mesquite tree months at a time, or a mailbox was falling off its post, or a front lawn had returned to desert.

Her heart sank when she found the address. She pulled into a long, rutted driveway that curled around a low-slung house to a huge shed that sat in the middle of an acre or two of messy gravel and discarded equipment. She parked the truck by the entrance and timidly walked into the shed. This was a different world. A man's world, for one thing, with machines—large, small, dirty, greasy and disorderly—and dozens of sculptures and parts of sculptures, both clay and bronze, which sat on the floor or on tables, the smaller ones on shelves.

Off in one corner four men in dirty jeans were leaning up against a counter in that vacant way men have when they talk shop, slouching, shuffling, speaking in half sentences, grunting responses and not wishing to be disturbed. A large, black dog sat at their feet, ears pointed straight up. It glared at Kate but didn't move a muscle. One of the men shot her an annoyed look, hesitated, and finally came forward. He was the huge man that Kate remembered seeing with Eldon during the ArtWalk. He hadn't shaved and Kate bet that he smelled bad downwind.

He took his time coming toward her, his eyes focused first on her chest, then on her hips. His hands went into his pockets as he planted himself in front of her. He jutted out his chin, cocked his head, and said, "Well, little lady, what can I do you for?"

She didn't want to look right at him because she sensed that he would take it as a come-on, so she frowned instead, glanced over at the far wall, and said vaguely, "I think this is where my father took his sculpture..."

"Your father, huh? What's his name, honey?"

"Russo, only he's..."

"Oh yeah, Russo. So you're Russo's daughter...Must say you're better looking than that daddy of yours. Haven't seen him for a while."

"Well, he's..."

"What's he doing letting a pretty thing like you come out here instead of dropping by himself?"

"I...I brought one of his sculptures..."

"Well, why dint you say so? Hal! C'mere." He turned and waved one of the men over. "Get over here, Hal. Let's unload this piece for the little lady."

Kate hesitated. This was not what she had expected. "Well, I'm not sure..." But it was too late. The two men were already hoisting the box out of the truck.

"Hell, this is one nice piece. Look at this, boys. A pretty little girl with a dog. My, my, ain't that sweet. Tell you what, honey, your daddy's the only guy I know who does this kind of stuff. No cowboys for him. No siree. Probably can't do horses worth shit. He sure dint grow up in Arizona, did he, fellas? Back east, right? Well, I guess things are different back east."

The men set the sculpture on a table and stared at it with suspicion. Kate glanced around and noticed that all the other sculptures were western themed—cowboys, Indians, horses, cattle drives. Some were huge, some were crudely done and awkwardly proportioned, some were really quite beautiful. There were a few of Derrick's and Kate had to admit they were the best of the lot.

"Why don't you hang around awhile?" He looked her over once again and grinned. "Always like to have a pretty thing hang around, isn't that right, boys?"

The boys didn't seem to agree on that. One of the men smiled at her appreciatively, but the others stared right through her, obviously wanting her gone.

"No, thanks. I've gotta go. Can you tell me how much..."

"Usual price. Tell your daddy it's the same as last time. He can mail me the deposit. I'll call him later, to get all the details. No use for you to bother that pretty head with all that stuff." He winked at one of the men. "Now, if you ain't gonna hang around and party a little, best be out of here. I got work to do." He turned his back to her and hitched up his jeans.

She had been dismissed! By this hunk of pathetic mankind. Dismissed. He had tried to make a fool of her, humiliate her. He even insulted her father. She wanted to pick up the sculpture and drive off, find another place to do business. But she'd have to ask for help to get it back into the truck, and she simply couldn't make herself do that. So she turned and left. When she started up the engine, she could see the men were still looking at her father's sculpture. One of them was laughing. The dog got up, walked out the entrance into the sunshine, and peed into a shrub.

Why had her father chosen to do business with that ugly, horrible man? And why had Eldon become friends with him? Didn't the man know about her father? Didn't he read the paper? You'd think Eldon would have told him that a mutual acquaintance had been murdered.

There was no question she had the right place. She had heard one of the men call him "Bones," and that was the name on her father's checks, "Bones Jones." And she had thought it so cute.

Back at the show, Kate checked her father's files. Yes, she had gotten the name and address correct. But she still felt sick, embarrassed somehow, like she had done something tremendously stupid by leaving the sculpture there. Perhaps she could ask Eldon about him. Besides, she needed to talk to him anyway, to find out if he had ever photographed *Mother and Child*.

Eldon was leaning on the counter, busy with bookwork, and barely looked up at her when she approached. Whatever happened to that intent gaze he had fixed on her when they first met?

"Did you ever take photos of *Mother and Child*?" she asked when she got his attention. "You know the one I mean?"

"No, I don't think so."

"Don't think you know the one I mean, or don't think you photographed it?"

"Don't think I photographed it. *Mother and Child*? No, never photographed it."

"Well, then, I'd like you to. No hurry, but some time this week, if you can."

"Sure thing." He put his pen down.

"Another question. You know your friend..."

"Sorry, Kate, I've got an appointment. We'll have to talk later." He closed his notebook, glanced up briefly, grabbed his cameras and was off.

Today must be her day to be dismissed.

Gretchen was busy with a customer, so was Vicki. Even Peter didn't have time to talk, although he did exchange earrings for her as usual. But when several customers crowded at his display, she moved away. She watched him glue a smile on his face and flirt with the customers. "What pretty pink ears, what a lovely neck." He looked depressed.

One of the comments made by the Sheriff's deputy yesterday had stuck with Tony. He had even written it down: all the saleswomen at the gem show remembered that the thief had a cute grin and nice clothes and brushed back their hair, telling them they had such pretty ears. Tony found it difficult to believe anyone would use a line like that, but he also remembered that Sophia had mentioned Peter brushing her hair back. He couldn't remember if there was any mention of ears.

And then, of course, late yesterday afternoon, when he learned that the murder weapon had been found in Peter's booth, it looked like a little bit of evidence might be piling up in his direction, so he had shifted his attention back to the jeweler.

But that was yesterday. Today he knew it couldn't have been Peter. His wife, Debra, had come to see him this morning. She was concerned that Peter was going to be arrested, she told him, and she wanted to supply proof that he was somewhere else.

"I think I know where he was that night," she had said, her eyes lowered, chin up, a large stylish pendant resting on her orange silk blouse. Her delicate hands rested quietly on her lap throughout her entire recitation and Tony thought she looked like royalty, like some princess from Thailand. She said she knew of Peter's adventures, knew also that he would rather get arrested for something he didn't do than admit to her that he was gay. She gave Tony some names, some phone numbers, some locations. Obviously she had spent quite a bit of money on detectives over the years. Then she made him promise not to let on to Peter what she knew.

A few phone calls later and Tony was speaking to Jason, a candle maker from Tubac, an art community south of Tucson. Yes, he said, he knew Peter. Yes, he had been with Peter that night. How could he be sure it was that night? Well, Jason said, Peter had suffered a severe asthma attack and had to be taken to the hospital. One call confirmed that Peter had been admitted to the emergency room at El Dorado Hospital in Tucson, and had not been released until Sunday morning.

That pretty much took care of Peter, so Tony yanked the now irrelevant blue 'Is Peter gay?' post-it off his monitor. Then he pulled off the one in pink that said 'missing sculpture?' St. Francis, after all, had been found. The orange one, 'Derrick's alibi-Eldon,' remained. Tony was waiting for J.D. to get Derrick's phone records.

It was now Monday afternoon and the only thing Tony was looking forward to was dinner at his mother's. She might scold him for not having solved the case, but at least he would eat well. His stomach was still churning from the three fast-food meals he had consumed yesterday. Stress didn't help, and spending almost an entire day with J.D. had tested both his patience and their friendship. He had almost thrown him out of the car when they got back to town. He certainly didn't want him around when he interviewed little Zach. He thought the interview had gone pretty well. Cute kid. Nice mother. Too bad it didn't amount to a hill of beans. Murder weapon, yes. Fingerprints, no.

What Tony was still trying to sort out was what they had learned from the Sheriff's deputy. There were no fingerprints at all on the abandoned vehicle other than those of its owner, Lydia Lopez. There were no footprints by the car, either, surrounded as it was by low brush and gravel and exposed to several hours of rain and wind. The only footprint was near where the body had been dumped, protected from the rainfall by an outcropping of rocks, but positioned right where the sandy soil was damp and could record and preserve a perfect size 12W Naturalizer. The wearer weighed either 300 pounds or 170, depending on whether or not he was carrying Lydia Lopez, who weighed 130. But whoever made the shoe print in the tents, Tony had learned, weighed only 145. That was Gretchen's weight, give or take a pound. It seemed evident, then, that the shoe prints were made by two different people. Could Gretchen have simply wandered innocently into Russo's booth that night, or even the next morning? Could the murderer have worn her *stolen* shoes, leaving a footprint in Casa Grande, but not in the tents?

But all of this might be totally irrelevant. The deputy, an ugly squat man with an ugly disposition, was convinced that the guilty party was being held at that very moment in El Cajon, California. The theory was that a guy named Benjamin Ghadi murdered Lopez after they had stolen the gems and then immediately took the nearby exit to Interstate 8, and went west toward San Diego. Ghadi, who weighed one eighty, had been picked up robbing a series of jewelry stores in El Cajon a few days after the murder. They had sent his photo to Tucson and already someone from the gem show had made a positive identification.

"What kind of jewelry stores did Ghadi hit?" Tony asked the deputy.

"Franchise stores...in the malls; he'd arrange to get there just at closing time and ask to see stuff."

"How much did he get away with?"

"Couple a hundred here, couple a hundred there," the ugly deputy said.

"Did he brush back the salesgirls' hair? Flirt with them?"

"What the hell do I care if he flirted with them?"

You ought to care, because he's not the right guy. Definitely not the right guy.

J.D. walked in. He looked tired. And very irritated. "You probably don't want to hear this. Derrick's phone records? Actually, Derrick's and Gretchen's phone records. Well, it seems that Gretchen called Derrick several times after she left the show that night. She called him once at 10:42, once at 11:04, and then again at 11:25. Each call lasted about five minutes."

Tony shook his head. "But his machine could have picked it

up. The calls don't prove he was in his apartment. He could have been anywhere."

"Not true. Derrick doesn't have an answering machine. Somebody really picked up the phone. No one shares the apartment."

"What's the driving time between the show and his apartment?"

"About fifteen minutes."

"Oh, great. A half-hour round trip. If he left the show right after Gretchen, say at 10:25, he'd be home for the first call. And that wouldn't leave him enough time to kill Russo. And there certainly wouldn't be enough time between any of the other calls, either."

Tony pulled off the last post-it and stuck it in the trash. His monitor was stripped bare.

"After all this time, J.D., you know what we've got? Nothing. All we know is that while Art Russo was getting his head bashed in, Jess was home with his mother watching TV, Eldon was in Flagstaff photographing a banquet, Peter was in an emergency room in Tucson, and Derrick was in his apartment talking to his girl friend on the phone. Maybe the Sheriff's right. Maybe a guy named Benjamin Ghadi killed Lopez. Maybe he killed Russo as well. If that's the case, I need to go find myself another line of work."

"You could be a cook in a Mexican restaurant," J.D. offered.

"Then what would you do?"

"Be your partner."

"But you don't like Mexican food."

"I like your mother's. Can I come to dinner this week? You haven't invited me since this case began. Your mother probably misses me."

"You can come to dinner if you tell me why Mohammed must come to the mountain."

"To get to the other side?"

"That's why the chicken crosses the road, stupid."

"I know, but I figure Mohammed's got to be at least as smart as the chicken."

TWENTY-NINE

The next morning Connie waved to Kate from the top of the office steps. "You've got some mail."

Kate opened the large manila envelope and pulled out a handful of glossy black and white photographs of a clay sculpture. Two figures—a 30-something man and a young girl—were standing by a headstone. There was a note attached, from Mark Von Steen, and a check for $5,000.

"Oh, look, Connie, look how beautiful!" she exclaimed, holding the pictures so they both could see. It was absolutely the best work her father had ever done. And how nice of that old man to send her the photographs. The little kindness brought tears to her eyes, reminding her that her emotions were still very close to the surface. All she could do was stand there and stare at the pictures through watery eyes, ignoring the sales staff walking by, the artists setting up for the day, the dozens of browsing customers.

Connie patted her shoulder. "Just think, now you have two wonderful portraits of yourself as a little girl, one with your mother and one with your father. You should frame the photographs and hang them side by side. Wouldn't that be nice?"

"But I don't have any photographs of *Mother and Child*. At least not yet."

"Sure you do. Your father showed them to me."

"Really? But Eldon said he didn't take any."

"But he did. Absolutely. Your father showed them to me at dinner that night, the night he... He had just gotten them and said they were the best photos Eldon had taken."

"But I asked Eldon yesterday." Kate tried to recall the conversation. "Maybe he forgot. But then where are they? They're not in Daddy's file box with all the others."

"Well, he definitely had them with him that night at dinner. Perhaps he left them in his truck."

"I think I would have seen them there by now, Connie. But I'll look for them this afternoon on my way home.

She filed the new photographs in the box with the others, dusted off the sculptures and went out into the sculpture garden to read the paper. She lifted her face to take in the cloudless sky and the smell of spring and contemplated life's contradictions: kindness and cruelty, grace and vulgarity, love and ...

Vicki plopped down beside her. "I have a present for you. Zach picked it out." She handed Kate a blue plastic truck. "He saw it in the store the other day and made me buy it. He told me it was for the nice lady with the blue truck and the popcorn."

"How sweet!"

"Well, he wouldn't be so sweet if he knew you were the one in his fort the other night. Why didn't you tell me it was you?"

"How'd you find out?" Kate asked.

"The detective interviewed us—interviewed Zach, that is—to find out how he got the statue of St. Francis."

"Well, how did he get it?"

"Didn't you hear? From under Peter's table."

Peter had hidden the murder weapon? He was the killer? She shook her head no. First, Peter was too finicky to do something so gruesome. Secondly, he was too smart to leave evidence hanging around.

Vicki leaned closer. "Did you really stay overnight? God, you're brave."

"No, not brave, just stupid," Kate said, wondering what she was going to do with the little blue truck.

"But why'd you do it, stay all night?"

"I told you, it was just stupid. I'm embarrassed I did it, so please keep it to yourself. Can we change the subject?"

"Well, sure...how'd it go yesterday at the foundry?" Vicki asked.

"It was awful. What a horrible man. Did Daddy ever talk to you about him?"

"You mean Bones? Bones Jones? Isn't that name a kick? Your father detested him, but said he did good work and was faster and cheaper than anyone else. Was he really that bad?"

"Horrible. A real creep." Kate put down her coffee and shielded her eyes, pulling the newspaper toward her. She looked down, and there he was, his fat face smiling at her. Bernard "Bones" Jones had been killed in his place of business!

"Oh my god, Vicki, look at this! He's dead. The creep is dead. Impaled on an anvil." She read some more. "Apparently there was a struggle."

"I'd say!"

Kate lowered her voice. "Is it wrong to call him a creep now that he's dead?"

"This happened last night? That sounds awfully suspicious, don't you think?" Vicki grabbed the paper to get a better look.

"Why, because I was there yesterday? You think I'm a jinx or something?"

"Oh, for Pete's sake, of course not. It just seems strange, that's all. Too much of a coincidence, don't you think, with your father's sculpture and all? You've got to tell the detective about this...that you were there yesterday."

"Call Tony? Not on your life." Why *should* she call him? Every time she got involved, he just made her feel ...

"He seems very nice," Vicki ventured.

"You can have him, Vicki. He's all yours."

"Zach liked him, too."

"Then the two of you can have him."

"You're sounding like a woman in love, Kate."

"Oh, for heaven's sake, Vicki. He's just a guy. He bullies. He yells. He's arrogant and..."

"He's sweet. He's also a hunk," Vicki finished.

Kate was irritated that someone else found him attractive and her irritation irritated her. But she didn't want to think about Tony right now. Her real concern was *Girl with Dog*. "What about the sculpture? Shouldn't I go get it? But what if the property is all taped off, like a crime scene. Then they probably wouldn't let me in."

"Well, that's one more reason to call Tony. See what he knows, see if he can get it for you."

"But it happened in Tempe, not Scottsdale."

"The two cities are neighbors, Kate, not foreign countries. I'm sure they speak to one another."

Of course Vicki was right. But if something had happened to the sculpture it would already be too late. She had accepted ten deposits, $700 each. She'd have to return all that money *plus* she'd lose out on the remaining balances, a thousand bucks each. $17,000. Dang, that was a lot of money! Then she felt ashamed that $17,000 was more important to her than someone's life.

She devoured the rest of the article to see if there were reports of damage to the premises or to the contents of the building but there was no more information. She should call Tony. No. Maybe later. Then she remembered Eldon. Creep or no, Bones was a friend of Eldon's, and Eldon had been nice to her when her father died. She should go down and give him her condolences.

Eldon wasn't in his booth but there was a pad of paper and a pen, so Kate scooted behind the counter to write him a note. That's when she came face to face with the Arizona "sunset" she had never really noticed before. How tacky! Even so, she couldn't resist looking closer at the postage-size images. Why do women always want to compare their bodies, she wondered, and see how they measure up to some guy's fantasy? There was a redhead, overweight, with a broad butt, shown lying on a bed facedown, faceup, twisted forward, backward and sideways. A skinny little brunette, with no chest at all, cavorted on a straight back chair in zen-like poses Kate couldn't even imagine attempting. An older woman, close to fifty, posed by a window, first standing, then sitting, looking out the window, then looking in. She had a tough, bored expression. There were others, one more pathetic than the next. Then she spotted a trim blonde, with a brave, smiling face: Lydia Lopez, multiplied by the dozen, was sunbathing on a huge rock, with the desert foothills in the distance.

Stunned, she made her way back to her booth and sat down at the desk. She tried to think. Eldon knew Lydia Lopez. Lydia Lopez was dead. Eldon knew Bones Jones, and he, too, was dead. How many people knew both Lydia and Bones? Kate guessed that Eldon was one of very few…maybe the only one. Did that mean what it seemed to mean? That she had been wrong about Derrick just as she had been wrong about Jess? That it was Eldon, instead? Gretchen had told her Eldon wasn't who he appeared to be. But Tony never seemed suspicious of him. In fact, Tony would probably think her a fool to suspect him. But the fact was that Eldon had lied to her about the photographs and that just didn't make sense.

She needed to make sure they weren't in the truck.

They weren't. She looked between the cushions, in the glove compartment and door pockets, under the floor mats, behind the visors. They simply weren't there. That meant not only that Eldon had lied but also that her father had brought them into the tents that night and some one had taken them. But why?

She returned to Eldon's booth. It was still empty. The painter next to him was busy with customers so Kate slipped behind the counter and scanned the two stacks of storage boxes. One on the top was labeled *artists' work.* The cover was loose so she nudged it off and peeked inside. The contents were filed alphabetically by artist. As soon as she spotted her father's name, between Kirk Randle and Bill Shaddix, she heard a voice call out, "Hey, Eldon, are my pictures ready yet?" And she heard Eldon reply, "Tomorrow."

She shot up, grabbed the pen and began writing on the pad,

Eldon, please don't forget to--- She kept her head down until she knew he was close, then looked up, pretending to be surprised. He was accompanied by a woman who looked very much like him. His sister? Didn't he say he had a sister? Hadn't he ordered a sculpture for her, in fact, the *Girl with Dog?*

Eldon looked puzzled. He smiled at her, but his eyes were cold. It took all the presence of mind she could muster to act as if it were the most natural thing to do, to stand there behind his counter.

"I was just leaving you a note. Nothing important." She finished writing *---photograph Mother and Child*, put down the pen and smiled up at the woman, saying sweetly, "Why, you must be Eldon's sister. Hi, I'm Kate." She held out her hand.

The woman smiled back stiffly. "Pleased to meet you. I'm Melody."

Kate skirted the counter, avoiding Eldon's face altogether, and focused only on the woman, on her flecked, hazel eyes and mascara-laden lashes, and said, still smiling, "Well, it's very nice to meet you, Melody. Perhaps I'll see you later. I sure hope you enjoy the show." And with that she handed Eldon the note and left the booth, determined not to walk fast, determined not to raise suspicion. She sauntered, she stopped and chatted with various artists, she smiled, she was as carefree as the beautiful spring day everyone was enjoying. Then she went out to the sculpture garden and sat on the bench by the bronze children.

The plan came to her fully formed. She knew where she would hide. She knew how she would dress. And she knew how she would remove her truck from the parking lot. She got up and walked out of the tents.

"Hey, Gretchen. Can you do me a favor? I'm stuck down here at Kierland Commons and my truck won't start. Can you come get me?"

Wasn't it convenient when people thought they owed you a favor? Actually, the shopping center was only two miles from the show and Gretchen said she didn't mind taking a break, although she wondered why Kate had gone shopping in the middle of a busy day. "Sale at Talbot's," Kate had replied. "Gotta take advantage, you know."

"Do you need me to drive you home tonight?" Gretchen asked on the way back to the show. "And who's taking care of your truck?"

"I made arrangements for the truck. They'll get it back to me tomorrow. And I'll have Vicki drive me home tonight," she lied.

THIRTY

It was the middle of the afternoon and the photographs were once again spread out across the table. J.D. was standing over to the side, arms crossed. His expression was one of deliberate boredom.

Tony glared at him. "C'mon, J.D. Help me out here."

"With what? We've been through this before."

Tony opened the envelope of negatives from the Saturday night banquet in Flagstaff and compared them to the prints. There was an extra negative, a scene of people gathered on the steps of a church, but all the rest matched. When he looked through the prints today, they didn't seem so amateurish. Why had he been so critical?

He opened the second envelope and pulled out the strips of negatives, but before he held them up to the light, he said, "J.D., something's wrong here."

"Wrong? You haven't even looked at them. How do you know they're wrong? You're holding them up like Carnak the Magician."

"I don't have to look at them." With his other hand he hurriedly reached for the envelope of negatives from the meeting in Williams and emptied the contents on the table.

"Take a look. Friday's events and Sunday's events were taken with a 35 mm camera. But these, from Saturday night, the better ones, they were taken with a medium- format camera—a Mamiya, or maybe a Hasselblad. The negatives are different, much larger, see?"

"So, he used a different camera on Saturday."

"But he doesn't have one of these. Remember? He said he sold his Bronica. These are not his. He got them from someone else."

J.D. came to attention, grabbed the newspaper clippings and his notebook, and waved them at Tony as he left the room. "I'll make some calls."

Tony pulled out the photos from the digital camera and lined them up according to the imprinted dates, starting with Thursday night. There were two sunset pictures of Camelback Mountain in Phoenix. From Friday there were a couple of shots of downtown Flagstaff, some pretty coeds on the university campus and several late afternoon shots of the Four Peaks Mountain area. Saturday there was one print of Four Peaks, backlit with the early morning sun, and a few close-ups of rocks and plants that could have been taken anywhere. The town of Williams, just 50 miles west of Flagstaff, appeared with Sunday's date. There were a few taken at noon, when the shadows looked like little puddles, and a few more later in the day, when the shadows stretched themselves out in the afternoon sun. Several shots of the train that brings visitors up to the Grand Canyon were taken in the early evening. The pictures dated after that were of little interest to Tony.

J.D. returned. "Spoke to Lars Weingold, a photographer for *The Arizona Daily Star*. Said he got a call from Eldon a few days after the banquet. Eldon wanted to buy his pictures. Would pay him five hundred bucks for the ones he hadn't used. Lars thought, what the hell, the event's long past, he wouldn't ever need them again and he could use the money. Said Eldon paid cash."

"Well, well, well. So Eldon wasn't in Flagstaff on Saturday night after all."

A phone call interrupted them. It was Vicki. Tony listened carefully, taking notes. He broke off the conversation briefly to ask J.D. to locate a copy of *The Arizona Republic*. When he found the article about Bernard Jones being murdered in his foundry, he asked Vicki a few questions and hung up.

"I think our guy's done it again," he said, poking his index finger at Bones' fat face.

The entrance to the shed was yellow-taped and the same crime scene team that Scottsdale used was now collecting evidence for the Tempe police. Tony and J.D. spoke to the officer in charge and walked in.

"Holy shit! Look at this mess," was J.D.'s reaction as he pulled out his notebook.

Small tools were scattered all over. An arc welder lay tipped against a forklift, and a sandblasting machine was capsized. Dozens of wax molds of heads, legs, and horse carcasses dangled from shelves and littered the floor.

A bloodied anvil stood in the center of what looked like a combat area, where the floor was cleared of debris for a 6-foot radius and then cluttered with objects that had been thrown or pushed aside in the struggle.

On a workbench nearby, several clay sculptures had been tipped over or bashed in. One of them was Russo's, its base gouged out on several sides, but otherwise intact. Tony checked to make sure the technicians had photographed the sculptures and gotten prints. They had.

It wasn't difficult to figure out what connected the three murders. What was difficult to figure out was what to do about it.

The Arizona night descended quickly and silently, without star or moon or cloud, and when it reached the desert floor beyond the sculpture garden, it spread out, erasing all evidence of rock or scrub. One tall saguaro remained visible because its silhouette stood taller than the range of hills that lay behind it.

Kate, dressed in black from head to toe, sat perfectly still on the bench beside the bronze children and watched the Indian scout,

20 feet away, dissolve into the darkness. Turning her head slightly to the right, she noticed that the stone lion, high on its pedestal, was disappearing too, as if a swath of black chiffon had drifted over it. The security light shone from behind her left shoulder and glittered provocatively on the tiny gold fig leaf that adorned one of the nudes. She couldn't see the other nude very well, because it was partially hidden from view by Jesus Christ, who seemed in command of the garden, not just because of who he was, but because he was so large and stood in the center, pale and majestic against the dark sky.

The security light caused long shadows to stretch from each of the sculptures and fan out across the dark green grass. The shadows, deepest at their source, dissipated as they floated outward, losing their definition until they became one with the rest of the lawn or climbed up the base of another sculpture.

Every hour, of course, the lights came on in the tents for about 10 minutes and she amused herself by watching the guard patrol first the south tent, then cross through the café to patrol the north. He probably shuffled through life the way he shuffled through the tents.

The temperature dropped as rapidly as the darkness and this caught her by surprise. She was afraid her breath might become visible, so she lowered her head very slowly and began breathing softly into her jacket. Otherwise, she remained just as she had been, sitting quietly with the children. Her only occupation had been to glance down at her watch without moving her head or rotating her wrists. It would be another half-hour before the security light would turn off and she could go about her business. Could she do it? She felt another wave of panic surge up from her gut. "Jesus, oh, sweet Jesus," she prayed as she swallowed it back.

She almost missed it, the figure emerging from behind the Indian scout, soft edged and fluid, like some beast squirming out of a host-body in a horror film. She watched the figure and its shadow slink sideways across the garden, sometimes merging with one of the shadows and at other times walking upright in the light. It finally slipped around the base of one of the floating silver discs, turned to the right, and disappeared.

She could barely breathe as another wave of panic hit her. She recognized the symptoms. Fight or flight. She went with flight, and slipped to the ground. Without waiting for the security light to go out, she crawled away through the dark, damp grass, toward the tent flap she had partially unlaced.

THIRTY-ONE

She nudged aside the silk plant that camouflaged where she had untied the flap, stuck her head into the tent, and breathed in the darkness as if gasping for air itself. The light from the sculpture garden slipped over her head and shoulders and plopped a triangular wedge of brightness half way across the asphalt aisle. Then, suddenly, the security light went out, erasing the triangle. Everything was dark.

For a moment she rested there, arms and shoulders in the tent, torso sprawled out on the grass. What a relief to be invisible, to be covered with a blanket of cool, black air. She waited until the headlights of a car slid across the grass and disappeared down the road before slowly pulling herself in by her elbows, slithering inch by inch, until only her feet remained outside.

She pushed her shoulders up and moved her knee forward, but suddenly the up-lights flooded the tent, stopping her cold. Of course! It was 10 o'clock and the guard would be making his rounds. How could she have forgotten? She quickly backed out of the tent and stretched out in the rut of dirt that had formed where the grass met the asphalt, holding the flap together with her fingertips. It would be almost impossible to see her from the inside, that she knew, but would the untied portion of the tent flap, with no plant to conceal it, be noticeable?

She watched the shadow of the guard as he made his way down the aisle in the glowing tents. She looked over her shoulder as he shuffled past and saw him reach the end and immediately turn around, heading back to where she lay. He paused briefly but didn't stop. Then she lost him as he proceeded back toward the lobby, but caught him again as he walked across the café and turned down the north tent. Before he reached the end, however, she was distracted by a figure moving in the café. The figure stopped, and his body language suggested he was talking to someone, someone she couldn't see. Just before the guard returned, the man in the café moved out of sight. Then the lights went out again.

Could that have been Jess? Or was it the person who had moved through the sculpture garden just minutes ago? And was that the same person she had seen the other night, the one with the strange shoes? She prayed it was Jess.

She lifted her face off the dirt and checked her pockets. Her new pen light was in her left pocket and her cell phone, turned off, was in her right. She had Tony's number on speed dial, but was determined to call him only in the direst emergency.

Once again, she parted the tent flaps. She entered silently, eased the plant back in place, and stood up, taking a moment to picture her surroundings. Directly in front of her would be Vicki's booth and Zach's fort. To the right of Vicki's booth were Penny's, then Daphne's, then Roger's, Gretchen's, Graydon's, and finally Eldon's. Each booth was 15 feet wide and ended with a wall that jutted a few inches into the aisle. If she counted out six paces and stopped, she could check her position with the penlight.

She estimated the distance to the center of the aisle, turned to the right, and began walking, slowly at first, her crepe-soled shoes silent on the asphalt. She counted six steps, flicked on the penlight and saw the end of Penny's booth. Gaining confidence, she took another step, but stopped when she heard voices back in the lobby. What if it was Jess and he had another job to do tonight? What if the lights came on right now, where could she hide? She panicked and spun around, counted seven steps, and entered Vicki's booth. She felt for the table, moved around to the other side, dropped to the floor and slipped into Zach's fort. Footsteps approached, accompanied by a flashlight that circled up and around and down again, scanning, searching for something. Then the person turned around and walked back to the lobby.

She sat still and listened. But nothing else happened. No lights, no conversation. How much longer should she wait? A little longer, just to be safe. But she didn't want to waste time and it sounded like only the guard remained, so she turned on the penlight and looked at her watch. There was a half-hour before the next rounds. That should be sufficient time. Zach's army caught the light. It was arranged as neatly as before, this time with Spiderman on top of the stack of raisin boxes. She smiled. How tempting it was to stay right here in the fort, safe and invisible. Instead, she gritted her teeth and crawled out.

This time she got all the way down the aisle with no interruptions, located the counter in Eldon's booth and slipped behind it. She shined the penlight on the storage boxes, searching for the one she had seen earlier. But the boxes were not in the same order, and it was difficult to read the tiny labels. She sat down on the cold floor and examined each one. There were containers labeled *filters, film, slides, sales records, portraits, special occasions*. Finally, at the bottom of one of the stacks, she found *artists' work*. She carefully removed the boxes stacked on top of it, creating another pile. Her hands were sweaty, and one of the boxes slipped from her fingers onto the floor. The sound startled her and she knew it would alert anyone who heard it, so she waited, not moving, to see if there was a reaction. There was only silence.

The plastic lid opened with a little pop. She placed it on the floor, pulled the box into her lap, and looked once again for her father's name. She held the penlight in her mouth and walked her fingers through the contents. But these were not photos at all! They were envelopes filled with strips of tiny negatives. There was no way she could examine such small images with a penlight, even if she stayed all night. She reached in, grabbed the lot of them, and shoved them in her pocket.

She put the boxes back in order and checked her watch. It was already two minutes to eleven. The guard would be coming down soon and she knew she was vulnerable where she was, huddled behind the counter. She pictured Graydon's booth next door, over-flowing with artwork. Paintings not hung on the wall were leaning against it, one in front of the other, and on his easel was an enor-mous landscape. She flashed her penlight in that direction and spot-ted his taboret, stacked with paint tubes and brushes, and decided to hide behind it in the confusion of supplies and half-finished can-vasses. She scurried over, sat down, and slid an unframed painting in front of her. The powerful smell of linseed oil and turpentine sur-prised her. Vicki's acrylics and Gretchen's watercolors were almost odorless, she realized, and then she wondered why she was thinking about such unimportant things as what paintings smelled like.

The lights came on. She heard the guard's footsteps approach but this time his step was firm and deliberate, and when he reached the end he took his time. Was he peering behind Eldon's counter? The turpentine fumes were overpowering, but she took shallow breaths and stayed absolutely still. After the guard moved on and she was certain he had finished with the south tent, she slid the painting aside and watched his shadowy shape go down the north tent. What was it about him that seemed different?

She had three choices now. She could stay where she was, she could return to the sculpture garden, or she could go back to Zach's fort. The fort won out. Easily.

As soon as the up-lights clicked off, she headed up the aisle, counting paces and checking her position with the penlight as she passed each booth. When she reached Daphne's booth, she knew she had only seconds to go, so she quickened her pace past Penny's, only to see a flashlight sweeping wide arcs as it turned the corner from the lobby and headed in her direction. She slipped into Vicki's booth and felt for the table, but the opening to the fort was on the opposite side. She looked up at the approaching flashlight, estimated the time it would take to circle the table, and decided against it. Instead, she felt her way along the back wall and into the opening to the storage area. She tried to remember what was in the space and how it was laid out. One wrong step and a ladder or a broom could fall on top of her.

Her adrenaline had kicked in and the sound of her own breathing alarmed her, each breath coming faster and deeper than the one before. The flashlight circled and darted about and twice flitted past the opening in the wall. And then, abruptly, the light went out. She listened for footsteps but couldn't hear anything over her own breathing.

She tried to focus on her surroundings. The ladder was on her left, leaning against the wall. She felt for it. The broom was usually stored behind it, along with Vicki's carpet sweeper. Yes, they were there. Boxes of pottery would be on her right. She felt for them with her foot, and then reached over with her hand. The top of the boxes came up to her waist and had collected an assortment of things hastily laid down and later forgotten. Her fingers found a coffee mug, an aerosol can, a measuring tape. Farther back on the wall, if she remembered correctly, there were several large frames hanging on hooks to keep them off the floor. She'd have to be careful not to bump her head on them if she moved. And way in the corner there would be a pile of blankets and quilts that Derrick and Gretchen had accumulated for their comfort.

She decided to spend the night where she was. When the up-lights came on the next time, she would move to the back corner and lay down on the blankets. At least she would be comfortable. And warm.

She estimated that 15 minutes went by before all her adrenaline had been released and her breathing returned to normal. In that time she had detected no other sound or movement or light, except there was the slightest...

Her phone sang out into the stillness. She felt her heart somersault in her chest. She was so stunned she couldn't move. Oh, Jesus, this couldn't be happening! She had to turn if off, and quickly. But the phone had already started on the second ring before her hand found its way to her pocket.

A muscular arm reached around her waist from behind, pinning her wrist to her pocket, while a hand, a big hand, covered her mouth. Her head was pulled back against strong shoulders and a leg wrapped around her shins. She couldn't move. She didn't *want* to move! The phone rang a third time. Her heart was exploding. Her eyes were opened wide but there was nothing to see.

A soft voice whispered into her neck, "Take the phone out of your pocket and put it on the boxes."

She didn't move. Her mind couldn't make sense of it.

"*Right now!*" The voice was urgent, and even though it still didn't make sense, she knew she would have to do it. She nodded her head. He loosened his grip. She removed the phone and placed it on top of the boxes, just as he had told her.

"Now we're going to back up," he whispered, "quick and quiet." He tightened his arm around her waist, lifted her off the floor and took three steps backward. They sank sideways onto the blanket-covered mattress, lying down one behind the other. She felt a heavy quilt float down through the air and cover her, face and all. She felt his warm breath on her neck. And then a silent kiss. Jesus!

Eyes still opened, she squinted into the void. Something was moving. A penlight shone into the closet. She could see it zigzag up the wall and along the floor just inches from her nose. She tried to see the shoes, but was blinded instead as the light momentarily found her eye on its path across the quilt. She didn't breathe. She could tell Tony wasn't breathing either. How long could she hold her breath? Two minutes? More? She couldn't remember. Long enough, apparently. The penlight steadied as the intruder picked up the phone, turned it off and put it back down. Then she felt a slight draft as he walked back through the opening.

She started to move, but Tony held her tight. His arm still encircled her, his hand cupping a breast, accidentally, she was sure. Once more she felt his breath on her neck. She remembered when they first met, how she hadn't wanted a detective breathing down her neck. Now, that was all she wanted, to have him hold her close, so close that her hips were locked into his. She wondered what there was about fear that triggered the shameless and inappropriate urges she was feeling. Damn libido.

One ear was burrowed into a pillow. With the other ear she heard two things: her heart beating and, more distant, a scraping. It was evident that Tony was listening, too, because his muscles were taut and his breathing shallow.

He put a finger to her lips, kissed the back of her neck again and slowly untangled himself. It was incredible, she thought, that a man his size could move with such grace and fluidity, but the next thing she knew he was standing above her and then he was drifting away into thin air. She knew exactly when he left the storage area because the loss of his body heat caused her to shiver under the covers.

The scraping continued. Then she heard voices and scuffling. Then grunts and a loud shout. What the hell was happening? She bolted out from under the covers and crawled toward the opening. Just as she reached it the up-lights came on, the brightness almost blinding her.

Tony was in her father's booth. He was struggling with another man and had gotten the upper hand, holding him in a vice-like grip. But then, just as quickly, a third man popped into view, from behind Zach's fort, and pointed a gun at Tony.

She stood up and screamed as loud as she could. "Tony! Watch out!"

Tony looked up at her, eyebrows raised, forehead creased, mouth opened. In an instant he lost just enough of his grip for the man to squirm free, push away and head toward the aisle. A sculpture fell from its stand, a chair toppled over, a dozen little marbles bounced and rolled all over the asphalt. Peter's display case crashed to the floor, causing shards of glass to sparkle and crackle under Tony's feet as he ran in pursuit. The third man, the one with the gun, yelled something, knocked a jar of scarlet paint off Vicki's worktable, and ran after them both.

Kate's feet were glued to the floor. She listened to objects crash and collide as the men ran down the aisle. She could hear them bump into walls as they raced and struggled with each other. They must be near the lobby now, she thought, forcing one foot in front of the other, stepping carefully around the glass and the paint and the fallen furnishings. But when she got to the aisle and heard a loud explosion—a gunshot—she raced ahead as fast as she could. Tony!

She rounded the corner into the lobby but immediately slowed down, afraid to see what lay ahead. But there was Tony, straddling the man, cuffing his wrists behind his back. The third man was still pointing his gun at them. Gary the Guard stood next to the man with the gun, eyes bulging, a satisfied grin on his beet-red face. Chunks of a broken television set were scattered on the floor.

Tony stood up and pulled the man to his feet. Then she heard the familiar words, "Eldon Melrose, you are under arrest for the murder of Art Russo. You have the right to..." Jesus, sweet Jesus. She'd been right, after all.

The third man put his gun away and was now talking quietly into his phone. The guard, sweating profusely and pointing to the broken television, was also on the phone, apparently notifying the Morrows, his voice high-pitched and giggling with excitement. Then red lights were blinking in the parking lot. Two uniformed officers, a man and a woman, appeared. After a short conversation with Tony, they left with Eldon securely between them. Their vehicle pulled out, and another arrived. More lights blinking. Just like a scene from *Law and Order*, she thought. And she hadn't wanted policemen in her life!

Tony looked at her and smiled. "You did pretty well until you screamed."

"But the gun! I thought..."

"Meet my partner, J.D."

She looked at J.D. Then she looked at Tony, and then back at J.D. again. Lord, what a mismatched pair!

J.D. grinned at Kate. "That was one hell of a scream," he said with admiration. To which Tony added, "I guess it shows how much she loves me."

You wish.

THIRTY-TWO

Tony looked at the little group that had assembled around one of the tables in the chilly café and wondered how much he should tell them. It was 2:30 in the morning and it was evident they wouldn't leave until they got some answers.

He was feeling a strange exhilaration and he knew that J.D. felt it, too—the thrill of the hunt, he supposed. But Kate looked numb. He had sat her down in the café, wrapped his jacket around her shoulders, kissed her gently and gotten to work. He checked on her from time to time, and offered to call her a cab, but she just shook her head and stared into the distance.

When the Morrows arrived, he relaxed a little. Mrs. Morrow sat with Kate while her husband, and then Jess—who had been called in to help—watched the evidence being collected. Afterwards they all cleaned up the mess, the shards of glass, the spilled paint, the toppled equipment. It was Jess who found the last of the diamonds in the puddle of red paint, quietly handing it to Tony, who put it in the plastic evidence bag with the other 16. Gary occupied himself with cleaning up the lobby and picking up the pieces of the smashed TV set that he had thrown at Eldon to slow him down. When the set exploded, sounding like a gunshot, Eldon had indeed slowed down, just long enough for Tony to grab him.

Mr. Morrow brought a pot of coffee and a can of Coke to the table. Mrs. Morrow followed with a big box of brownies. Tony watched Gary and Jess grab for the brownies, but Kate sat very still, hands in her lap.

J.D. had his notebook out, pencil in one hand, brownie in the other, and was ready to write down any new information gleaned from the conversation.

Tony sipped his coffee, looked around the table and began. "This is only an overview. You won't be hearing a lot of details because some of it is just supposition, some is still unknown and some can't be told because of the nature of the evidence and how it might be used to prosecute the case."

"Good brownies," said J.D.

Tony ignored him.

Right away Kate asked, "Why did Eldon want to kill my father?" It was the first time she had spoken since right after Eldon had been hauled away.

The question was so simple that everyone went quiet. J.D. was reaching for another brownie and stopped mid motion.

"Your father was killed, Kate, because he got in the way. Just as I suspected from the beginning. He came here to do some work, that much we know. We also know that Eldon was in the process of hiding a 35mm film container filled with seventeen diamonds in the base of one of your father's clay sculptures. Your father must have surprised him."

"Are these the seventeen diamonds stolen from Tucson? The ones in the newspaper?" asked Mrs. Morrow.

Tony nodded. "Apparently Eldon heard about the Tucson Gem Show from Peter, who's been there plenty of times and knows the ropes. By the way, Eldon's mannerisms at the gem show were perfect imitations of things Peter said and did right here—you know, the way Peter brushed back the ladies' hair and told them they had such pretty ears? At any rate, it appears Eldon and a gal named Lydia Lopez, the one you read about in the paper, stole the diamonds. He did away with her and then wanted to park the stones somewhere safe."

"But why hide them here? Surely, he could have found an easier place to put them," Mrs. Morrow asked.

She was right, thought Tony. There would be many easier places to hide them. "While Eldon was hanging around Peter's booth, learning all about the gem show and studying his sales techniques, he would have seen Art working with clay in the next booth. He must have figured that no one would ever think to look in a clay sculpture. It was a very creative solution, you have to give him credit for that. And he also befriended Bones so that if he couldn't retrieve the stones here, he could collect them at the foundry.

"He kept asking when I would send the *Girl with Dog* to the foundry. He even ordered one for his sister," Kate added. "Now I'm wondering if he faked some of the other sales just to hurry things along. Was his sister involved, do you think?"

"We think so. Or at least she knew what was going on. We know they've worked together before. Criminal siblings. Must have made their parents proud."

J.D. was busy writing and stopped chewing long enough to say, "I still don't understand why he got confused and followed the wrong sculpture to the foundry."

"I know why," said Jess.

Everyone turned to look at Jess. He was sitting at the table with his chair turned sideways, looking at the rest of them out of the corner of his eye, head down and peeling dried red paint from his fingers.

"What do you mean?" asked Tony.

"The booth got changed. The sculptures were moved," he said.

"That's right!" Kate agreed. "The first day I got here, I rearranged Daddy's booth because it didn't look right. Vicki and Peter helped me change things around and we switched the two clay pieces."

Tony looked over at Kate. It was good to see her alert and involved again. She was simply amazing, he thought, even with her hair in her face, circles under her eyes and no make up. But why...? He couldn't wait any longer. "Kate, why in heaven's name were you here tonight?"

"I won't tell you unless you promise not to give me any flak. I'm in no mood to get yelled at."

"I give you my word. No flak."

"Eldon lied to me for no apparent reason. It was one of those little things that just didn't make sense, didn't fit in with everything else I knew about him. He had always been so direct, with a kind of in-your-face style, and suddenly he was vague and evasive." She pulled the envelopes of negatives out of her pocket and handed them to Tony. "Somewhere in those envelopes are negatives of the *Mother and Child*. He took the pictures and gave them to Daddy, who showed them to Connie when they were out to dinner that night. But Eldon denied taking the photos. Not only that, I couldn't find them in Daddy's box of photos, or in his truck. I figured someone must have taken them that night and they might have something to do with what happened to Daddy. So, I guess I just wanted to find out if Eldon was lying and why."

"Is this what you were looking for?" Tony retrieved the picture he had kept tucked in his notebook since the investigation began.

"Yes, that's it! *Mother and Child*."

"That's *it*?" Tony repeated. "He lied to you about photographs and you risked your life to..." His voice rose. He told himself to calm down.

"You promised you wouldn't yell."

"I know. But, is that really *it*?"

"No. That's not the only thing. I knew that Eldon knew Bones. I saw them together at the ArtWalk."

"Lots of people would know Bones," Mrs. Morrow said.

"Yes, but I also found out that he knew Lydia Lopez..."

"How the hell did you know that? Why didn't you tell me?" Tony's voice went up a notch.

"Why should I tell you?" Kate's voice rose as well. "I didn't think there was any connection till yesterday afternoon when I saw her photographs plastered all over that stupid sunset..."

"Lydia Lopez is in the sunset picture?"

"Yeah, dozens of times. And I figured that anyone who knew both Lydia and Bones..."

Tony was impressed. "That's very good, Kate. Really observant. I overlooked that entirely." His voice returned to normal. He knew that the sunset picture would be valuable evidence and he also knew he would never have looked at the thing carefully enough to find Lydia Lopez, although he suspected J.D. would have examined every square inch of it.

As if to confirm his suspicions, J.D. put down his brownie and stood up. "I'm gonna go take a look at that sunset."

"Sit down, J.D."

"But I still don't understand why Eldon thought he had to lie about the photographs," said Kate.

"Well, this one was sticking out from under the wall in your father's booth, so they probably fell to the ground when Eldon assaulted your father—and Eldon wouldn't want to leave them there because that would be a connection he wouldn't want any one to make." Besides, thought Tony, they might have been spattered with blood. "It looks like he took all the time he needed—retrieved the photographs, unlaced the tent flaps, dragged your father outside, laced the flaps back up—and then very carefully hid the diamonds in the base of the sculpture. He obviously used one of those sculpture tools, just like your father did, on the edge of the base, so there wouldn't be any fingerprints in the clay. Cool as a cucumber."

"I have another question," said Kate. "Why the stupid shoes? I saw them the other night and again tonight. What's that all about?"

J.D. said, "He stole Gretchen's shoes."

"He stole *shoes*? Why?"

"I'm betting it was a form of extortion - just to say *I know what you're doing here at night, so you better do what I ask...*" And then it became clear. It was *Eldon* who got Derrick to provide an alibi for him, not the other way around. "But then he figured he might as well wear the shoes. Don't forget, it had been raining for days when this all happened and the ground was wet. He must have thought he'd confuse the investigation wearing women's shoes." Then Tony remembered how slowly and deliberately Eldon had walked across the living room of his apartment. Were the damn brogues deliberately oversized?

"You know, now that I think of it, Eldon has a lot of characteristics of a very creative, antisocial mastermind." Kate frowned in concentration, tucking a little crease, like an exclamation mark, between her eyebrows. Tony was so enchanted he almost didn't pay attention to what she was saying. "Masterminds are really smart, absolutely amoral and cool-headed. They have a cruel streak, too. And they're good actors, able to change their demeanor to fit the occasion."

"He was always very polite to me," volunteered Gary.

"Yes, well that's just it. He was polite to you, buddy-buddy with Peter, sympathetic to me, cruel to Gretchen..."

"...charming to the women he conned at the gem show," added Tony.

"...and very professional with us," said Mrs. Morrow.

"Exactly. He also improvised," Kate added. "He made last-minute decisions as needed, and the ability to do that comes from having loads of self-confidence. These people are often able to see a complex plan as a whole and then adapt quickly if something goes wrong with any part of it."

"Wow," said J.D., obviously impressed.

Kate leaned forward, apparently caught up in the subject. "The one thing they really know how to do is to manipulate, to use the weaknesses of others to their own advantage—a little praise to satisfy one person's ego, a little threat to play on someone else's fears, a little charm to convince the weak or undecided, that kind of thing. Also, these people are definitely greedy, and you can't get much greedier than stealing seventeen diamonds."

Tony thought about Kate's analysis and pretty much agreed. Mastermind personality. He'd have to remember that. Trouble was, that kind of analysis only worked in hindsight.

"So what happened to Bones?" Mr. Morrow asked Tony.

"Two possibilities. Bones was either some kind of partner and

Eldon decided to eliminate him, just like he eliminated Lydia Lopez—or else Bones simply got in the way, like Kate's father did. We'll find out which pretty soon."

Tony added the envelopes of negatives to the collection of objects on the table next to them. The sculpture of *Old Man Reading*, with a gouge out of its ample base, stood slightly askew on its wooden platform. There was also a sculptor's tool, a film container with bits of clay stuck to it, a plastic bag of diamonds speckled with red paint, a penlight and a pair of gloves. Before they left the premises, Tony and J.D. would empty out Eldon's booth, with special attention to the infamous sunset.

Tony stood up and stretched. He was tired and wanted to signal that it was time to go home.

"Detective Bannigan," Mr. Morrow said firmly, indicating for him to sit down again. Tony hesitated and then complied. What the hell.

"Sir?"

"How did you know it was Eldon?"

"Yeah," asked Gary. "How'd you know?"

"Process of elimination."

Everyone leaned forward to listen. Tony hated this. He was used to giving police reports to professionals who could understand the combination of reasoning, evidence, hunches and just plain good luck. This was a more difficult audience and he had to be careful not to say too much.

"We had several suspects. You needn't know who was on that list. But in the end, there was only one alibi that didn't hold up, and that was Eldon's."

He also wanted to give credit where it was due. "But the person who helped pull it altogether was Vicki. She called to tell me that Kate had brought a sculpture to Bones' place the day before he was killed. I had seen the article about him in the newspaper but had no reason to make a connection until Vicki called. When we got to the foundry it was obvious that the murderer had expected to find something in the base of Russo's sculpture. I had a hunch it was the diamonds, and that if he didn't find them *there*, he'd come *here*. So we just came and waited."

"Weren't you afraid you'd scare him off?" asked Mrs. Morrow. "All the noise driving in…?"

"We left two officers down the drive to watch out for him. We knew he'd come on foot, so that's the way we came."

"You know, Tony," said Kate, teasing, "the way that all came to you, as a kind of complete idea, it reminds me of the mastermind personality…good planning, yet very improvisational…"

"And what about you? What about hiding in Zach's fort? Or hiding behind the back walls? That's improvisational."

"You hid in Zach's fort?" asked Gary, looking totally amazed.

"That would be a great place to hide," said Jess, a small smile flitting across his face. "He's got the neatest toys in there."

"How'd you know that?" Mr. Morrow demanded, eyebrows raised.

Jess frowned at his fingernails. "I looked. I like the kid. I kinda watch out for him."

"Well, I'll tell you this," Kate told the group, "I liked hiding in Zach's fort a lot better than in the storage area." Then she looked at Tony. "By the way, how'd you know it was me back there? It was pitch black."

"Your fragrance, first. And your damn phone, of course." Then he grinned. "But I thought it was a neat place to hide and I got the impression that you liked it, too, all cuddled up in the blankets…"

She stood up quickly, flustered. "I'm going home, now."

"And how do you plan to get there?"

"Oh, the truck! I keep forgetting I don't have the truck."

Mr. Morrow looked up at Kate and gestured emphatically to her chair. "Sit down, young lady." She smiled at Tony, shrugged her shoulders and sat down, just as he had done.

"How did you get into the tents? Before we closed up tonight, I searched Zach's fort and the restrooms, even the storage area, and no one was there. Where were you?"

"Do I really have to tell you?"

"Yes, you really have to tell me."

"I sat with the children. Outside, on the bench."

The children? Tony didn't get it. No one seemed to get it.

But then J.D. smiled at her. "With the statues? Wow! I'm really impressed."

Kate smiled back. "Why thank you, J.D."

Tony pictured her sitting outside in the cold sculpture garden waiting for darkness to come just so she could find out if Eldon lied about the photographs. He marveled at how brave she was. After all, she knew the real dangers better than anyone else. Except her father, of course. Her father would be very proud of her. Tony was proud of her, too, but more than anything, he was glad she was safe.

Mr. Morrow shook his head, got up from his chair, and said to his wife, "Come on, let's drive Kate home."

"I'm going home, too" mumbled Jess.

"I'll stay here and guard the evidence," said Gary.

"I'm going to look at the sunset," said J.D.

THIRTY-THREE

The poblano chiles were seeded, stuffed with jack cheese and lined up on the breadboard in three neat rows. Next to the board sat a bowl of beaten egg whites, and on the stovetop, a pan of heated oil. Tony was beating the egg yolks in a second bowl, adding just enough flour to assure the coating would be fluffy, yet crisp. Then he carefully folded the yolk mixture into the egg whites.

Tony loved to cook the chiles, a fact his mother found difficult to appreciate because he always insisted she leave the kitchen. He simply needed to keep things organized. The need for an organized kitchen escaped Inez.

What appealed to Tony about cooking was that it was a straightforward kind of job. It had a beginning, a middle and an end, and when the job was done you got to enjoy the results immediately. There was nothing murky or vague or uncertain about it. You either got it right or you didn't.

With detective work there was always a certain amount of ambiguity: false leads, unintended consequences, inconclusive evidence, to say nothing of the sloppy way the justice system often worked when it was all over.

He thought about the case. What had he left undone? What did he still not understand? Had he collected all the evidence, uncontaminated, and secured it for the prosecution?

He picked the chiles up by their stems and dipped them one by one, first into the egg batter and then into the heated oil. The sizzle focused his attention on the work at hand, so he grabbed the tongs, ready to turn the chiles over at the precise moment. When he heard a car stop, he looked out the window and saw J.D. get out, carrying a big bouquet of flowers and a six-pack of beer and smiling from ear to ear.

He glanced back at the pan just in time, turned the chiles over and reached for the platter his mother had set aside for him. Another car stopped and parked across the street. Connie got out, her Chrysler convertible and country club looks slightly out of place in the neighborhood. Finally a blue truck pulled into the driveway, and there was Kate, her hair catching the light from the setting sun. Vicki was with her, and little Zach.

He was working on the second batch and wanted to rush the job now that Kate was in the house. He wondered how she felt, if she had caught up with her sleep. He certainly hadn't. There had been so much work to do after returning to the station that he wasn't able to disengage until a few hours ago. He was exhausted, but it didn't matter. It was time to celebrate.

He had convinced his mother that this Wednesday's dinner party should be outside, like a little fiesta with twinkling lights, colored tablecloths, lots of margaritas and perhaps Emilio playing the guitar. Angela and Angelina thought it was a great idea and had transformed the patio, rearranging the potted plants, borrowing tables and chairs and cleaning off the grill. Inez hadn't liked the idea at all. She told Tony she felt she was "at fives and sixes." Tony understood why: Inez hated to give up the control she exercised in the dining room, where she sat at the head of the table like a grand matriarch. He would try to think of some way to make her feel important tonight.

The second batch of chiles was transferred onto the platter. He had started on the next when Sophia walked in.

"Hey, how's my hotshot brother doing tonight? Congratulations.

You got your guy in jail and now I bet you're looking forward to his conviction, to say nothing of his execution." She gave him a kiss.

"Of course I am. Why not? He murdered *three people*, Sophia. That's a sizable chunk of the population. I say, he deserves to die."

"You better check with Kate before you start leading the parade to death row. She might not want that to happen, you know. Have you asked her?"

"She's entitled to her opinion, and I'm entitled to mine." This was not the conversation they should be having tonight. "Listen, Sophia, can't we just celebrate the fact that we caught the guy—the right guy—and agree that that's a good thing?"

"Yeah. I agree. That's a very good thing. It's just that I want you to be careful, Tonio. If you start getting too heavy handed with that get-tough, redneck attitude of yours, you might scare her away."

"Well, if her attitudes are as liberal as yours, she might scare *me* away!"

Sophia lined a basket with a bright red napkin, filled it with warm tortillas, and put another napkin on top. She grinned at Tony. "Have you two slept together yet?"

"Sophia! For heaven's sake, back off, will you?"

"Why should Sophia back off?" He hadn't seen Kate walk into the kitchen. She looked rested but with the vague and slightly puffy look of someone who just woke up from a very long nap.

"He's always telling me to back off," Sophia said before giving Kate a hug. "But he's still my big brother. And just look at these wonderful *chiles rellenos*. Aren't they beautiful?"

"They are beautiful, but I have no idea what *chiles rellenos* are."

"Tell you what," Sophia said, "I'll go outside and make sure everyone's got something to drink and Tony can tell you all about his chiles." She headed for the door and called over her shoulder, "You two look so cute together."

Tony watched her leave and shook his head. "I'm sorry. Sophia can be a real pain."

"Don't be sorry. She's not a pain, and it's nice to know we look cute. It's kind of innocent, like high school, don't you think?"

"If there's one thing Sophia isn't, it's innocent! She wants us making mad passionate love. Not that I disagree with her..." He looked at her hopefully.

"Maybe I'm not ready for mad, passionate love."

"I thought you were last night. Under the quilt. I detected a certain..."

"That's not fair! That was an unusual circumstance..."

"Then I'll have to think up another unusual circumstance." He kissed her cheek. "In the meantime, hold on to the platter while I get the enchiladas out of the oven."

They carried the food out through the living room to the back patio where the party was getting off to a good start. Tony looked around and smiled at the scene, wishing he had remembered to bring his camera. There was Uncle Manny telling his stories to Connie and Vicki, who actually looked interested. Emilio was strumming his guitar, his sleeves rolled up to reveal a gang insignia on one arm and the Virgin of Guadalupe on the other. Angela and Angelina were fussing with the food on the buffet table. Father Miguel was attending to the steaks on the grill. J.D. was trying, unsuccessfully, to amuse Sophia, while little Zach and Spiderman were under the far table by the acacia tree. A gaggle of aunts and widows sat demurely at a table devouring taquitos as fast as they could, hoping Inez wasn't watching. Inez stood in the middle of the patio, shot an offended look in their direction, and tried to quiet everyone down.

"It's time to say grace," she was saying, tapping a glass with her spoon. She tapped again, but no one paid attention. She frowned at the priest and said, loud and clear, "Please, Father Miguel, say grace!"

Instead, Emilio strummed a beautiful, rich chord. "Amazing grace," he sang out, "how sweet the sound..." Everyone stopped and looked at him, even Zach. He sang the hymn straight through and no one moved until he finished.

Tony put his arm around his mother's shoulder. "That was a great idea, Ma, to ask Emilio to sing the blessing."

Inez shrugged. "Emilio is a blessing in a disguise."

~~~~~~~~~~~~~~~~~~~~~~~~~~~~~~~~~

Kate stood alone on the gentle rise and looked out across the vast lawn of grass and stone markers, past the parking lot and red-roofed neighborhoods, to the blue-gray hills on the horizon. The scene pleased her. Even in the silence she could hear the mariachi music, haunting and bittersweet.

So much had changed in one short month. She needed time for reflection, but that was not to be. The show had closed and she was flying back to New Jersey tomorrow. Once there, she would have to deal with her grief and with Martin and with her job at the clinic. And also with the pain of separation from her new friends. From Tony.

One month ago her father was alive and she was engaged to a man she didn't love. One month ago she had been afraid to drive a truck and afraid to talk to God. One month ago she had no courage, little self-confidence, and almost no sense of who she was or what she was capable of. A tragic and amazing month. And, along with everything else, some time during the month she had fallen in love.

She sat down on the grass, rummaged deep in her tote bag, and pulled out the items to place on the grave. She knew they would be picked up and discarded in a day or two when they were discovered by the landscaping crew she could see working in the distance. What in the world would they think of such a memorial, she wondered.

She saw Tony pull into the parking lot and followed him with her eyes as he wandered up the path. Her heart fluttered at the sight of him, and that worried her.

"Do you mind?" he asked, eyebrows raised, waiting for her permission before sitting down.

"How did you know I was here?"

"Sophia."

"I should have known." She patted the grass next to her, glad he had come.

"It must be hard to say goodbye to your father," he said. "Maybe it's hard for him, too. Have you thought that he might not want you to go?"

"I have to go."

"I don't see why. It's obvious you like it here in Arizona. And you and I…"

"I have a life in New Jersey, Tony. I have an apartment, a car. I have a job waiting for me."

"And Martin."

"Martin may be waiting, but I'm not interested. You know that."

"He keeps calling you. Almost got you killed."

"I can't help that he calls."

Tony put his arm around her. "Why don't you think of it this way: out here, instead of an apartment you have your father's house, instead of a car you have your father's truck. And as far as a job, you could easily…"

"No, I have to go back." The idea of staying in Arizona both attracted and frightened her. "I've put Daddy's house on the market, you know, and I've brought all his sculptures down to the Long Gallery. Except the ones I'm keeping for myself."

"And the truck?"

"I was hoping to keep it, but selling it makes more sense."

"I'll buy it from you."

"Really?"

"Yeah. I've always wanted a truck, and it'll remind me of you. And when my son comes to visit, I can drive him around in the truck, maybe up in the mountains to fish, and he'll think that's real cool." He kissed the back of her neck. "Besides, when you decide to come back, the truck will be here waiting for you."

He pointed to the makeshift memorial. "Speaking of trucks, most people bring flowers to cemeteries," he said, smiling. "You want to tell me about all this?"

"Well, Zach gave me the little blue truck…"

"And St. Francis? That's a pretty ugly St. Francis."

"But he's got personality, don't you think? I got him at the

Franciscan Renewal Center, you know that place on Lincoln Drive? I've passed there nearly every day this month, so today I went in to have a look. Have you been out in the back, with those tall trees and all the birds singing and the roses blooming? It's amazing, tucked right behind Camelback Mountain. Anyway, I went into the gift shop and saw this little guy. I looked at the stupid blue bird he was holding and the blue reminded me of the blue truck and somehow the vision just came to me, all at once—St. Francis riding over the hills in the bed of the little blue truck." She suddenly felt embarrassed, less confident than a moment ago. "It's *symbolic*."

"It's also very creative. He'll probably like it better out here than in the bathroom."

"Funny, very funny."

"Your father must have liked St. Francis."

"You're the second person who's said that. St. Francis was Italian, and that probably appealed to Daddy. And he was a man of peace, and that would definitely appeal to him." Peace, oh, how she prayed her father was at peace. Her throat tightened, but she refused to cry. "Daddy wouldn't want his killer executed, you know. He just wouldn't. He didn't believe in capital punishment. I thought I should tell you that."

"But Eldon killed two other people and their families might feel differently."

"I know."

"He's not a good guy, Kate. He was part of the Hollywood paparazzi, got into extortion and ended up in jail. Then he moved to Vegas and branched out big time—gambling, more extortion, probably murder. They were about to close in on him so he moved here to lay low as a photographer. He wrecked people's lives, Kate. And he killed three people for a bunch of diamonds. I mean, that's really evil, don't you think?"

"It is, truly evil. But I'm not going to feel any better if he's executed. Daddy will still be dead. And so will Lydia. And Bones."

Tony moved closer, so she leaned her head on his shoulder. She wanted to kiss him, but was hesitant to make the first move. Her heart tumbled when he lifted her face up to his, but just then her phone rang. She felt him stiffen and heard his quiet *damn*. Then he reached into her bag and pulled out the phone. He stood up and slowly scanned the cemetery, looking for a target, arm back, ready to pitch.

She shot up. "No, don't do that! Please, Tony, give it to me."

He handed it to her reluctantly, clearly irritated by her request. But she smiled at him, a truly happy smile. Then she looked in the direction of his target, swung her arm back the way she remembered pitching softball at summer camp, and let the phone go. It arced across the blue sky, playing its little tune until it landed in a crimson bougainvillea bush. There was a rustling, and two white wing doves fluttered out and flew away.

EPILOGUE

Kate moved back to Scottsdale. She lives in her father's house and works at the Desert Mountain Clinic. She also volunteers at the Franciscan Renewal Center as a grief and bereavement counselor.

Tony is working on two new cases with J.D. He recently purchased a Hasselblad camera and is taking a class in photography at Phoenix College. He never tires of photographing Kate.

Peter moved to Tubac to live with Jason. He designs jewelry for several galleries and boutiques in Tucson.

Derrick returned to Idaho, where he is working on the sculpture commissioned by the Northern Arizona Insurance Company. Gretchen has moved in with him.

Eldon is in the Madison Street jail in Phoenix. He has also been charged with the murders of Lydia Lopez and Bernard "Bones" Jones. His sister has agreed to testify for the prosecution.

Girl with Dog and *Old Man Reading* were repaired by sculptor Martha Pettigrew and cast into bronze at another foundry.

Jess moved out of Connie's house and is now working at an animal shelter.

Mark Von Steen suffered a stroke and died in the care of his loving daughter. He left millions of dollars to the Art Department at Northern Arizona University.

Vicki took Zach to Disneyland where he bought the entire collection of figures from the Pirates of the Caribbean. He has forgotten all about the King.

Gary the Guard retired and moved with his wife to Sun City.

Mr. and Mrs. Morrow celebrated a successful show by cruising the Greek islands. They are making plans to enhance the security system.

Sophia graduated from law school and is studying for the bar exam. She works for the Arizona Chapter of the ACLU.

Inez decided to write a cookbook. The working title is *The Whole Enchilada.*